**Deschutes
Public Library**

I1053007

BEOWULF

BEOWULF

STEPHEN MITCHELL

Yale UNIVERSITY PRESS

New Haven and London

Copyright © 2017 by Stephen Mitchell.
Map copyright © 2017 by Jeffrey L. Ward.
All rights reserved. This book may not be reproduced, in whole or in part, including illustrations, in any form (beyond that copying permitted by Sections 107 and 108 of the U.S. Copyright Law and except by reviewers for the public press), without written permission from the publishers.

Yale University Press books may be purchased in quantity for educational, business, or promotional use. For information, please e-mail sales.press@yale.edu (U.S. office) or sales@yaleup.co.uk (U.K. office).

Designed by Mary Valencia.
Set in Minion type by Tseng Information Systems, Inc.
Printed in the United States of America.

Grateful acknowledgment is made to the University of Toronto Press for permission to reprint the Old English text from *Klaeber's Beowulf and The Fight at Finnsberg,* edited, with an introduction, commentary, appendices, glossary, and bibliography, by R. D. Fulk, Robert E. Bjork, and John D. Niles, fourth edition, copyright © University of Toronto Press Incorporated 2008. Reprinted by permission of the University of Toronto Press.

Library of Congress Control Number: 2017938421
ISBN 978-0-300-22888-5 (hardcover : alk. paper)

A catalogue record for this book is available from the British Library.

This paper meets the requirements of ANSI/NISO Z39.48-1992
(Permanence of Paper).

10 9 8 7 6 5 4 3 2 1

By Stephen Mitchell

Poetry
Parables and Portraits

Fiction
The Frog Prince
Meetings with the Archangel

Nonfiction
A Mind at Home with Itself *(with Byron Katie)*
A Thousand Names for Joy *(with Byron Katie)*
Loving What Is *(with Byron Katie)*
The Gospel According to Jesus

Translations and Adaptations
Beowulf
The Odyssey
The Iliad
Duino Elegies & The Sonnets to Orpheus
The Second Book of the Tao
Gilgamesh
Bhagavad Gita
Full Woman, Fleshly Apple, Hot Moon: Selected Poems of Pablo Neruda
Genesis
Ahead of All Parting: The Selected Poetry and Prose of Rainer Maria Rilke
A Book of Psalms
The Selected Poetry of Dan Pagis
Tao Te Ching
The Book of Job
The Selected Poetry of Yehuda Amichai *(with Chana Bloch)*
The Sonnets to Orpheus
The Lay of the Love and Death of Cornet Christoph Rilke
Letters to a Young Poet
The Notebooks of Malte Laurids Brigge
The Selected Poetry of Rainer Maria Rilke

Edited by Stephen Mitchell
Question Your Thinking, Change the World: Quotations from Byron Katie
The Essence of Wisdom
Bestiary: An Anthology of Poems about Animals
Song of Myself
Into the Garden: A Wedding Anthology *(with Robert Hass)*
The Enlightened Mind: An Anthology of Sacred Prose
The Enlightened Heart: An Anthology of Sacred Poetry
Dropping Ashes on the Buddha: The Teaching of Zen Master Seung Sahn

For Children
The Ugly Duckling, by Hans Christian Andersen
Iron Hans
Genies, Meanies, and Magic Rings
The Tinderbox, by Hans Christian Andersen
The Wishing Bone and Other Poems
The Nightingale, by Hans Christian Andersen
Jesus: What He Really Said and Did
The Creation

To Paul Muldoon

Contents

Introduction

It's something of a miracle that any of our ancient literary master-pieces survived the downfall or shift of civilizations, since they all might easily have been lost. Of Heraclitus's profound insights, we have only tantalizing fragments. Of Sappho's nine books, there remain just four poems and scattered verses of incomparable love-liness. Of Aeschylus, six out of ninety plays; of Sophocles, seven out of 123. *Gilgamesh,* the oldest of our masterpieces (its final version was written around 1200 BCE), disappeared for two thousand years: the baked clay tablets on which it was inscribed in cuneiform characters lay buried in the rubble of cities across the ancient Near East, and it wasn't until 1850 that the first fragments were discovered among the ruins of Nineveh.

Beowulf too dropped out of existence for centuries. It was probably unread after 1066 CE, when the Norman Conquest changed the nature of the English language. The single manuscript in which it survives, copied onto vellum around the year 1000, sat on the shelf of a monastic library until it found its way into the collection of Sir Robert Cotton (1571–1631), an antiquarian and a member of Parliament. In 1731, a fire broke out in the building where the collection was being stored, destroying a quarter of its books and manuscripts. Before the *Beowulf* manuscript was saved (someone tossed it out a window), the top and the outside edge of each leaf were badly scorched. In 1787, an Icelandic historian named Grímur Jónsson Thorkelin prudently commissioned a transcript. Even as the transcriber copied it, the charred edges of the leaves were crumbling away; many of his readings go unrecorded in Thorkelin's own, later transcription, and scholars estimate that nearly two thousand letters lost in the manuscript as a result of fire damage can be restored on the basis of these transcriptions. Finally, in 1845, librarians mounted the leaves on paper frames and re-bound them, thus putting an end to any further deterioration. Thorkelin published the first edition in 1815, and the poem began to be studied and translated during the following decades. But it wasn't until J. R. R. Tolkien published his famous paper "*Beowulf*: The Monsters and the Critics" in 1936 that readers began to recognize its status as a great literary work of art.

No one knows who the author of *Beowulf* was, or when he wrote it, or precisely where in England. Among historians and literary scholars, opinions on the date of its composition have ranged anywhere from 650 to 1025, while most linguists and archaeologists date it between 700 and 750.

The poem's story is simple. Beowulf is the nephew of the king of the Geats, a people who lived in southern Sweden. When he hears that an allied people, the Danes, have been attacked by Grendel, a huge, cannibalistic ogre, he volunteers to help them, sails to Denmark, and single-handedly kills Grendel and Grendel's equally murderous mother. The second part of the poem takes place fifty years later, after Beowulf has become the king of the Geats. A slave steals a gold cup from a dragon's hoard, and in retaliation the monster goes on a fiery rampage, destroying people, buildings, and the whole countryside. Beowulf kills the dragon, but in the fight he himself is mortally wounded. The poem ends with his funeral and eulogy.

The poet who wrote *Beowulf* may have believed that these Geats, Danes, and other neighboring Germanic tribes were like his own ancestors, Angles, Saxons, and Jutes who had migrated from Denmark and northwest Germany and conquered Britain in the fifth and sixth centuries and whose language had mostly supplanted the Celtic of the British inhabitants. Two or three centuries later, the Anglo-Saxon nobility enjoyed special civil liberties and patronage in comparison with commoners and slaves.

Christianity had come to England in the second or third century, and by the end of the seventh century most of the island was nominally Christian. The great majority of scholars today believe that *Beowulf* is a Christian poem. But the poet's Christianity is peculiar. His only biblical references are to the book of Genesis; he never refers to the Gospels. Nor does he make any mention of Jesus or of the fundamental beliefs that differentiate Christianity from Judaism, though it would have been natural for him to do so. For example, in the only doctrinaire passage in the poem—a passage so atypical that Tolkien was convinced that it must have been interpolated or altered by a reviser—the poet mentions that some Danes, in despair over the horrors of Grendel's attacks, were driven to idolatry:

> Some of them even prayed to idols,
> made pagan sacrifices, and pledged
> themselves to the Slayer of Souls, to gain
> help from this horror. That was the thing
> those heathens hoped for; deep in their hearts
> they served the devil. They did not know
> God Almighty, the Judge of Men,
> and could not give praise to the Prince of Heaven,
> the King of the World. (167–75 in this translation)

It would have been easy to insert a Christian reference in this passage, something on the order of

> They did not know
> God Almighty, the Judge of Men,
> and could not be saved by Jesus Christ,
> His only son, who died for our sins.

By contrast, the ninth- or tenth-century author of the Old English poem *Judith* doesn't hesitate to use anachronistic Christian expressions about the Jewish heroine ("the Savior's servant") and the Babylonian villain Holofernes ("despised by the Savior"), and he calls God "God of creation, Spirit of comfort, Son of God, . . . glory of the Trinity" (83–86).

In *Beowulf*, though the poet or his characters refer to God more than four dozen times, there is never any mention of a savior. And though these characters often give thanks to God and express their trust in his omnipotence, they are portrayed as clearly pagan. Scyld Scefing, the founder of the Danish royal house, is buried in a pagan funeral ship; the Geatish elders consult omens, contrary to Christian law; both Danes and Geats practice the burning of the dead, which was prohibited by the Church. Not only pagan practices but pagans themselves, along with Jews and other unbelievers, were unambiguously condemned by Christian doctrine, in such New Testament verses as "Whoever does not believe [in the only begotten Son of God] is condemned already" (John 3:18) and "There is no salvation in anyone else [but Jesus]" (Acts 4:12). At around the same time that the *Beowulf* poet was active, the English scholar and theologian Alcuin of York (735–804) wrote, "What has Ingeld [an ancient Germanic hero] to do with Christ? The house is narrow, it cannot hold them both. The King of Heaven will have no fellowship with so-called kings who are pagan and damned, for the Eternal King reigns in Heaven, while the pagan is damned and laments in Hell."

The *Beowulf* poet was having none of this. For him, the virtuous actions of his ancestors were enough to earn them a place in heaven. Beowulf himself is consistently magnanimous, loyal to his superiors, generous to his inferiors, as eager for fame, revenge, and gold as a noble pagan should be, a king who always puts his people's welfare before his own, a warrior who is impeccably fair even to the demonic Grendel, declining to use weapons because the monster has none—he is, in short, the embodiment of all the aristocratic virtues. There is no sense in the poem that the hero or anyone else is in jeopardy because he hasn't heard about Jesus. The poet implies this when he mentions the deaths of Scyld Scefing, who "went forth, / still strong, into the Lord's safekeeping" (24–25), and of two other heroes peripheral to the main story. Queen Wealhtheow confidently speaks of her husband's "go[ing] forth to face God's judgment" (1124). King Hrothgar later urges Beowulf to turn away from unseemly pride and "choose the better way: / eternal rewards" (1685–86). Beowulf himself, in his death speech, says that he has no fear of God's judgment:

> For fifty years
> I ruled this country. Not one king
> of any neighboring nation dared
> attack me with troops or even threaten
> war against me. I stood my ground,
> took what fate brought, defended my people,
> never stirred up a quarrel or swore
> a false oath. I can still find joy
> in this, although my wound is mortal.

> Once the life-spirit has left my flesh,
> the eternal Lord has no cause to condemn me
> for the murder of kinsmen. (2627–38)

After Beowulf's last words, the poet affirms that

> soon from his breast his soul departed
> to seek the glory God holds for the just. (2713–14)

It is touching to see how a fundamental point of Christian doctrine has been reshaped in such a radical way. *Beowulf* is a deeply pious poem, but it is so bold in its reverence for a virtuous pagan past that it teeters on the edge of heresy. The poet may have thought that he was an orthodox Christian, but from the evidence of *Beowulf*, he was what we might call an ethical monotheist, and his religion could have come straight out of Ben Franklin's sketch of the credo of a reasonable human being: "That there is one God, who made all things. That he governs the world by his providence. That he ought to be worshiped by adoration, prayer, and thanksgiving. But that the most acceptable service to God is doing good to man [which, for the poet, may entail killing your enemies]. That the soul is immortal. And that God will certainly reward virtue and punish vice, either here or hereafter." Given the mainstream rabbinic doctrine that "righteous gentiles have a place in the world to come," one might also, not entirely facetiously, call the *Beowulf* poet an *anima naturaliter judaica*.

It is this faith in God's justice that tempers the melancholy of the poem's end, when it is clear that after Beowulf's death all his people will be killed or enslaved by their enemies. Certainly there is a sense of pathos here, but it is nowhere near as intense as the pathos of a pagan poem like the *Iliad*—as, for example, in the famous, heartbreakingly tender scene between Hector and Andromache when the Trojan hero envisions the future enslavement of his wife and the mass slaughter of his people. For a poet who believes in the afterlife, life is filled with suffering, but the suffering is as transitory as life itself, and all good people will have their reward in heaven. Whatever despair there is in the hearts of Beowulf's mourners, there seems to be none in the poet himself. And since *Beowulf* is for the most part a celebration of its hero's life, it ends with a kind of triumph, death in victory, the most glorious death that a warrior could wish for. If one allows for the difference between a martial and a pastoral culture, the ending even has the tone of serenity that we hear in the deaths of the biblical patriarchs, who were "old and full of days."

However Christian the poet may have thought himself, he was the heir to a long tradition of oral pagan poetry, and he knew many formulaic phrases that bards had developed to carry on the momentum as they improvised their verses. There are several scenes in *Beowulf* where the poet describes a warrior or a professional bard reciting or improvising "for people's delight":

> At times a warrior gifted with words,
> who kept in his memory many ancient
> tales and sagas, composed a new song
> in praise of Beowulf's brilliant deed,
> his stirring language skillfully fashioned,
> each word correctly linked to the rest. (826–31)

In a moment of celebration, even the Danish king, Hrothgar, takes up the harp and sings:

> "When he who had once been bold in battle
> touched the harp-strings, they trembled with joy,
> and then he began to sing a story

> that was true and mournful, or he would tell
> a wonder-tale in just the right way. . . .
> And so, in Heorot, that whole day
> we feasted and laughed . . ." (2024–28, 2033–34)

This was aristocratic poetry, usually performed at court, and the setting was not very different from the Phaeacian court in the *Odyssey*, where the blind bard Demodocus sings "of the glorious deeds of heroes." Odysseus's appreciation of the performance must have been similar to the emotion of the warriors at the Danish court in *Beowulf*:

> "It is a fine thing to be listening to a poet
> such as this, who is like the immortals in speech.
> For I think that there is no more complete fulfillment
> than when joy takes over an audience in the great hall,
> and the banqueters are sitting next to each other
> listening to the poet, and beside them the tables
> are loaded with bread and meat, and the steward carries
> the drawn wine around and fills their cups to the brim.
> This seems to me the most beautiful thing in the world."

Like the Homeric tradition, though with a language cruder than the infinitely elegant ancient Greek, the *Beowulf* poet's was a tradition of public speech. Not only courage and loyalty were expected of a great warrior; he also had to be eloquent, and the audience must have delighted in the intricate courtesy and pride of his speeches. (When, out of a sense of duty, I watched Robert Zemeckis's film *Beowulf*, which stars computer-generated likenesses of Ray Winstone, Anthony Hopkins, and—it must be said—Angelina Jolie as Grendel's mother, I was struck by the inarticulateness of the characters, who speak in a coarse comic-book vernacular.)

Throughout *Beowulf* there are passages of great emotional power, which draw us into a scene with the vividness and enchantment that only poetry can achieve. Here, for example, the poet writes of Beowulf's voyage to Denmark to kill Grendel:

> Time moved quickly. The ship was moored
> under the cliffs; the warriors, eager,
> climbed aboard it, the surf crashed
> onto the sand, the men stowed
> weapons and war-gear, then shoved off
> with oars out into the open sea.
> Over the waves, with the wind in her sails
> and her prow in foam, she flew like a bird
> till in due time on the second day
> the bold seafarers sighted land:
> shimmering cliffs, sheer crags,
> and jutting headlands. The journey was done.
> Lightly they leaped out onto the shore
> and secured the ship with a strong cable.
> Then they shook out their heavy mail-shirts
> and battle-gear, and gave thanks to God
> for the smooth crossing on a calm sea. (200–216)

Once Beowulf arrives in Denmark, Grendel again attacks the great golden mead-hall of Heorot:

> He stood there, seething,
> maddened with rage, then he ripped open
> the hall's mouth and hurried across
> the patterned floor. From his fierce eyes
> an evil light flared like two flames.
> He saw the young men in the mead-hall, sleeping

close together, a troop of kinfolk,
and his heart laughed; before dawn's light
he intended to tear the life from each body
and devour the flesh in a gruesome feast. . . .
                        [Then,] in a flash
he lunged and seized a warrior sleeping,
tore him apart, gnawed bones, drank blood
gushing from veins, gorged on gobbets
of flesh, and soon had devoured the victim
utterly, even his hands and feet. (691–700, 704–9)

Later in the poem, there is a chilling description of Grendel's home:

They live in the hidden land, high country
where the wolf hunts on windy headlands,
treacherous marsh-paths where mountain torrents
plunge down cloud-covered cliffs to form
an underground river. That lake lies
not many miles from this mead-hall; boughs
heavy with frost hang all around it,
and a root-thick wood looms over the water.
Each night something uncanny occurs:
the water burns. Not even the wisest
man alive knows the lake's bottom.
The strong-horned stag who is pursued
by a pack of hounds, though he seeks safety
desperately, would much rather die
on the shore of that lake than save his life
by plunging in. It is a foul place. (1299–1314)

And finally, in one of the many digressions that are a feature of the poem's allusive style, we hear the lament of the last survivor of an ancient race.

> "Death claimed all my kinfolk in battle;
> every last one has left this world,
> never again to know its pleasures.
> Now there is not even one remaining
> to carry the sword or bear the cup;
> all those warriors—hurried away.
> The hardened helmet must lose the gold trim
> that now adorns it; the stewards sleep
> who used to burnish the battle-masks;
> so too the mail-shirt that marched to war,
> a shelter behind the thick shields crashing
> as the blades bit; it decays like the body,
> and the linked chains cannot travel along
> with the commander beside his men;
> no longer is there delight from the harp,
> surges of joy from the singing wood;
> no well-trained hawk now flies through the hall,
> and the swift horse does not stamp in the courtyard.
> Savage death has silenced them all." (2165–83)

Our pleasure in *Beowulf* doesn't come only from great passages like these; it comes from the whole dense texture of the poem. From beginning to end, we feel that we are in the hands of a master poet, whose joy is to re-create his ancestors' virtues in "stirring language skillfully fashioned" that can still move us today, after more than a thousand years.

About This Translation

The robust masculine music of Old English verse entered the world of the modern reader in 1912, when Ezra Pound published *Ripostes*, which includes his brilliant, quirky translation of "The Seafarer." To an ear tuned to the genteel verse of the Georgians, these jagged four-beat lines must have sounded almost as barbaric as Stravinsky's *Sacre du printemps* did to an indignant Parisian audience at its first performance the following year. The music of Pound's translation startles us less now, though it is no less thrilling.

There are two ways of trying to re-create *Beowulf* in contemporary English verse. One is to stay as close as possible to the word order and the full, three-pronged alliteration of the original text, the "rum, ram, ruf" of it. The other is to adopt a lighter mode of alliteration and find a diction that is midway between the formal and the colloquial: a contemporary language that seems natural and alive.

Here, for example, is the Old English text's powerful description of corpses being burned on a funeral pyre:

wand tō wolcnum;   wælfȳra   mǣst
Curled to clouds   funeral fire greatest

hlynode for   hlāwe.   Hafelan multon,
roared   before burial-mound.   Heads   melted,

benġeato   burston   ðonne blōd ætspranc,
wound-openings burst   while blood spurted out,

lāðbite   līċes;   līġ ealle forswealg,
hostile bites (= wounds) bodies';   fire all   swallowed up,

gǣsta ġīfrost,   þāra ðe þǣr gūð fornam
spirit greediest,   those who there war took away

bēġa   folces.   Wæs hira blǣd scacen.
of both peoples.   Was their glory departed.

If your main priority is to re-create the music of the original at all costs, you might translate this as follows, somewhat à la Pound:

> Spun to sky smoke of death-flames,
> howled on hillock; heads melted,
> wound-gates burst, gore gushed
> from bodies' hate-bites. Blazing fire,
> greediest spirit, swallowed unspared
> of two tribes; their triumph fled.

Despite its oddness, this kind of translation has its virtues: compression, weight, a kind of unsparing dignity. But for me, the oddness quickly palls, and the unrelenting beat of the alliteration becomes tedious. No wonder Joyce parodied it in *Ulysses:* "Before born babe bliss had. Within womb won he worship."

Like most translators, I have used the second method. Here is how the passage turned out for me:

Smoke rose up and spiraled to heaven,
the flames in front of the burial mound
roared, wounds burst, heads melted, blood
bubbled and gushed. That greedy spirit,
fire, consumed the slain of both tribes,
and their glory was gone from the earth forever. (1062–67)

To someone who has the music of the Old English text resounding in his ear, the disadvantage of this is all those pesky little prepositions and definite articles running around, trying to pull the lines into too regular a rhythm of anapests or dactyls. On the other hand, the language sounds natural and emotionally believable, and two alliterating letters per line is quite enough to maintain a sense of the form.

Here are the rules I have played by in my translation:

• Every line has four beats, and alliteration is a structural element; it is always present in every line, but as unobtrusively as I could manage. Occasionally, there are three alliterating letters to a line, but I have kept these instances to a minimum. (Sometimes, arbitrarily, it turned out that two different letters alliterate in a single line — for example, "and their glóry was góne from the eárth foréver.")

• Words alliterate as sounded, not as spelled. For example, "who" alliterates with "hall," not "wall"; "one" alliterates with "war," not "oar"; "generous" alliterates with "joy," not "gift." "Sh" doesn't alliterate with "s," while "sl," "sp," and other such combinations do. "Wh" is considered equivalent to "w." As in Old English, all vowels alliterate with one another.

• The alliterating letters occur at accented syllables. Occasionally, when I was having trouble finding a synonym, I cheated on this rule and sneaked an alliterating letter onto an unaccented syllable. (Examples: "for twélve long wínters, while the Dánes' lórd," "térror óver the foúl níght-fiend," "Tíme moved quíckly. The shíp was moóred," "Béowulf, it múst be becaúse.")

• The alliterating letters can occur at any place in the line, whereas in Old English verse the fourth beat never alliterates.

• The lines are usually end-stopped, with a caesura in the middle, though sometimes a line may be unbalanced or enjambed for dramatic effect.

Though Pound's "Seafarer" is still often delicious, its archaisms and inversions have not aged well—to my ear, at least. I have tuned my diction to a more colloquial, though still slightly elevated, level. This has meant, among other things, not trying to re-create the many compound nouns of the original text and its synonyms for "sword," "battle," "king," and so forth. It has also meant disregarding or unpacking the Old English kennings. Thus, *ofer hronrād* (over whale-road) becomes "over the waves where the whales ride," and *ganotes bæð* (gannet's bath) becomes "the broad sea where the gannet bathes."

My goal throughout has been to make the language of this translation seem transparent and to let the poetry of the original text shine through in the language of today.

About the Text

The text I have translated is *Klaeber's Beowulf,* fourth edition, ed. R. D. Fulk, Robert E. Bjork, and John D. Niles. I have not followed its use of italics or of certain diacritical marks. All other divergences are indicated below.

The line numbers of Klaeber's Old English text do not correspond to the line numbers of the translation, which, since I value concision, turned out to be 117 lines shorter than the original.

1, *Hwæt we:* Wrenn. Klaeber⁴ punctuates *Hwæt, we.* See Walkden.

62, *Ȳrse wæs Onelan:* conjecture Clarke. Klaeber⁴ reads *[. . . . . . wæs On]elan.* See Klaeber⁴, pp. 117–18.

149, *sōna:* conjecture Holthausen. Klaeber⁴ reads *[ġesȳne].*

389b–390a, *Þā tō dura healle / Wulfgār ēode:* conjecture von Schaubert. Klaeber⁴ reads * * * / *[Wedera lēodum].*

420, *fīfel:* conjecture Grein. Klaeber⁴ reads *fīfe.* See Tolkien, *Beowulf,* p. 231.

457, *For gewyrhtum:* conjecture Trautmann. Klaeber⁴ reads *Fore †fyhtum.* See Dobbie, pp. 140–41.

588, *healle:* Klaeber⁴ reads *helle.* See Mitchell and Robinson, p. 67.

600, *ond sǣndeþ:* Klaeber⁴ reads *ondsendeþ.* See Mitchell and Robinson, p. 68.

758, *mōdga:* conjecture Bliss. Klaeber⁴ reads *gōda.* See Klaeber⁴, p. 160.

1066: *healgamen:* Klaeber³, etc. Klaeber⁴ reads *Healgamen.*

1537, *feaxe:* conjecture Stanley. Klaeber⁴ reads *eaxle.* See Klaeber⁴, p. 207.

1932, *fremu:* Klaeber³, etc. Klaeber⁴ reads *Fremu.*

2001, *micel:* conjecture Klaeber³. Klaeber⁴ reads *mǣru.* See Kiernan.

2276, *hord on:* conjecture Zupitza. Klaeber⁴ reads *(hear)r(h on).*

2341, *lǣn:* Klaeber³, etc. Klaeber⁴ reads *(lī)þend.*

2791, *wætere sweorfan:* conjecture Rieger. Klaeber⁴ reads *wæteres weorpan.* See Bammesberger; Klaeber⁴, p. 256.

A Note on Pronunciation

The accent in Old English names always falls on the first syllable. Initial H before r and n is a strongly breathed sound. The combination *sc* has the value of *sh,* and the combination *cg* has the value of *dg* in "edge." The combination *kh* in the pronunciation column has the value of the sound of *ch* in the Scottish "loch."

In the following list of characters, place-names, and tribes, I have omitted names that are obviously pronounced as written (e.g., Grendel, Wulfgar).

Aelfhere	Alf'-heh-ruh
Aeschere	Ash'-heh-ruh
Beowulf	Bay'-o-wulf
Daeghrefn	Day'-hre-ven
Eadgils	Ay'-ad-gils *(hard* g)
Eanmund	Ay'-an-mund
Ecglaf	Edge'-lahf
Ecgtheow	Edge'-thay-oh
Eofor	Ay'-uh-vor
Eomer	Ay'-uh-mair
Eormanric	Ay'-uhr-mahn-rich
Fitela	Fit'-e-la

Freawaru	Fray'-uh-wah-roo
Geat	Geet *(hard g; in Old English this is pronounced* Yay-at*)*
Giftha	Yif'-thah
Guthlaf	Gooth'-lahf
Haereth	Ha'-reth
Haethcyn	Hath'-kin
Halga	Hahl'-gah
Handscioh	Hahnd'-shee-oh
Healfdene	Hahlf'-deh-nuh *(the* l *is pronounced)*
Heardred	Hay'-ar-dred
Heatholaf	Hay'-uh-thuh-lahf
Heathoream	Hay'-uh-thuh-ray-uhm
Hengest	Hen'-gest *(hard g)*
Heorogar	Hay'-ar-uh-gar
Heorot	Hair'-oht
Heoroweard	Hay'-uh-ruh-way-uhrd
Herebeald	Heh'-ruh-bay-uld
Heremod	Heh'-ruh-mode
Hetware	Het'-wah-ruh
Hildeburh	Hil'-duh-burkh
Hnaef	Hnaf
Hrethel	Hray'-thel
Hrethric	Hraith'-rich
Hrothmund	Hrothe'-mund
Hrothulf	Hrothe'-uhlf
Huga	Hoo'-gah
Hunlaf	Hoon'-lahf
Hygd	Heegd *(hard g)*
Hygelac	Hee'-yuh-lahk
Naegling	Nay'-ling
Ohthere	Okht'-heh-ruh

Onela	Oh'-neh-lah
Ongentheow	On'-gen-thay-oh *(hard* g*)*
Oslaf	Ohs'-lahf
Scefing	Shay'-ving
Scyld	Shield
Scylding	Shield'-ing
Sigemund	See'-uh-mund
Unferth	Oon'-fairth
Waegmunding	Way'-mund-ing
Wealhtheow	Way'-uhlkh-thay-oh
Weohstan	Way'-uhkh-stahn
Wiglaf	Wee'-lahf
Withergyld	With'-er-yild
Wonred	Wone'-rad
Wylfing	Will'-ving
Yrmenlaf	Ir'-men-lahf
Yrse	Ir'-suh

THE GEOGRAPHY OF *BEOWULF*

Heathoreams

Swedes

North Sea

Geats

Jutes

Baltic Sea

Danes

•Heorot

Angles

Gifthas

Vandals?

Heathobards

Wylfings?

Frisians

Weser

Elbe

Vistula

Ems

Hetware

Oder

Franks

Meuse

Rhine

0 Miles   100   200

0 Kilometers   200

© 2017 Jeffrey L. Ward

BEOWULF

Hwæt wē Gār-Dena   in ġeārdagum,
þēodcyninga   þrym ġefrūnon,
hū ðā æþelingas   ellen fremedon.
    Oft Scyld Scēfing   sceaþena þrēatum,
monegum mæġþum   meodosetla oftēah,
eġsode eorl[as],   syððan ǣrest wearð
fēasceaft funden.   Hē þæs frōfre ġebād:
wēox under wolcnum,   weorðmyndum þāh,
oð þæt him ǣġhwylċ   þāra ymbsittendra
10   ofer hronrāde   hȳran scolde,
gomban ġyldan.   Þæt wæs gōd cyning.
    Ðǣm eafera wæs   æfter cenned
ġeong in ġeardum,   þone God sende
folce tō frōfre;   fyrenðearfe onġeat—
þæt hīe ǣr drugon   aldor(l)ēase
lange hwīle.   Him þæs līffrea,
wuldres wealdend   woroldāre forġeaf:
Bēow wæs brēme   —blǣd wīde sprang—
Scyldes eafera   Scedelandum in.
20   Swā sceal ġe(ong) guma   gōde ġewyrċean,
fromum feohġiftum   on fæder (bea)rme,
þæt hine on ylde   eft ġewuniġen
wilġesīþas,   þonne wīġ cume,
lēode ġelǣsten;   lofdǣdum sceal
in mǣġþa ġehwǣre   man ġeþeon.
    Him ðā Scyld ġewāt   tō ġescæphwīle
felahrōr fēran   on frēan wǣre.
Hī hyne þā ætbǣron   tō brimes faroðe,
swǣse ġesīþas,   swā hē selfa bæd
30   þenden wordum wēold.   Wine Scyldinga,
lēof landfruma   lange āhte—
þǣr æt hȳðe stōd,   hrinġedstefna

OF THE STRENGTH OF THE SPEAR-DANES in days gone by
we have heard, and of their hero-kings:
the prodigious deeds those princes performed!
Often Scyld Scefing shattered the ranks
of hostile tribes and filled them with terror.
He began as a foundling but flourished later
and grew to glory beneath the sky,
until the countries on every coast
over the waves where the whales ride
yielded to him with yearly tribute   10
to keep the peace. He was a good king.

    Afterward he was granted an offspring;
God sent a son to console the people,
for He knew their anguish, how they ached
from lack of a leader. The Lord therefore
bestowed great honor on Beow, Scyld's son.
The fame of this man spread far and wide,
reaching throughout the northern realms.
Thus, to be powerful, a prince
should hand out gifts of his father's gold,   20
in order that someday, when enemies strike,
his friends and vassals will stand at his side.
Through praiseworthy deeds a young man prospers.

    Scyld went forth at the fated moment,
still strong, into the Lord's safekeeping.
His close companions carried him down
to the edge of the sea, as he had ordered
when in his long reign over the land
he had governed them as their great protector.
In the harbor the king's ship stood with curved prow,   30

īsiġ ond ūtfūs— æþelinges fær;
ālēdon þā   lēofne þēoden,
bēaga bryttan   on bearm scipes,
mǣrne be mǣste.   Þǣr wæs mādma fela
of feorwegum   frætwa ġelǣded.
Ne hȳrde iċ cȳmlicor   ċēol ġeġyrwan
hildewǣpnum   ond heaðowǣdum,
40   billum ond byrnum;   him on bearme læġ
mādma mæniġo,   þā him mid scoldon
on flōdes ǣht   feor ġewītan.
Nalæs hī hine lǣssan   lācum tēodan,
þēodġestrēonum,   þonne þā dydon
þē hine æt frumsceafte   forð onsendon
ǣnne ofer ȳðe   umborwesende.
Þā ġȳt hīe him āsetton   seġen gy(l)denne
hēah ofer hēafod,   lēton holm beran,
ġēafon on gārsecg;   him wæs ġeōmor sefa,
50   murnende mōd.   Men ne cunnon
secgan tō sōðe,   selerǣdende,
hæleð under heofenum,   hwā þǣm hlæste onfēng.
   Ðā wæs on burgum   Bēow Scyldinga,
lēof lēodcyning   longe þrāge
folcum ġefrǣġe   —fæder ellor hwearf,
aldor of earde—   oþ þæt him eft onwōc
hēah Healfdene;   hēold þenden lifde
gamol ond gūðrēouw   glæde Scyldingas.
   Ðǣm fēower bearn   forðġerīmed
60   in worold wōcun,   weoroda rǣswa[n],
Heorogār ond Hrōðgār   ond Hālga til;
hȳrde iċ þæt Ȳrse   wæs Onelan cwēn,
Heaðo-Scilfingas   healsġebedda.
   Þā wæs Hrōðgāre   herespēd ġyfen,

ice-laden and eager to sail.
They laid him down, their belovèd lord,
the giver of gold, on the ship's deck,
majestic beside the mast. Great wealth
was piled around him, from faraway places—
I have never heard of a ship so heavy
with warrior's gear and battle weapons,
chain-mail and swords; on his chest lay
massive treasures to travel with him
far out into the ocean's realm—   40
much more lavish now than the little
they bestowed on him when he was sent forth
alone, as a child, on the chill waves.
High up they placed a golden pennant,
then offered him to the encircling sea
with heavy hearts. No one can tell—
wise man or warrior—where that ship landed.

    Then Beow took over, and for a long time
he ruled the nation, greatly renowned,
admired by his men. To him was born   50
the large-hearted Healfdene, who all his life,
fearsome in war, defended his people.
He fathered four children into the world:
Heorogar, Hrothgar, Halga the Good,
and Yrse, who was Onela's queen,
the bedfellow of that battle-fierce Swede.
    Then Hrothgar too was granted such glory

wīġes weorðmynd,   þæt him his winemāgas
ġeorne hȳrdon,   oðð þæt sēo ġeogoð ġewēox,
magodriht miċel.   Him on mōd bearn
þæt healreċed   hātan wolde,
medoærn miċel   men ġewyrċean
70 þon[n]e yldo bearn   ǣfre ġefrūnon,
ond þǣr on innan   eall ġedǣlan
ġeongum ond ealdum   swylċ him God sealde,
būton folcscare   ond feorum gumena.
Ðā iċ wīde ġefræġn   weorc ġebannan
maniġre mǣġþe   ġeond þisne middanġeard,
folcstede frætwan.   Him on fyrste ġelomp,
ǣdre mid yldum,   þæt hit wearð eal ġearo,
healærna mǣst;   scōp him Heort naman
sē þe his wordes ġeweald   wīde hæfde.
80 Hē bēot ne ālēh: bēagas dǣlde,
sinċ æt symle.   Sele hlīfade
hēah ond hornġēap;   heaðowylma bād,
lāðan līġes—   ne wæs hit lenġe þā ġēn
þæt se ecghete   āþumswēoran
æfter wælnīðe   wæcnan scolde.
    Ðā se ellengǣst   earfoðlīċe
þrāge ġeþolode,   sē þe in þȳstrum bād,
þæt hē dōgora ġehwām   drēam ġehȳrde
hlūdne in healle.   Þǣr wæs hearpan swēġ,
90 swutol sang scopes.   Sæġde sē þe cūþe
frumsceaft fīra   feorran reċċan,
cwæð þæt se ælmihtiga   eorðan worh(te),
wlitebeorhtne wang,   swā wæter bebūgeð,
ġesette siġehrēþiġ   sunnan ond mōnan,
lēoman tō lēohte   landbūendum,
ond ġefrætwade   foldan sċēatas

6

and fortune in war that his friends and kinsmen
eagerly served him—strong young soldiers
who became a mighty army of men.   60
And then the ring-giver gave the order
to build a mighty mead-hall whose fame
would last forever while mortals lived,
and within that hall he would hand out
to young and old all that he had,
whatever God might grant him, except
for the common land and the lives of men.
Then, I have heard, all over the earth
the command was announced to many nations
that they should adorn it. And in due time—   70
quickly, as people count—it was finished,
the greatest of halls. He called it "Heorot,"
that king who ruled wide lands with his words.
And keeping his promise, he portioned out golden
bracelets and rings. The hall towered high
with wide-arched gables, awaiting the fire
that would devastate it; the days approached
when his son-in-law's hatred and sword-sharp rage
would flare up, rekindling a deadly feud.

THEN THE FIERCE DEMON who prowled in darkness   80
suffered torment: it tore at his heart
to hear rejoicing inside the hall,
the sound of the harp, and the bard singing
day after day for people's delight,
telling how humankind was created,
how the Almighty made the earth
a glistening plain girded by water
and in triumph set the sun and the moon
as lamps for earth-dwellers, adorned the world

leomum ond lēafum,   līf ēac ġesceōp
cynna ġehwylcum   þāra ðe cwice hwyrfaþ.
Swā ðā drihtguman   drēamum lifdon,
100   ēadiġlīċe,   oð ðæt ān ongan
fyrene fre(m)man   fēond on helle;
wæs se grimma gǣst   Grendel hāten,
mǣre mearcstapa,   sē þe mōras hēold,
fen ond fæsten;   fīfelcynnes eard
wonsǣlī wer   weardode hwīle,
siþðan him scyppen   forscrifen hæfde
in Cāines cynne—   þone cwealm ġewræc
ēċe drihten,   þæs þe hē Ābel slōg;
ne ġefeah hē þǣre fǣhðe,   ac hē hine feor forwræc,
110   metod for þȳ māne   mancynne fram.
Þanon untȳdras   ealle onwōcon,
eotenas ond ylfe   ond orcneas,
swylċe ġī(ga)ntas,   þā wið Gode wunnon
lange þrāge;   hē him ðæs lēan forġeald.

Ġewāt ða nēosian,   syþðan niht becōm,
hean hūses,   hū hit Hring-Dene
æfter bēorþeġe   ġebūn hæfdon.
Fand þā ðǣr inne   æþelinga ġedriht
swefan æfter symble;   sorge ne cūðon,
120   wonsceaft wera.   Wiht unhǣlo,
grim ond grǣdiġ,   ġearo sōna wæs,
rēoc ond rēþe,   ond on ræste ġenam
þrītiġ þeġna;   þanon eft ġewāt
hūðe hrēmiġ   tō hām faran,
mid þǣre wælfylle   wīca nēosan.
Ðā wæs on ūhtan   mid ǣrdæġe
Grendles gūðcræft   gumum undyrne;

8

with branches and leaves, and then gave life   90
to every being under the sky.

    The warriors lived in joy and laughter
until one creature unleashed his crimes.
"Grendel" they called that grim spirit,
a hellish fiend who haunted the wasteland,
unhappy soul, and stalked the fens.
He had lived long in the land of monsters,
condemned by the Lord with all Cain's clan
in revenge for the vicious murder of Abel.
Cain had no joy of that crime; the Creator   100
banished the brute far from mankind.
From him sprang many evil spirits,
ogres, elves, and the savage undead,
giants as well, who warred against God
until He killed them and all their kin.

    Grendel went forth when darkness had fallen
to see how the Ring-Danes in the high hall
had bedded down when their beer-feast was done.
He found the noblemen on the floor
sound asleep, knowing no sadness   110
or human pain. That God-cursed creature
hurried over and horribly grabbed
thirty thanes; then he strode back
gloating, glutted with blood and slaughter,
dragging the dead to his dank lair.

    In the dim light just before daybreak,
his violence was revealed to men.

þā wæs æfter wiste   wōp up āhafen,
miċel morgenswēġ.   Mǣre þēoden,
130   æþeling ǣrgōd,   unblīðe sæt,
þolode ðrȳðswȳð,   þeġnsorge drēah,
syðþan hīe þæs lāðan   lāst scēawedon,
werġan gāstes;   wæs þæt ġewin tō strang,
lāð ond longsum.   Næs hit lengra fyrst,
ac ymb āne niht   eft ġefremede
morðbeala māre,   ond nō mearn fore,
fǣhðe ond fyrene;   wæs tō fæst on þām.
Þā wæs ēaðfynde   þē him elles hwǣr
ġerūmlicor   ræste [sōhte],
140   bed æfter būrum,   ðā him ġebēacnod wæs,
ġesæġd sōðlīċe   sweotolan tācne
healðeġnes hete;   hēold hyne syðþan
fyr ond fæstor   sē þǣm fēonde ætwand.
Swā rīxode   ond wið rihte wan,
āna wið eallum,   oð þæt īdel stōd
hūsa sēlest.   Wæs sēo hwīl miċel:
twelf wintra tīd   torn ġeþolode
wine Scyldinga,   wēana ġehwelcne,
sīdra sorga.   Forðām sōna wearð
150   ylda bearnum,   undyrne cūð
ġyddum ġeōmore   þætte Grendel wan
hwīle wið Hrōþgār,   hetenīðas wæġ,
fyrene ond fǣhðe   fela missera,
singāle sæce;   sibbe ne wolde
wið manna hwone   mæġenes Deniġa,
feorhbealo feorran,   fēa þingian,

Lamentation arose, loud wailing,
cries of horror. The king of the Danes
sat there stunned, stricken with grief,   120
overwhelmed by the loss of his liegemen,
with a blank stare at the bloody footprints
of that ghastly fiend—a hardship too great
for a man to endure. On the next day,
at nightfall, the monster returned, remorseless;
again he committed a savage slaughter,
without a grain of guilt for his crimes.
Afterward many went to sleep elsewhere,
out in the huts, when the bitter hatred
of the vicious hall-raider was fully revealed.   130
Whoever could escape from his clutches
kept far away from Hrothgar's hall.

So Grendel ruled and fought what was right,
one against all, till that tall house
stood there empty. It stayed deserted
for twelve long winters, while the Danes' lord
suffered from inconsolable grief,
an anguish beyond all human endurance.
The news soon spread to neighboring lands;
bards sang songs that were filled with sorrow,   140
telling of Grendel's gruesome acts,
how that dark spirit, malice-driven,
had fought against Hrothgar with cruel fury
and ravaged the kingdom, committing crimes
unmatched in ghastliness, drenched with gore,
not wishing peace with any person
in the Danish host, nor wanting to halt
his butchery or make blood-payment.

nē þǣr nǣniġ witena   wēnan þorfte
beorhtre bōte   tō banan folmum,
(ac se) ǣġlǣċa   ēhtende wæs,
160   deorc dēaþscua,   duguþe ond ġeogoþe,
seomade ond syrede;   sinnihte hēold,
mistiġe mōras;   men ne cunnon
hwyder helrūnan   hwyrftum scrīþað.
Swā fela fyrena   fēond mancynnes,
atol āngenġea   oft ġefremede,
heardra hȳnða;   Heorot eardode,
sinċfāge sel   sweartum nihtum.
Nō hē þone ġifstōl   grētan mōste,
māþðum for metode,   nē his myne wisse.
170   Þæt wæs wræc miċel   wine Scyldinga,
mōdes brecða.   Moniġ oft ġesæt,
rīċe tō rūne;   rǣd eahtedon,
hwæt swīðferhðum   sēlest wǣre
wið fǣrgryrum   tō ġefremmanne.
Hwīlum hīe ġehēton   æt hærgtrafum
wīġweorþunga,   wordum bǣdon
þæt him gāstbona   ġēoce ġefremede
wið þēodþrēaum.   Swylċ wæs þēaw hyra,
hǣþenra hyht;   helle ġemundon
180   in mōdsefan,   metod hīe ne cūþon,
dǣda dēmend,   ne wiston hīe drihten God,
nē hīe hūru heofena helm   herian ne cūþon,
wuldres waldend.   Wā bið þǣm ðe sceal
þurh slīðne nīð   sāwle bescūfan
in fȳres fæþm,   frōfre ne wēnan,
wihte ġewendan;   wēl bið þǣm þe mōt
æfter dēaðdæġe   drihten sēċean
ond tō fæder fæþmum   freoðo wilnian.

No counselor had cause to expect
a man-price from that murderer's hands;   150
the monster kept up his crimes, devouring
young and old, a dark death-shadow
slinking through the mists of the moorland
in the long nights. Men cannot know
where hell's servants hover and roam.
   So Grendel continued his vile attacks,
stalking the fens alone, inflicting
hideous pain on all the people.
He took over Heorot's jewel-rich hall
and camped there during the hours of darkness   160
(because he was cast out from God's love
he could not approach the precious throne).
This caused the king of the Danes great torment
and heart-heaviness. Many wise men
worried over what should be done
to save the land from these savage onslaughts.
Some of them even prayed to idols,
made pagan sacrifices, and pledged
themselves to the Slayer of Souls, to gain
help from this horror. That was the thing   170
those heathens hoped for; deep in their hearts
they served the devil. They did not know
God Almighty, the Judge of Men,
and could not give praise to the Prince of Heaven,
the King of the World. Woe unto him
who in times of turmoil has thrust his soul
into the fire's embrace, not begging
for heaven's mercy. But blessed is he
who after his death-day goes to God
and finds peace in the Father's bosom.   180

Swā ðā mǣlċeare   maga Healfdenes
190 singāla sēað;   ne mihte snotor hæleð
wēan onwendan;   wæs þæt ġewin tō swȳð,
lāþ ond longsum,   þē on ðā lēode becōm,
nȳdwracu nīþgrim,   nihtbealwa mǣst.
Þæt fram hām ġefræġn   Hiġelāces þeġn
gōd mid Ġēatum,   Grendles dǣda;
sē wæs moncynnes   mæġenes strenġest
on þǣm dæġe   þysses līfes,
æþele ond ēacen.   Hēt him ȳðlidan
gōdne ġeġyrwan;   cwæð, hē gūðcyning
200 ofer swanrāde   sēċean wolde,
mǣrne þēoden,   þā him wæs manna þearf.
Ðone sīðfæt him   snotere ċeorlas
lȳthwōn lōgon,   þēah hē him lēof wǣre;
hwetton hiġe(r)ōfne,   hǣl scēawedon.
Hæfde se gōda   Ġēata lēoda
cempan ġecorone,   þāra þe hē cēnoste
findan mihte.   Fīftȳna sum
sundwudu sōhte;   secg wīsade,
lagucræftiġ mon   landġemyrċu.
210 Fyrst forð ġewāt;   flota wæs on ȳðum,
bāt under beorge.   Beornas ġearwe
on stefn stigon.   Strēamas wundon,
sund wið sande.   Secgas bǣron
on bearm nacan   beorhte frætwe,
gūðsearo ġeatoliċ;   guman ūt scufon,
weras on wilsīð   wudu bundenne.
Ġewāt þā ofer wǣġholm   winde ġefȳsed
flota fāmīheals   fugle ġelīcost,
oð þæt ymb āntīd   ōþres dōgores
220 wundenstefna   ġewaden hæfde,

14

The son of Healfdene ceaselessly brooded
over his cares, nor was that king
able to ward off anguish; too deep
was the pain endured by his people, an endless
terror caused by the foul night-fiend.

FAR OFF IN HIS HOMELAND, Hygelac's thane,
the Geats' champion, heard about Grendel.
He was the mightiest man of that age,
tall, brave, and noble in bearing.
He told his men to make a ship ready;   190
over the sea where the swans ride
he would fight on behalf of that harried king.
The councilmen approved of the plan;
they were well aware of its danger, but when
they inspected the omens, they urged him on.
The great man chose fourteen of the Geats,
the boldest fighters that he could find,
and then that commander skilled in seaways
marched his valiant men to the shore.
    Time moved quickly. The ship was moored   200
under the cliffs; the warriors, eager,
climbed aboard it, the surf crashed
onto the sand, the men stowed
weapons and war-gear, then shoved off
with oars out into the open sea.
Over the waves, with the wind in her sails
and her prow in foam, she flew like a bird
till in due time on the second day

þæt ðā līðende   land ġesāwon,
brimclifu blīcan,   beorgas stēape,
sīde sænæssas;   þā wæs sund liden,
eoletes æt ende.   Þanon up hraðe
Wedera lēode   on wang stigon,
sæwudu sældon,   syrċan hrysedon,
gūðġewædo;   Gode þancedon
þæs þe him ȳþlāde   ēaðe wurdon.

    Þā of wealle ġeseah   weard Scildinga,
230   sē þe holmclifu   healdan scolde,
beran ofer bolcan   beorhte randas,
fyrdsearu fūslicu;   hine fyrwyt bræc
mōdġehyġdum   hwæt þā men wæron.
Ġewāt him þā tō waroðe   wicge rīdan
þeġn Hrōðgāres,   þrymmum cwehte
mæġenwudu mundum,   meþelwordum fræġn:
'Hwæt syndon ġē   searohæbbendra,
byrnum werede,   þē þus brontne ċēol
ofer lagustræte   lædan cwōmon,
240   hider ofer holmas?   [Iċ hwī]le wæs
endesæta,   æġwearde hēold,
þē on land Dena   lāðra næniġ
mid scipherġe   sceðþan ne meahte.
Nō hēr cūðlicor   cuman ongunnon
lindhæbbende,   nē ġē lēafnesword
gūðfremmendra   ġearwe ne wisson,
māga ġemēdu.   Næfre iċ māran ġeseah
eorla ofer eorþan   ðonne is ēower sum,
secg on searwum;   nis þæt seldguma,
250   wæpnum ġeweorðad,   næfne him his wlite lēoge,
ænliċ ansȳn.   Nū iċ ēower sceal
frumcyn witan,   ær ġē fyr heonan

the bold seafarers sighted land:
shimmering cliffs, sheer crags,   210
and jutting headlands. The journey was done.
Lightly they leaped out onto the shore
and secured the ship with a strong cable.
Then they shook out their heavy mail-shirts
and battle-gear, and gave thanks to God
for the smooth crossing on a calm sea.

FROM THE HIGH SHORE the Scyldings' lookout,
whose duty it was to watch the coast,
saw them unload their sparkling weapons
over the gangway. Anxiety gripped   220
his heart, as he wondered who they might be.
So Hrothgar's watchman mounted his horse,
and riding down to the beach, he brandished
his mighty spear-shaft and spoke this challenge:
"Who are you, strangers, who come here armed,
sailing your tall ship over the sea-roads?
I have long kept my watch at land's-end
so that no raiders who reach our shore
should pillage and plunder the Danish homeland.
Never have armed men come to this coast   230
so impudently, without a password
or the permission of king and court.
Nor have I seen a mightier man
on this wide earth than one of you is;
he must be not just a simple soldier
wielding a nobleman's weapons, unless
his princely look and manner are lies.
But before I permit you to move along
I must learn your lineage and your intent.

lēasscēaweras   on land Dena
furþur fēran.   Nū ġē feorbūend,
merelīðende,   mīn[n]e ġehȳrað
ānfealdne ġeþōht: ofost is sēlest
tō ġecȳðanne   hwanan ēowre cyme syndon.'

Him se yldesta   andswarode,
werodes wīsa,   wordhord onlēac:
'Wē synt gumcynnes   Ġēata lēode
ond Hiġelāces   heorðġenēatas.
Wæs mīn fæder   folcum ġecȳþed,
æþele ordfruma,   Ecgþēow hāten;
ġebād wintra worn,   ǣr hē on weġ hwurfe,
gamol of ġeardum;   hine ġearwe ġeman
witena wēlhwylċ   wīde ġeond eorþan.
Wē þurh holdne hiġe   hlāford þīnne,
sunu Healfdenes   sēċean cwōmon,
lēodġebyrġean.   Wes þū ūs lārena gōd.
Habbað wē tō þǣm mǣran   miċel ǣrende
Deniġa frean.   Ne sceal þǣr dyrne sum
wesan, þæs iċ wēne: þū wāst, ġif hit is
swā wē sōþlīċe   secgan hȳrdon,
þæt mid Scyldingum   sceaðona iċ nāt hwylċ,
dēogol dǣdhata   deorcum nihtum
ēaweð þurh eġsan   uncūðne nīð,
hȳnðu ond hrāfyl.   Iċ þæs Hrōðgār mæġ
þurh rūmne sefan   rǣd ġelǣran
hū hē frōd ond gōd   fēond oferswȳðeþ—
ġyf him edwenden   ǣfre scolde
bealuwa bisigu,   bōt eft cuman—
ond þā ċearwylmas   cōlran wurðaþ;
oððe ā syþðan   earfoðþrāge,

260

270

280

You may be spies. Quickly now, state   240
why you have sailed here across the sea.
The sooner you tell me the truth, the better."
    The warrior then unlocked his word-hoard:
"We are all Geats by birth and breeding,
hearth-companions of Hygelac.
My father was famous far and wide,
the bravest man in the battle lines.
His name was Ecgtheow; after many
winters he took his leave from the world.
Everywhere men remember his deeds   250
and think kindly of him. We come in good faith,
with loyal intentions, to see your lord,
Hrothgar, the Danes' fearless defender.
Trust us now. We will try to help you;
we have come to fight for your noble king.
There is no mystery to our mission;
we can answer any questions you ask.
So tell us if what we have heard is true:
that some deadly thing is slaughtering Danes,
a hidden hater in the dark night   260
who brings you terror, a brute's rage,
and sudden death. I am here to save you.
I will offer all my strength to your king;
I will conquer this cruel fiend for him
and assuage the heartache that burns in his breast—
if any man can ever assuage it.
Otherwise he will suffer untold

þrēanȳd þolað   þenden þǣr wunað
on hēahstede   hūsa sēlest.'
　　Weard maþelode   ðǣr on wicge sæt,
ombeht unforht: 'Ǣġhwæþres sceal
scearp scyldwiga   ġescād witan,
worda ond worca,   sē þe wēl þenċeð.
290　Iċ þæt ġehȳre,   þæt þis is hold weorod
frēan Scyldinga.   Ġewītaþ forð beran
wǣpen ond ġewǣdu;   iċ ēow wīsiġe.
Swylċe iċ maguþeġnas   mīne hāte
wið fēonda ġehwone   flotan ēowerne,
nīwtyrwydne   nacan on sande
ārum healdan,   oþ ðæt eft byreð
ofer lagustrēamas   lēofne mannan
wudu wundenhals   tō Wedermearce,
gōdfremmendra   swylcum ġifeþe bið
300　þæt þone hilderǣs   hāl ġedīġeð.'
　　Ġewiton him þā fēran;   flota stille bād,
seomode on sāle   sīdfæþmed scip,
on ancre fæst;   eoforlīċ scionon
ofer hlēorber[g]an   ġehroden golde,
fāh ond fȳrheard;   ferhwearde hēold
gūþmōd grīmmon.   Guman ōnetton,
sigon ætsomne,   oþ þæt hȳ [s]æl timbred
ġeatoliċ ond goldfāh   onġyton mihton;
þæt wæs foremǣrost   foldbūendum
310　reċeda under roderum,   on þǣm se rīċa bād;
līxte se lēoma   ofer landa fela.
Him þā hildedēor   [h]of mōdiġra
torht ġetǣhte,   þæt hīe him tō mihton
ġeġnum gangan;   gūðbeorna sum
wicg ġewende,   word æfter cwæð:

anguish of spirit, ceaseless torment,
for as long as Heorot remains on its heights."

    Astride his horse, the officer answered, 270
"A clear-minded questioner always knows
when a man's words and deeds are one.
I believe what you told me: that your troop
is loyal to the lord of the Scyldings.
So I will permit you to move along
with your weapons and war-gear. I will lead you,
and also I will tell my retainers
to stand on the shore and guard your ship,
keeping her safe until the time comes
for her to sail home over the sea-roads, 280
bearing the warrior back to his land.
A man so noble will never fail
to return unharmed from the harshest battle."

    So they all left, while the ship lay there
riding its mooring-rope close to shore.
Boar-figures glittered above their cheek-guards,
inlaid intricately with gold,
fire-hardened, on the fierce war-masks
that guarded their lives. The company quickly
strode on together until they saw 290
the hall where the king lived, with its high timbers,
the noblest house under the heavens;
its golden light shone through the land.
Then the guard who had guided them there
pointed them toward that bright building,
wheeled on his horse, and spoke these words:

'Mæl is mē tō fēran;   fæder alwalda
mid ārstafum   ēowiċ ġehealde
sīða ġesunde.   Iċ tō sǣ wille,
wið wrāð werod   wearde healdan.'

320   Strǣt wæs stānfāh,   stīġ wīsode
gumum ætgædere.   Gūðbyrne scān
heard hondlocen;   hrinġīren scīr
song in searwum.   Þā hīe tō sele furðum
in hyra gryreġeatwum   gangan cwōmon,
setton sǣmēþe   sīde scyldas,
rondas reġnhearde   wið þæs reċedes weal;
bugon þā tō benċe.   Byrnan hringdon,
gūðsearo gumena;   gāras stōdon,
sǣmanna searo   samod ætgædere,
330   æscholt ufan grǣġ;   wæs se īrenþrēat
wǣpnum ġewurþad.
                                Þā ðǣr wlonc hæleð
ōretmecgas   æfter æþelum frǣġn:
'Hwanon feriġeað ġē   fǣtte scyldas,
grǣġe syrċan,   ond grīmhelmas,
heresceafta hēap?   Iċ eom Hrōðgāres
ār ond ombiht.   Ne seah iċ elþēodiġe
þus maniġe men   mōdiġlīcran.
Wēn' iċ þæt ġē for wlenċo,   nalles for wræcsīðum
ac for hiġeþrymmum,   Hrōðgār sōhton.'
340   Hīm þā ellenrōf   andswarode,
wlanc Wedera lēod,   word æfter spræc
heard under helme: 'Wē synt Hiġelāces
bēodġenēatas;   Bēowulf is mīn nama.
Wille iċ āsecgan   sunu Healfdenes,
mǣrum þēodne   mīn ǣrende,

"I must go now, friends. May the Father Almighty
grant you His grace in your bold venture.
I am going back to the beach at land's-end
to take up my guard against sea-raiders."   300

THE ROAD WAS STONE-PAVED, and its straight path
led the men to the hall. Their mail-shirts
gleamed in the sunlight, solid, hand-linked,
and the rings rattled. As they marched in
through the door in their dreadful armor,
the sea-weary voyagers stacked their shields
of metal-hard wood against the wall
and sat down on benches, their bright mail clanging.
Spears stood upright with their steel points,
a grove of gray ash-trees; those Geatish men   310
were powerfully armed. A proud retainer,
Wulfgar by name, spoke these words:
"Where have you come from, carrying shields
rounded with gold, an array of spears,
iron-gray mail-shirts, and thick mask-helmets?
I, Hrothgar's herald and spokesman,
never have seen a troop of strangers
bolder in bearing. It must be courage,
not exile from home, that has brought you here
to the golden mead-hall of our great king."   320
     To him the gallant prince of the Geats,
that brave warrior, spoke these words,
stern in his helmet: "We are Hygelac's
bench-friends. Beowulf is my name.
I wish to make known my mission here
to the son of Healfdene, the hero-king,

aldre þīnum,   ġif hē ūs ġeunnan wile
þæt wē hine swā gōdne   grētan mōton.'
Wulfgār maþelode;   þæt wæs Wendla lēod;
wæs his mōdsefa   manegum ġecȳðed,
350   wīġ ond wīsdōm: 'Iċ þæs wine Deniġa,
frēan Scildinga   frīnan wille,
bēaga bryttan,   swā þū bēna eart,
þēoden mǣrne   ymb þīnne sīð,
ond þē þā andsware   ǣdre ġecȳðan
ðē mē se gōda   āġifan þenċeð.'
   Hwearf þā hrædlīċe   þǣr Hrōðgār sæt
eald ond anhār   mid his eorla ġedriht;
ēode ellenrōf,   þæt hē for eaxlum ġestōd
Deniġa frean;   cūþe hē duguðe þēaw.
360   Wulfgār maðelode   tō his winedrihtne:
'Hēr syndon ġeferede,   feorran cumene
ofer ġeofenes begang   Ġēata lēode;
þone yldestan   ōretmecgas
Bēowulf nemnað.   Hȳ bēnan synt
þæt hīe, þēoden mīn,   wið þē mōton
wordum wrixlan.   Nō ðū him wearne ġetēoh
ðīnra ġeġncwida,   glædman Hrōðgār.
Hȳ on wīġġetawum   wyrðe þinċeað
eorla ġeæhtlan;   hūru se aldor dēah,
370   sē þǣm heaðorincum   hider wīsade.

   Hrōðgār maþelode,   helm Scyldinga:
'Iċ hine cūðe   cnihtwesende;
wæs his ealdfæder   Ecgþēo hāten,
ðǣm tō hām forġeaf   Hrēþel Ġēata
āngan dohtor;   is his eafora nū
heard hēr cumen,   sōhte holdne wine.

your gracious lord, if it please him to grant
that we may approach his royal presence."
    Wulfgar answered (he was a Wendel;
his noble spirit was known to many,   330
and his valor and wisdom): "The wish you made
I will deliver to our dear lord,
the Scyldings' ruler, our giver of rings.
I will tell him that your troop has arrived,
and I will come back, bringing such answer
as he in his goodness sees fit to give."
    Swiftly he strode to where Hrothgar sat,
old, white-bearded, his best men around him,
and in front of the famous king he waited,
knowing the customs of courtly men.   340
After some time he spoke to his lord:
"From the other side of the vast sea
some loyal Geats have sailed to our land.
Their chief is named Beowulf, and they beg
an audience to state their errand.
Do not refuse to speak with them, Sire.
From their weapons and gear, they seem most worthy,
and it is clear that their noble captain
is of great mettle, a leader of men."
    Then Hrothgar, the Scyldings' sovereign, spoke: 350
"I knew this Beowulf in his boyhood.
Ecgtheow was his honored father,
to whom King Hrethel granted the hand
of his only daughter. Now Ecgtheow's son
is paying a call on a proven friend.

Ðonne sæġdon þæt   sǣlīþende,
þā ðe ġifsceattas   Ġēata fyredon
þyder tō þance,   þæt hē þrītiġes
manna mæġencræft   on his mundgripe

380 heaþorōf hæbbe.   Hine hāliġ God
for ārstafum   ūs onsende,
tō West-Denum,   þæs iċ wēn hæbbe,
wið Grendles gryre.   Iċ þǣm gōdan sceal
for his mōdþræce   māðmas bēodan.
Bēo ðū on ofeste,   hāt in gan
sēon sibbeġedriht   samod ætgædere;
ġesaga him ēac wordum,   þæt hīe sint wilcuman
Deniġa lēodum.'   Þā tō dura healle

390 Wulfgār ēode   word inne ābēad:
'Ēow hēt secgan   siġedrihten mīn,
aldor Ēast-Dena,   þæt hē ēower æþelu can,
ond ġē him syndon   ofer sǣwylmas
heardhicgende   hider wilcuman.
Nū ġē mōton gangan   in ēowrum gūðġetawum
under heregrīman   Hrōðgār ġesēon;
lǣtað hildebord   hēr onbīdan,
wudu wælsceaftas   worda ġeþinġes.'
    Ārās þā se rīċa,   ymb hine rinċ maniġ,

400 þrȳðliċ þeġna hēap;   sume þǣr bidon,
heaðorēaf hēoldon,   swā him se hearda bebēad.
Snyredon ætsomne,   þā secg wīsode,
under Heorotes hrōf;   [ēode hildedēor]
hear(d) under helme,   þæt hē on heo[r]ðe ġestōd.
Bēowulf maðelode;   on him byrne scān,
searonet seowed   smiþes orþancum:
'Wæs þū, Hrōðgār, hāl!   Iċ eom Hiġelāces
mǣġ ond magoðeġn;   hæbbe iċ mǣrða fela

Also, seamen who carried splendid
treasure chests as gifts to the Geats,
in token of our respect, have told me
that Beowulf has become a hero,
with the might of thirty men in each hand.   360
God in His grace has surely sent him
to rescue us now from Grendel's rage.
I will offer him some excellent gifts
to reward his courage in coming here.
Hurry, summon these men to the hall
to meet my noble retainers. Tell them
that they will be greeted as welcome guests."

  Then Wulfgar stood inside the hall's door
and, speaking to Beowulf, said these words:
"My dread lord Hrothgar, king of the Danes,   370
says that he knows your noble descent,
that you and your worthy men are welcome,
who have sailed so bravely across the sea.
You may come close now, clad in your armor,
wearing your helmets, to look upon Hrothgar;
but leave your shields and your deadly shafts
in place, until his pleasure is known."

  The prince arose, and his warriors with him.
Some of them stayed to guard the war-gear
as he had commanded. Quickly they marched   380
through Heorot with the hero leading,
stern in his helmet, until he stood
upon the hearth, close to the king,
then greeted him; his mail-shirt glistened,
the ring-net sewn by the smiths' art.
"Good health to you, Hrothgar! I am a thane
and kinsman of Hygelac. I have accomplished

ongunnen on ġeogoþe.   Mē wearð Grendles þinġ
410 on mīnre ēþeltyrf   undyrne cūð;
secgað sǣliðend   þæt þæs sele stande,
reċed sēlesta   rinca ġehwylcum
īdel ond unnyt,   siðð̄an ǣfenlēoht
under heofenes haðor   beholen weorþeð.
Þā mē þæt ġelǣrdon   lēode mīne
þā sēlestan,   snotere ċeorlas,
þēoden Hrōðgār,   þæt iċ þē sōhte,
forþan hīe mæġenes cræft   mīn[n]e cūþon;
selfe ofersāwon   ðā iċ of searwum cwōm
420 fāh from fēondum,   þǣr iċ fīfel ġeband,
ȳðde eotena cyn,   ond on ȳðum slōg
niceras nihtes,   nearoþearfe drēah,
wræc Wedera nīð   —wēan āhsodon—
forgrand gramum;   ond nū wið Grendel sceal,
wið þām āglǣċan   āna ġehēġan
ðinġ wið þyrse.   Iċ þē nūða,
brego Beorht-Dena,   biddan wille,
eodor Scyldinga,   ānre bēne,
þæt ðū mē ne forwyrne,   wīġendra hlēo,
430 frēowine folca,   nū iċ þus feorran cōm,
þæt iċ mōte āna,   mīnra eorla ġedryht,
ond þes hearda hēap   Heorot fǣlsian.
Hæbbe iċ ēac ġeāhsod   þæt se ǣġlǣċa
for his wonhȳdum   wǣpna ne reċċeð;
iċ þæt þonne forhicge,   swā mē Hiġelāc sīe,
mīn mondrihten   mōdes blīðe,
þæt iċ sweord bere   oþðe sīdne scyld,
ġeolorand tō gūþe,   ac iċ mid grāpe sceal
fōn wið fēonde   ond ymb feorh sacan,
440 lāð wið lāþum;   ðǣr ġelȳfan sceal

great things, though I am young in years.
Rumors of Grendel have reached my land;
seafarers say that this noble hall,   390
the finest building on earth, stands empty,
useless to you and to your people
when daylight fades beneath heaven's dome.
Our worthiest men, the wisest among us,
counseled me to go to your court
and offer my service, honored king.
They know my strength; they have all seen it
tested in combat when I came back
blood-stained after I beat down trolls,
flushed out and finished off one of their clans,   400
and later that night I slew sea-monsters.
I have borne much pain to avenge our people
on heartless foes who did us great harm.
Now I will go face Grendel alone
and pay him back for his brutal crimes.
Therefore, lord of the Scyldings, allow me
this one request—since I have come
from so far away, do not refuse me:
to rid your radiant house of this evil
without the help of my own men.   410
I have been told that your attacker
in his wild recklessness scorns all weapons.
Therefore, to gladden Hygelac's heart,
I too renounce weapons and war-gear;
I will not proceed with sword or shield
into the battle, but with bare hands
I will face the monster and fight him here.
Whomever death takes will have to trust

dryhtnes dōme   sē þe hine dēað nimeð.
Wēn' iċ þæt hē wille,   ġif hē wealdan mōt,
in þǣm gūðsele   Ġēatena lēode
etan unforhte,   swā hē oft dyde
mæġenhrēð manna.   Nā þū mīnne þearft
hafalan hȳdan,   ac hē mē habban wile
d[r]ēore fāhne,   ġif meċ dēað nimeð:
byreð blōdiġ wæl,   byrġean þenċeð,
eteð āngenġa   unmurnlīċe,
450   mearcað mōrhopu—   nō ðū ymb mīnes ne þearft
līċes feorme   lenġ sorgian.
Onsend Hiġelāce,   ġif meċ hild nime,
beaduscrūda betst   þæt mīne brēost wereð,
hræġla sēlest;   þæt is Hrǣdlan lāf,
Wēlandes ġeweorc.   Gǣð ā wyrd swā hīo scel.'
     Hrōðgār maþelode,   helm Scyldinga:
'For gewyrhtum þū,   wine mīn Bēowulf,
ond for ārstafum   ūsiċ sōhtest.
Ġeslōh þīn fæder   fǣhðe mǣste;
460   wearþ hē Heaþolāfe   tō handbonan
mid Wilfingum;   ðā hine Wedera cyn
for herebrōgan   habban ne mihte.
Þanon hē ġesōhte   Sūð-Dena folc
ofer ȳða ġewealc,   Ār-Scyldinga;
ðā iċ furþum wēold   folce Deniġa
ond on ġeogoðe hēold   ġinne rīċe,
hordburh hæleþa,   ðā wæs Heregār dēad,
mīn yldra mǣġ   unlifiġende,
bearn Healfdenes;   sē wæs betera ðonne iċ!
470   Siððan þā fǣhðe   fēo þingode:
sende iċ Wylfingum   ofer wæteres hrycg
ealde mādmas;   hē mē āþas swōr.

30

that it is God's judgment. If Grendel wins,
this hall will be steeped in blood and horror,   420
corpses will cover the floor, and that ghoul
will gorge on the flesh of my Geatish men.
You will not need to bury my body;
the beast will devour it, bones and all;
he will drag my bloody corpse to his den
and gnaw on my face. No need to bother
about providing me burial rites.
But if I am slain, send Hygelac
this splendid mail-shirt that shields my heart;
the best of my war-gear, forged by Wayland—   430
Hrethel's gift. Fate moves as it must."
    Then Hrothgar, the Scyldings' sovereign, spoke:
"Beowulf, it must be because
of the favors I did for your father once
that you wish to help us. He, when he killed
the Wylfings' great warrior Heatholaf,
single-handed, set off a feud.
The Geats refused to grant him asylum—
they feared a war—so he fled from his home
and sailed over the surging waves   440
to seek asylum with us, when first
I began to rule this glorious land,
this stronghold of heroes. Heorogar
had died, my elder brother, a better
man than I was. I ended that feud
by sending blood-gold across the sea
to the Wylfings. Then Ecgtheow swore me an oath.

Sorh is mē tō secganne   on sefan mīnum
gumena ǣngum   hwæt mē Grendel hafað
hȳnðo on Heorote   mid his heteþancum,
fǣrnīða ġefremed;   is mīn fletwerod,
wīġhēap ġewanod;   hīe wyrd forswēop
on Grendles gryre.   God ēaþe mæġ
þone dolscaðan   dǣda ġetwǣfan!
480   Ful oft ġebēotedon   bēore druncne
ofer ealowǣġe   ōretmecgas
þæt hīe in bēorsele   bīdan woldon
Grendles gūþe   mid gryrum ecga.
Ðonne wæs þēos medoheal   on morgentīd,
drihtsele drēorfāh   þonne dæġ līxte,
eal benċþelu   blōde bestȳmed,
heall heorudrēore;   āhte iċ holdra þȳ lǣs,
dēorre duguðe,   þē þā dēað fornam.
Site nū tō symle   ond onsǣl meoto,
490   siġehrēð secgum,   swā þīn sefa hwette.'
    Þā wæs Ġēatmæcgum   ġeador ætsomne
on bēorsele   benċ ġerȳmed;
þǣr swīðferhþe   sittan ēodon,
þrȳðum dealle.   Þeġn nytte behēold,
sē þe on handa bær   hroden ealowǣġe,
scencte scīr wered.   Scop hwīlum sang
hādor on Heorote.   Þǣr wæs hæleða drēam,
duguð unlȳtel   Dena ond Wedera.

    Ūnferð maþelode,   Ecglāfes bearn,
500   þē æt fōtum sæt   frēan Scyldinga,
onband beadurūne.   Wæs him Bēowulfes sīð,
mōdġes merefaran,   miċel æfþunca,
forþon þe hē ne ūþe   þæt ǣniġ ōðer man

My heart is heavy with grief when I tell
any man of these dreadful onslaughts,
the shame and horror that Grendel has heaped   450
upon me here, the unending pain
that his cruelty and malice have caused.
In the last years I have lost so many
whom fate swept into Grendel's grasp.
Only God would be able to stop
this hideous slaughter. Time after time
my best men, when they were flushed with beer
at the banquet table, vowed to take on
Grendel's rage with a rush of their swords.
But at dawn the hall would be drenched in gore,   460
the benches smashed, dripping with blood,
the floor awash in it, warriors mangled —
battle-scarred soldiers dear to my heart.
But sit on this bench now and join our banquet.
Afterward, if your mind should still urge you,
you can focus upon the coming fight."

  A place was cleared for the Geatish cohort,
and the stout-hearted warriors took their seats.
A steward approached and from golden pitchers
he served the mead. The song of the bard   470
rang through the ranks. Joy and laughter
brightened the banquet of Geats and Danes.

THEN UNFERTH, THE SON of Ecglaf, spoke,
who sat at the feet of the Danes' defender.
He unbound a buried thought in his breast.
Beowulf's venture vexed him sorely;
he would never allow that another man

æfre mærða þon mā   middanġeardes
ġehēdde under heofenum   þonne hē sylfa:
'Eart þū se Bēowulf,   sē þe wið Brecan wunne
on sīdne sǣ,   ymb sund flite,
ðǣr ġit for wlenċe   wada cunnedon
ond for dolġilpe   on dēop wæter
510   aldrum nēþdon?   Nā inċ æniġ mon,
nē lēof nē lāð,   belēan mihte
sorhfullne sīð,   þā ġit on sund reon.
Þǣr ġit ēagorstrēam   earmum þehton,
mǣton merestrǣta,   mundum brugdon,
glidon ofer gārsecg;   ġeofon ȳþum wēol,
wintrys wylm[um].   Ġit on wæteres æht
seofonniht swuncon;   hē þē æt sunde oferflāt,
hæfde māre mæġen.   Þā hine on morgentīd
on Heaþo-Rǣmes   holm up ætbær;
520   ðonon hē ġesōhte   swǣsne ēþel,
lēof his lēodum,   lond Brondinga,
freoðoburh fæġere,   þǣr hē folc āhte,
burh ond bēagas.   Bēot eal wið þē
sunu Bēanstānes   sō(ð)e ġelǣste.
Ðonne wēne iċ tō þē   wyrsan ġeþinġea,
ðēah þū heaðorǣsa   ġehwǣr dohte,
grimre gūðe,   ġif þū Grendles dearst
nihtlongne fyrst   nean bīdan.'
Bēowulf maþelode,   bearn Ecgþeowes:
530   'Hwæt, þū worn fela,   wine mīn Ūnferð,
bēore druncen   ymb Brecan sprǣce,
sæġdest from his sīðe.   Sōð iċ taliġe,
þæt iċ merestrenġo   māran āhte,
eafeþo on ȳþum,   ðonne æniġ ōþer man.
Wit þæt ġecwǣdon   cnihtwesende

should gain more glory for any deed
under the heavens than he himself.
"Are you the Beowulf who with Breca   480
strove in a swimming match on the sea?
Nothing but vanity urged your venture
to cross the sea-roads single-handed:
rash boasts that risked your lives on the deep.
Nobody, friend or foe, could dissuade
either of you from that foolish exploit.
You recklessly rowed across the waves,
wrapping the ocean tides in your arms,
moving by means of your hand-strokes, gliding
on a sea swollen with winter floods.   490
For seven days the two of you toiled
alone on the waves. He won that contest
decisively; he was stronger than you.
He was cast up on the Heathoreams' coast,
then traveled back to the Brondings' land,
where he favored his people with fortresses
and ring-giving. He had proved himself right
when he boasted that he was the better man.
Now I forecast a far worse result—
however bravely you may have acted   500
in the uproar of battle—if you should dare
to stay here awaiting Grendel's assault."
    Then Beowulf, son of Ecgtheow, spoke:
"What a great deal of beer you have drunk,
Unferth, my friend, and what foolish lies
you have told about Breca! The truth is this:
that amid the shattering waves I showed
far more strength than that other fellow.
We two had vowed—we were very young—

ond ġebēotedon   —wǣron bēġen þā ġīt
on ġeogoðfēore—   þæt wit on gārsecg ūt
aldrum nēðdon,   ond þæt ġeæfndon swā.
Hæfdon swurd nacod,   þā wit on sund reon,
540   heard on handa;   wit unc wið hronfixas
werian þōhton.   Nō hē wiht fram mē
flōdýþum feor   flēotan meahte,
hraþor on holme,   nō iċ fram him wolde.
Ðā wit ætsomne   on sǣ wǣron
fīfnihta fyrst,   oþ þæt unc flōd tōdrāf,
wado weallende,   wedera ċealdost,
nīpende niht,   ond norþan wind
heaðogrim ondhwearf;   hrēo wǣron ýþa.
Wæs merefixa   mōd onhrēred;
550   þǣr mē wið lāðum   līċsyrċe mīn
heard hondlocen   helpe ġefremede;
beadohræġl brōden   on brēostum læġ
golde ġeġyrwed.   Mē tō grunde tēah
fāh fēondscaða,   fæste hæfde
grim on grāpe;   hwæþre mē ġyfeþe wearð
þæt iċ āglǣcan   orde ġerǣhte,
hildebille;   heaþorǣs fornam
mihtiġ meredēor   þurh mīne hand.

Swā meċ ġelōme   lāðġetēonan
560   þrēatedon þearle.   Iċ him þēnode
dēoran sweorde,   swā hit ġedēfe wæs.
Næs hīe ðǣre fylle   ġefēan hæfdon,
mānfordǣdlan,   þæt hīe mē þēgon,
symbel ymbsǣton   sǣgrunde nēah,
ac on merġenne   mēċum wunde
be ýðlāfe   uppe lǣgon,

that we would swim out and stake our lives   510
on the vast deep, and we did as we said,
keeping our bare swords close beside us
to defend ourselves from any sea-beasts.
He lacked the power to pull ahead
on the pounding sea, nor for my part
did I wish to hurry and leave him behind.
For five days and nights the two of us tossed
on the raging deep, till it drove us apart.
The coldest of tempests turned against us;
night came and the north wind   520
crashed down on us, whipping the water
till the waves boiled and angry beasts
were stirred from the bottom. Then my strong armor
saved my life; my linked chain-mail,
gold-inwoven, guarded my breast
as suddenly a huge sea-monster
dragged me downward into the depths
in its tight grip. But by God's grace
my sword was able to stab the brute
and pierce its thick hide with a fatal thrust.   530
Time and again horrid attackers
menaced me, but they met their fate
by the edge of my blade, as was only fitting.
Those monstrous man-eaters did not have
the pleasure of gnawing my flesh and picking
my bones at a feast on the sea's bottom.
In morning's light, they lay on the beach
dead, mangled; my sword had slashed

sweo[r]dum āswefede, þæt syðþan nā
ymb brontne ford brimlīðende
lāde ne letton. Lēoht ēastan cōm,
570 beorht bēacen Godes, brimu swaþredon,
þæt iċ sǣnæssas ġesēon mihte,
windiġe weallas. Wyrd oft nereð
unfǣġne eorl, þonne his ellen dēah!
Hwæþere mē ġesǣlde þæt iċ mid sweorde ofslōh
niceras nigene. Nō iċ on niht ġefræġn
under heofones hwealf heardran feohtan,
nē on ēgstrēamum earmran mannon;
hwæþere iċ fāra fenġ fēore ġedīġde,
sīþes wēriġ. Ðā meċ sǣ oþbær,
580 flōd æfter faroðe on Finna land,
wadu weallendu. Nō iċ wiht fram þē
swylcra searonīða secgan hȳrde,
billa brōgan. Breca nǣfre ġīt
æt heaðolāce, nē ġehwæþer inċer,
swā dēorliċe dǣd ġefremede
fāgum sweordum —nō iċ þæs [fela] ġylpe—
þēah ðū þīnum brōðrum tō banan wurde,
hēafodmǣgum; þæs þū in healle scealt
werhðo drēogan, þēah þīn wit duge.
590 Secge iċ þē tō sōðe, sunu Ecglāfes,
þæt nǣfre Gre[n]del swā fela gryra ġefremede,
atol ǣġlǣċa, ealdre þīnum,
hȳnðo on Heorote, ġif þīn hiġe wǣre,
sefa swā searogrim swā þū self talast;
ac hē hafað onfunden þæt hē þā fǣhðe ne þearf,
atole ecgþræce ēower lēode
swīðe onsittan, Siġe-Scyldinga;
nymeð nȳdbāde, nǣnegum ārað

38

deep gashes into them. Never again
would they mar the passage of men who sail   540
over the waves. Light came from the east—
God's bright beacon. The broad sea calmed,
and at last there was land ahead of me: cliffs
and a wind-swept shore. Thus fate will shelter
a steadfast man, if only his strength
does not fail. There were nine fierce
sea-beasts who charged me, and with my sword
I hacked them apart. I have never heard
of such night-valor beneath the sky's vault,
nor of someone so hard-pressed upon the sea.   550
Yet I escaped from these creatures' grasp,
exhausted. The current carried me off
and washed me up in the Lapps' land.
Unferth, I have never heard any
tales about *your* triumphs in war.
Never did Breca or you bring forth
daring deeds or show much prowess
with your bright swords in the play of battle.
But you killed your own brothers, your nearest kin;
for this one act you deserve all men's   560
condemnation, though you are so clever.
The truth is, friend, that the fiend would not
have committed such crimes against your king
and brought such horror to Heorot if
your spirit were half as strong as you say.
But Grendel found that he need not fear
revenge in a terrible storm of spears
from you and your comrades. He plunders, kills,
brings doom to the Danes, showing no mercy,

lēode Deniġa,   ac hē lust wiġeð,
600   swefeð ond sǽndeþ,   seċċe ne wēneþ
tō Gār-Denum.   Ac iċ him Ġeata sceal
eafoð ond ellen   unġeāra nū,
gūþe ġebēodan.   Gǽþ eft sē þe mōt
tō medo mōdiġ,   siþþan morgenlēoht
ofer ylda bearn   ōþres dōgores,
sunne sweġlwered   sūþan scīneð.'
      Þā wæs on sālum   sinċes brytta
gamolfeax ond gūðrōf;   ġēoce ġelȳfde
brego Beorht-Dena;   ġehȳrde on Bēowulfe
610   folces hyrde   fæstrǽdne ġeþōht.
      Ðǣr wæs hæleþa hleahtor,   hlyn swynsode,
word wǣron wynsume.   Ēode Wealhþēo forð,
cwēn Hrōðgāres   cynna ġemyndiġ,
grētte goldhroden   guman on healle,
ond þā frēoliċ wīf   ful ġesealde
ǣrest Ēast-Dena   eþelwearde,
bæd hine blīðne   æt þǣre bēorþeġe,
lēodum lēofne;   hē on lust ġeþeah
symbel ond seleful,   siġerōf kyning.
620   Ymbēode þā   ides Helminga
duguþe ond ġeogoþe   dǣl ǣġhwylcne,
sinċfato sealde,   oþ þæt sǣl ālamp
þæt hīo Bēowulfe,   bēaghroden cwēn
mōde ġeþungen   medoful ætbær;
grētte Ġeata lēod,   Gode þancode
wīsfæst wordum   þæs ðe hire se willa ġelamp
þæt hēo on ǣniġne   eorl ġelȳfde
fyrena frōfre.   Hē þæt ful ġeþeah,
wælrēow wiga   æt Wealhþeon,
630   ond þā ġyddode   gūþe ġefȳsed.

takes pleasure in ripping your men apart,   570
devouring their flesh, and knows that his fury
will go unpunished by your brave people.
But very soon I will set before him
the courage and strength of the Geats in combat.
Whoever wishes may walk to the banquet
high-spirited when the morning sun,
clothed in radiance, rises tomorrow
and shines from the south on the sons of men."
    The treasure-giver was greatly pleased,
the gray-bearded, war-bold lord of the Danes;   580
he saw that in Beowulf help was at hand
and heard in him an unmoving purpose.
Warriors laughed; they talked with loud voices,
and their words were joyous. Wealhtheow rose,
Hrothgar's queen, who was versed in court manners;
gold-adorned, she greeted the men
and gave the first cup to the king, saying
how dear he was to the Danish people,
then bade him savor the evening's banquet.
He drank deep of the foaming cup,   590
and for many hours he ate and made merry.
The Helming-born lady went round the hall,
jewel-rich, with a generous heart,
giving the ornate golden goblet
to old and young, till in due time
she brought it to Beowulf. Standing before him,
she welcomed him to the king's court
and thanked God that her wish had been granted:
a hero had come to help the people—
someone to count on. He took the cup,   600
that warrior, from Wealhtheow's hand,

Bēowulf maþelode,   bearn Ecgþeowes:
'Iċ þæt hogode,   þā iċ on holm ġestāh,
sǣbāt ġesæt   mid mīnra secga ġedriht,
þæt iċ ānunga   ēowra lēoda
willan ġeworhte   oþðe on wæl crunge
fēondgrāpum fæst.   Iċ ġefremman sceal
eorliċ ellen,   oþðe endedæġ
on þisse meoduhealle   mīnne ġebīdan.'
Ðām wīfe þā word   wēl līcodon,
640   ġilpcwide Ġēates;   ēode goldhroden
frēolicu folccwēn   tō hire frēan sittan.

   Þā wæs eft swā ǣr   inne on healle
þrȳðword sprecen,   ðēod on sǣlum,
siġefolca swēġ,   oþ þæt semninga
sunu Healfdenes   sēċean wolde
ǣfenræste;   wiste þǣm āhlǣċan
tō þǣm hēahsele   hilde ġeþinġed,
siððan hīe sunnan lēoht   ġesēon meahton
oþ ðe nīpende   niht ofer ealle,
650   scaduhelma ġesceapu   scrīðan cwōman
wan under wolcnum.   Werod eall ārās.
[Ġe]grētte þā   guma ōþerne,
Hrōðgār Bēowulf,   ond him hǣl ābēad,
wīnærnes ġeweald,   ond þæt word ācwæð:
'Nǣfre iċ ǣnegum men   ǣr ālȳfde,
siþðan iċ hond ond rond   hebban mihte,
ðrȳþærn Dena   būton þē nūða.
Hafa nū ond ġeheald   hūsa sēlest,
ġemyne mǣrþo,   mæġenellen cȳð,
660   waca wið wrāþum!   Ne bið þē wilna gād
ġif þū þæt ellenweorc   aldre ġedīġest.'

and, eager to start the battle, he said:
"I made up my mind when I set out,
boarding the ship with my band of men,
that I would do what your people have prayed for—
kill the demon—or else I would die
in his cruel grip. I have come to fulfill
my decision and do a heroic deed
here in Heorot, and if I fail,
I will lose my life defending your people."   610
    Beowulf's proudly uttered boast
lifted the heart of the noble lady,
who sat down, gold-bright, beside her lord.
    Then again gladness filled the great hall,
laughter, the sound of liegemen rejoicing
in toasts and stories of triumph, till
the son of Healfdene said that he wished
to retire for the night. He knew that the hero
was planning to fight the fierce assailant
when the sun had sunk below the horizon,   620
after the darkening sky descended
over them all, and shadowy night-shapes
slunk out secretly under the clouds.
The company rose, and the old king
wished Beowulf good luck and gave him
mastery of the mead-hall, then said:
"Never since I shouldered a shield
have I given over the Danes' great hall
to anyone else. I give it to you now.
Guard and protect this glorious house.   630
Remember your fame and your battle-fierceness,
and watch for the foe. This valorous work
will bring you great glory, if you survive."

Đā him Hrōþgār ġewāt   mid his hæleþa ġedryht,
eodur Scyldinga   ūt of healle;
wolde wīġfruma   Wealhþēo sēċan,
cwēn tō ġebeddan.   Hæfde kyningwuldor
Grendle tōġēanes,   swā guman ġefrungon,
seleweard āseted;   sundornytte behēold
ymb aldor Dena,   eotonweard' ābēad.
Hūru Ġēata lēod   ġeorne truwode
670   mōdgan mæġnes,   metodes hyldo.
Đā hē him of dyde   īsernbyrnan,
helm of hafelan,   sealde his hyrsted sweord,
īrena cyst,   ombihtþeġne,
ond ġehealdan hēt   hildeġeatwe.
Ġespræc þā se gōda   ġylpworda sum,
Bēowulf Ġēata,   ǣr hē on bed stiġe:
'No iċ mē an herewǣsmun   hnāgran taliġe
gūþġeweorca   þonne Grendel hine;
forþan iċ hine sweorde   swebban nelle,
680   aldre benēotan,   þēah iċ eal mæġe.
Nāt hē þāra gōda   þæt hē mē onġēan slea,
rand ġehēawe,   þēah ðe hē rōf sie
nīþġeweorca;   ac wit on niht sculon
secge ofersittan   ġif hē ġesēċean dear
wīġ ofer wǣpen,   ond siþðan wītiġ God
on swā hwæþere hond,   hāliġ dryhten
mǣrðo dēme,   swā him ġemet þinċe.'
Hylde hine þā heahþodēor,   hlēorbolster onfēng
eorles andwlitan,   ond hine ymb moniġ
690   snelliċ sǣrinċ   selereste ġebēah.
Nǣniġ heora þōhte   þæt hē þanon scolde
eft eardlufan   ǣfre ġesēċean,
folc oþðe frēoburh   þǣr hē āfēded wæs;

THEN HROTHGAR GOT UP and left the hall,
and his warriors followed. He went to find
Wealhtheow, his wife and bed-companion,
having appointed a powerful guard
to defend Heorot (as people heard)
from Grendel's rage—a match for the monster,
a hero to do great deeds for the Danes.   640
    Beowulf trusted totally
in his great strength and in God's favor.
He lifted off his helmet and armor
and gave his sword, inlaid with gold,
the best of blades, to his body servant
and told him to take good care of them all.
And before the great man lay down on his mat,
he stood and spoke these confident words:
"When it comes to combat, I think that my skill
is as good as Grendel's; I need not carry   650
a sword to slay him, although I could.
Of the warrior's art he knows nothing—
of thrusting, hacking, or hewing a shield—
though he shows a cruel strength in his crimes.
Therefore I too will take no weapons;
I will face him unarmed if he dares to fight,
and God in His grace will give the triumph
to whichever side suits Him the best."
    The hero lay down, and the pillow held
his manly cheek, and around him many   660
warriors lay down to sleep as well.
No man imagined that he would ever
return from Heorot to his own homeland,
the people and place that had nurtured him;

ac hīe hæfdon ġefrūnen   þæt hīe ǣr tō fela micles
in þǣm wīnsele   wældēað fornam,
Deniġea lēode.   Ac him dryhten forġeaf
wīġspēda ġewiofu,   Wedera lēodum,
frōfor ond fultum,   þæt hīe fēond heora
ðurh ānes cræft   ealle ofercōmon,
700   selfes mihtum.   Sōð is ġecȳþed
þæt mihtiġ God   manna cynnes
wēold (w)īdeferhð.

                      Cōm on wanre niht
scrīðan sceadugenġa.   Scēotend swǣfon,
þā þæt hornreċed   healdan scoldon,
ealle būton ānum   —þæt wæs yldum cūþ
þæt hīe ne mōste,   þā metod nolde,
se s[c]ynscaþa   under sceadu breġdan—
ac hē wæċċende   wrāþum on andan
bād bolgenmōd   beadwa ġeþinġes.

710   Ðā cōm of mōre   under misthleoþum
Grendel gongan,   Godes yrre bær;
mynte se mānscaða   manna cynnes
sumne besyrwan   in sele þām hēan.
Wōd under wol(c)num   tō þæs þe hē wīnreċed,
goldsele gumena   ġearwost wisse
fǣtum fāhne;   ne wæs þæt forma sið
þæt hē Hrōþgāres   hām ġesōhte;
nǣfre hē on aldordagum   ǣr nē siþðan
heardran hǣle,   healðeġnas fand.
720   Cōm þā tō reċede   rinċ sīðian
drēamum bedǣled.   Duru sōna onarn
fȳrbendum fæst,   syþðan hē hire folmum (æt)hrān;
onbrǣd þā bealohȳdiġ,   ðā (hē ġe)bolgen wæs,

46

they had all heard how the fiend's frenzy
had seized and slaughtered too many Danes
in that great hall. But the Lord granted
fortune in battle to the brave Geats,
giving them aid to utterly
destroy the demon through one man's strength.   670
For God in his mercy has ruled mankind
through all the ages.
       Out of the night
came the dark stalker. The warriors slept—
all but one. They knew full well
that without God's will, the fiend was unable
to drag them off to his shadowy den.
Wakeful, Beowulf watched for the beast,
awaiting the fight with a heart in fury.
 Then up from the moor, in a veil of mist,
Grendel came slouching. He bore God's wrath.   680
The evil brute intended to trap
and eat some human in the great hall.
Under the clouds he crept, until
he saw the mead-hall, glistening with gold.
It was not the first time he had called on the king,
but never before had he found bad luck:
a fearless warrior waiting for him.
The creature, exiled from all man's joys,
came to the hall; the heavy door,
though bound with iron, burst from its hinges   690
as soon as he touched it. He stood there, seething,
maddened with rage, then he ripped open
the hall's mouth and hurried across

receóes mūþan.   Raþe æfter þon
on fāgne flōr   fēond treddode,
ēode yrremōd;   him of ēagum stōd
liġġe ġelīcost   lēoht unfæġer.
Ġeseah hē in receóe   rinca maniġe,
swefan sibbeġedriht   samod ætgædere,
730   magorinca hēap.   Þā his mōd āhlōg;
mynte þæt hē ġedælde,   ær þon dæġ cwōme,
atol āglǣċa   ānra ġehwylċes
līf wið līċe,   þā him ālumpen wæs
wistfylle wēn.   Ne wæs þæt wyrd þā ġēn
þæt hē mā mōste   manna cynnes
ðicgean ofer þā niht.   Þrȳðswȳð behēold
mǣġ Hiġelāces   hū se mānscaða
under fǣrgripum   ġefaran wolde.
Nē þæt se āglǣċa   yldan þōhte,
740   ac hē ġefēng hraðe   forman sīðe
slǣpendne rinċ,   slāt unwearnum,
bāt bānlocan,   blōd ēdrum dranc,
synsnǣdum swealh;   sōna hæfde
unlyfiġendes   eal ġefeormod,
fēt ond folma.   Forð nēar ætstōp,
nam þā mid handa   hiġeþīhtiġne
rinċ on ræste.   Hē hi(m) rǣhte onġēan,
fēond mid folme;   hē onfēng hraþe
inwitþancum   ond wið earm ġesæt.
750   Sōna þæt onfunde   fyrena hyrde,
þæt hē ne mētte   middanġeardes,
eorþan sċēata   on elran men
mundgripe māran.   Hē on mōde wearð

the patterned floor. From his fierce eyes
an evil light flared like two flames.
He saw the young men in the mead-hall, sleeping
close together, a troop of kinfolk,
and his heart laughed; before dawn's light
he intended to tear the life from each body
and devour the flesh in a gruesome feast.   700
It was not his fate, though, to feed on mankind
after this onslaught.
             Beowulf watched
to see where the killer would strike first.
And the demon did not delay; in a flash
he lunged and seized a warrior sleeping,
tore him apart, gnawed bones, drank blood
gushing from veins, gorged on gobbets
of flesh, and soon had devoured the victim
utterly, even his hands and feet.
He strode to where Beowulf lay in bed   710
and grasped at him. But the hero's grip
took his hand and tightened around it
as he leaned on one arm and sat up straight.
The evil creature instantly knew
that in no man he had ever met
on the face of the earth had he confronted
such a hand-grip. His heart froze;

forht on ferhðe;   nō þȳ ǣr fram meahte.

Hyġe wæs him hinfūs,   wolde on heolster flēon,

sēċan dēofla ġedrǣġ;   ne wæs his drohtoð þǣr

swylċe hē on ealderdagum   ǣr ġemette.

Ġemunde þā se mōdga,   mǣġ Hiġelāces,

æfensprǣċe,   uplang āstōd

760   ond him fæste wiðfēng;   fingras burston;

eoten wæs ūtweard,   eorl furþur stōp.

Mynte se mǣra   (hw)ǣr hē meahte swā

wīdre ġewindan   ond on weġ þanon

flēon on fenhopu;   wiste his fingra ġeweald

on grames grāpum.   Þæt wæs ġēocor sīð

þæt se hearmscaþa   tō Heorute ātēah.

Dryhtsele dynede;   Denum eallum wearð,

ċeasterbūendum,   cēnra ġehwylcum,

eorlum ealuscerwen.   Yrre wǣron bēġen,

770   rēþe renweardas.   Reċed hlynsode.

Þā wæs wundor miċel   þæt se wīnsele

wiðhæfde heaþodēorum,   þæt hē on hrūsan ne fēol,

fǣġer foldbold;   ac hē þæs fæste wæs

innan ond ūtan   īrenbendum

searoþoncum besmiþod.   Þǣr fram sylle ābēag

medubenċ moniġ,   mīne ġefrǣġe,

golde ġereġnad,   þǣr þā graman wunnon.

Þæs ne wēndon ǣr   witan Scyldinga

þæt hit ā mid ġemete   manna ǣniġ

780   betliċ ond bānfāg   tōbrecan meahte,

listum tōlūcan,   nymþe līġes fæþm

swulge on swaþule.   Sweġ up āstāg

nīwe ġeneahhe;   Norð-Denum stōd

ateliċ eġesa,   ānra ġehwylcum

þāra þe of wealle   wōp ġehȳrdon,

fear shook his bones, but he could not flee.
He longed to break loose, into the darkness,
and return to the tumult of demons. Never 720
in his whole life had he been greeted
as harshly as this. Then Hygelac's kinsman
remembered his evening speech, stood up,
and grappled him close. Fingers cracked.
With his uttermost strength Grendel was straining
to pull away, but the warrior held him.
The foul thing thought that he might be able
to run from there to his dismal den,
but he felt his finger-bones being crushed
in Beowulf's grip. The king's house groaned; 730
all who heard it were harrowed with fear.
Both huge wrestlers, raging, reeled
and crashed through the hall. Timbers clattered;
it was a wonder that Heorot withstood
the fight and did not fall to the ground,
that beautiful building; but smiths had forged
strong iron bands to brace its walls
both inside and out. Many mead-benches
with golden fittings were smashed to the floor,
so I have heard, as the two struggled. 740
Before this combat no counselor,
even the wisest, would have believed
that there was anybody on earth
who could destroy that splendid house
with its horn-trimmed fixtures, unless some fire
swallowed it in consuming flames.
An uncanny cry came through the walls.
Dread descended on every Dane
who was there to hear that horrible shriek—

gryrelēoð galan   Godes andsacan,
siġelēasne sang,   sār wāniġean
helle hæfton.   Hēold hine fæste
sē þe manna wæs   mæġene strenġest
790 on þǣm dæġe   þysses līfes.

Nolde eorla hlēo   æniġe þinga
þone cwealmcuman   cwicne forlǣtan,
nē his līfdagas   lēoda ængum
nytte tealde.   Þǣr ġenehost brægd
eorl Bēowulfes   ealde lāfe,
wolde frēadrihtnes   feorh ealgian,
mǣres þēodnes,   ðǣr hīe meahton swā.
Hīe þæt ne wiston,   þā hīe ġewin drugon,
heardhicgende   hildemecgas,
800 ond on healfa ġehwone   hēawan þōhton,
sāwle sēċan: þone synscaðan
æniġ ofer eorþan   īrenna cyst,
gūðbilla nān,   grētan nolde,
ac hē siġewǣpnum   forsworen hæfde,
ecga ġehwylcre.   Scolde his aldorġedāl
on ðǣm dæġe   þysses līfes
earmliċ wurðan,   ond se ellorgāst
on fēonda ġeweald   feor sīðian.
Ðā þæt onfunde   sē þe fela ǣror
810 mōdes myrðe   manna cynne,
fyrene ġefremede   —hē [wæs] fāg wið God—
þæt him se līċhoma   lǣstan nolde,
ac hine se mōdega   mǣġ Hyġelāces
hæfde be honda;   wæs ġehwæþer ōðrum
lifiġende lāð.   Līċsār ġebād
atol ǣġlǣċa;   him on eaxle wearð

52

God's enemy singing his terror song,   750
a howl of defeat, hell's prisoner
bewailing his wound. But he was held tight
by that mighty hero, the strongest man
who ever lived on the wide earth.
    The noble warrior would not allow
his evil guest ever to leave;
he was convinced that the vicious thing
should be quickly killed. His comrades-in-arms
drew their ancient ancestral swords;
they wished to defend the famous captain,   760
their belovèd lord, however they could.
But they did not know, those noble retainers,
as they stepped forward to join the fray—
to strike the enemy from all sides
and cut him down—that the wicked creature
could not be wounded by any weapon;
no sword on earth, not even the finest,
could kill him, for he had cast a spell
to blunt all blades. But he was doomed
to be slain that night; his alien spirit   770
would journey far to the fiends' realm.
    Then he who had broken the hearts of so many
and inflicted such misery on mankind
with foul crimes in his fight against God
found that his body's strength was failing.
Beowulf, that boldhearted man,
held his arm fast; hateful to each
was the life of the other. That loathsome thing
felt a pain-flash. A huge wound gaped

syndolh sweotol, seonowe onsprungon,
burston bānlocan. Bēowulfe wearð
gūðhrēð ġyfeþe. Scolde Grendel þonan
820 feorhsēoc fleon under fenhleoðu,
sēċean wynlēas wīċ; wiste þē ġeornor
þæt his aldres wæs ende ġegongen,
dōgera dæġrīm. Denum eallum wearð
æfter þām wælrǣse willa ġelumpen:
hæfde þā ġefǣlsod sā þe ǣr feorran cōm,
snotor ond swȳðferhð, sele Hrōðgāres,
ġenered wið nīðe. Nihtweorce ġefeh,
ellenmǣrþum. Hæfde Ēast-Denum
Ġēatmecga lēod ġilp ġelǣsted,
830 swylċe onċȳþðe ealle ġebētte,
inwidsorge þe hīe ǣr drugon
ond for þrēanȳdum þolian scoldon,
torn unlȳtel. Þæt wæs tācen sweotol
syþðan hildedēor hond āleġde,
earm ond eaxle —þǣr wæs eal ġeador
Grendles grāpe— under ġēapne hr(ōf).

Ðā wæs on morgen mīne ġefrǣġe
ymb þā ġifhealle guðrinċ moniġ;
fērdon folctogan feorran ond nean
840 ġeond wīdwegas wundor sċēawian,
lāþes lāstas. Nō his līfġedāl
sārliċ þūhte secga ǣnegum
þāra þe tīrlēases trode sċēawode,
hū hē wēriġmōd on weġ þanon,
nīða ofercumen, on nicera mere
fǣġe ond ġeflȳmed feorhlāstas bær.
Ðǣr wæs on blōde brim weallende;

in his shoulder, sinews split, and muscles   780
burst from the bone. The victory
was granted to Beowulf. Grendel fled
with a mortal wound, under the moor-hills
to his joyless den. During that journey
he knew that his end was near, his hours
numbered. The dearest wish of all Danes
had been fulfilled in that deadly fight.

    The warrior from far away,
that proud hero who had just purged
Hrothgar's hall and saved it from evil,   790
gloried in the night's great achievement;
he had kept his daring pledge to the Danes
and relieved them at last of their long torment,
the devastation they had endured,
the agony each had had to suffer.
And as a sign, the hero hung
Grendel's whole arm—hand to shoulder—
from one of the rafters in the high roof.

MANY WARRIORS gathered that morning
around the gift-hall, so I have heard.   800
Clan-chieftains came from near and far,
on wide-branching ways, to see the wonder
of the fiend's footprints. They felt great joy
as they heard how he had lurched away
sick at heart, desperate, dying,
to the lake of sea-monsters, leaving a spoor
of red as he went. The water surged
and boiled with blood, the waves heaved

atol ȳða ġeswinġ   eal ġemenġed
hāton heolfre   heorodrēore wēol.
850 Dēaðfǣġe dēog   siððan drēama lēas
in fenfreoðo   feorh āleġde,
hæþene sāwle;   þǣr him hel onfēng.
    Þanon eft ġewiton   ealdġesīðas
swylċe ġeong maniġ   of gomenwāþe
fram mere mōdġe   mēarum rīdan,
beornas on blancum.   Ðǣr wæs Bēowulfes
mǣrðo mǣned;   moniġ oft ġecwæð
þætte sūð nē norð   be sǣm twēonum
ofer eormengrund   ōþer nǣniġ
860 under sweġles begong   sēlra nǣre
rondhæbbendra,   rīċes wyrðra.
Nē hīe hūru winedrihten   wiht ne lōgon,
glædne Hrōðgār,   ac þæt wæs gōd cyning.
Hwīlum heaþorōfe   hlēapan lēton,
on ġeflit faran   fealwe mēaras,
ðǣr him foldwegas   fæġere þūhton,
cystum cūðe.   Hwīlum cyninges þeġn,
guma ġilphlæden,   ġidda ġemyndiġ,
sē ðe eal fela   ealdġeseġena
870 worn ġemunde,   word ōþer fand
sōðe ġebunden;   secg eft ongan
sīð Bēowulfes   snyttrum styrian
ond on spēd wrecan   spel ġerāde,
wordum wrixlan;   wēlhwylċ ġecwæð
þæt hē fram Siġemunde[s]   secgan hȳrde
ellendǣdum,   uncūþes fela,
Wælsinges ġewin,   wīde sīðas,
þāra þe gumena bearn   ġearwe ne wiston,
fǣhðe ond fyrena,   būton Fitela mid hine,

with the hot gore that gushed from his wounds.
He had dived in, doomed, and wretchedly   810
in his dank marsh-den had given up
his heathen soul. Hell had received him.

    Then back to the hall the whole throng came,
young and old, on a joyous journey,
in the highest spirits on their gray horses.
Many men praised Beowulf's prowess;
nowhere, they said, to the north or south,
across the broad earth and under the heavens,
was there a man more masterful
or one more worthy to rule a kingdom,   820
though they found no fault with their own lord,
the gracious Hrothgar, who was a good king.

    At times some of them let their steeds
gallop ahead in gleeful races
wherever the footpath was broad and firm.
At times a warrior gifted with words,
who kept in his memory many ancient
tales and sagas, composed a new song
in praise of Beowulf's brilliant deed,
his stirring language skillfully fashioned,   830
each word correctly linked to the rest.

        He told all he knew of Sigemund's triumphs,
        strange tales of that hero's struggles,
        of distant journeys unknown to any
        except to Fitela, feuds, foul crimes

880 þonne hē swulċes hwæt   secgan wolde,
eam his nefan,   swā hīe ā wǣron
æt nīða ġehwām   nȳdġesteallan;
hæfdon eal fela   eotena cynnes
sweordum ġesǣġed.   Siġemunde ġesprong
æfter dēaðdæġe   dōm unlȳtel
syþðan wīġes heard   wyrm ācwealde,
hordes hyrde.   Hē under hārne stān,
æþelinges bearn,   āna ġenēðde
frēcne dǣde,   nē wæs him Fitela mid;
890 hwæþre him ġesǣlde   ðæt þæt swurd þurhwōd
wrǣtlicne wyrm,   þæt hit on wealle ætstōd,
dryhtliċ īren;   draca morðre swealt.
Hæfde āglǣċa   elne ġegongen
þæt hē bēahhordes   brūcan mōste
selfes dōme;   sǣbāt ġehlēod,
bær on bearm scipes   beorhte frætwa
Wælses eafera;   wyrm hāt ġemealt.
    Sē wæs wreċċena   wīde mǣrost
ofer werþēode,   wīġendra hlēo,
900 ellendǣdum   —hē þæs ǣr onðāh—
siððan Heremōdes   hild sweðrode,
eafoð ond ellen.   Hē mid Ēotenum wearð
on fēonda ġeweald   forð forlācen,
snūde forsended.   Hine sorhwylmas
lemedon tō lange;   hē his lēodum wearð,
eallum æþellingum   tō aldorċeare;
swylċe oft bemearn   ǣrran mǣlum
swīðferhþes sīð   snotor ċeorl moniġ,
sē þe him bealwa tō   bōte ġelȳfde,
910 þæt þæt ðēodnes bearn   ġeþēon scolde,
fæderæþelum onfōn,   folc ġehealdan,

and certain valiant acts of revenge.
They had always been allies, those two men,
close companions in every combat;
they had slain giants with their swift swords—
more than a few. Many men heard   840
of Sigemund's deeds, and after his death
his fame spread, for he had slain a dragon
who guarded a treasure. Beneath gray rocks
he proceeded alone, that prince's son,
then thrust his sword and drove it straight through
the wondrous serpent; the blade stuck
in the cave's wall, and the dragon died.
The hero had by his high courage
gained as much gold as he could have wished,
the whole huge hoard, and then he carried   850
the dazzling treasures down to his boat
and put the golden piles on the deck.
The dragon dissolved in its boiling blood.

    Sigemund was by far the most famous
adventurer of that time; his valor
was known to all nations, and he was a great
bulwark in battle to his dear friends
when Heremod's prowess had proven vain.
Later on, in the land of the Jutes,
Heremod was betrayed and handed   860
to enemy princes, then put to death.
A long dejection had loomed in his mind
and made him a shame and a grief to the Scyldings.
Many men lamented the reign
of that headstrong king; they had counted on him
to defend them from harm when his father died
and had trusted that he would protect the people

hord ond hlēoburh,   hæleþa rīċe,
ēþel Scyldinga.   Hē þǣr eallum wearð,
mǣġ Hiġelāces,   manna cynne,
frēondum ġefǣġra;   hine fyren onwōd.
    Hwīlum flītende   fealwe strǣte
mēarum mǣton.   Ðā wæs morgenlēoht
scofen ond scynded.   Ēode scealc moniġ
swīðhicgende   tō sele þām hēan
searowundor sēon;   swylċe self cyning
of brȳdbūre,   bēahhorda weard,
tryddode tīrfæst   ġetrume micle,
cystum ġecȳþed,   ond his cwēn mid him
medostiġġe mæt   mæġþa hōse.

    Hrōðgār maþelode—   hē tō healle ġēong,
stōd on stapole,   ġeseah stēapne hrōf
golde fāhne,   ond Grendles hond:
'Ðisse ansȳne   alwealdan þanc
lungre ġelimpe.   Fela iċ lāþes ġebād,
grynna æt Grendle;   ā mæġ God wyrċan
wunder æfter wundre,   wuldres hyrde.
Ðæt wæs unġeāra   þæt iċ ǣniġra mē
wēana ne wēnde   tō wīdan feore
bōte ġebīdan,   þonne blōde fāh
hūsa sēlest   heorodrēoriġ stōd,
wēa wīdscofen   witena ġehwylcum,
ðāra þe ne wēndon   þæt hīe wīdeferhð
lēoda landġeweorc   lāþum beweredon
scuccum ond scinnum.   Nū scealc hafað
þurh drihtnes miht   dǣd ġefremede
ðē wē ealle   ǣr ne meahton
snyttrum besyrwan.   Hwæt, þæt secgan mæġ

and princes in that homeland of heroes;
but sin had corrupted Heremod's soul.
So Beowulf was even better esteemed   870
among his friends and by all men.
   Sometimes, again, on the sandy road
they raced their horses. The sun had risen
and was climbing the sky. A large crowd
had gathered by now in the gabled hall
to see the wonder. The king himself,
the treasure-guardian, famed for his giving,
majestically walked from the women's chambers
across to the mead-hall with many men,
accompanied by the queen and her maids.   880
   Hrothgar stood on the hall's steps,
gazed at Grendel's gigantic arm
as it hung from the steep gold roof, and said:
"For this sight, may thanks sincerely be given
to the Almighty. I have borne much
savage abuse and many sorrows
from Grendel; but God is always prepared
to work great wonders, if so be His will.
Not long ago I had given up hope
of any relief from all my afflictions,   890
when the great house stood dripping with gore,
a grief that weighed on our wisest men;
we could not imagine how our hall
could be defended from Grendel's fury.
And now one man, through the Lord's might,
has accomplished what none of us ever could
with all our wisdom. The woman who bore
a son such as this among mankind

efne swā hwylċ mæġþa   swā ðone magan cende
æfter gumcynnum,   ġyf hēo ġȳt lyfað,
þæt hyre ealdmetod   ēste wǣre
bearnġebyrdo.   Nū iċ, Bēowulf, þeċ,
secg bet[e]sta,   mē for sunu wylle
frēoġan on ferhþe;   heald forð tela
nīwe sibbe.   Ne bið þē [n]æniġre gād
950   worolde wilna   þe iċ ġeweald hæbbe.
Ful oft iċ for lǣssan   lēan teohhode,
hordweorþunge   hnāhran rinċe,
sǣmran æt sæcce.   Þū þē self hafast
dǣdum ġefremed   þæt þīn [dōm] lyfað
āwa tō aldre.   Alwalda þeċ
gōde forġylde,   swā hē nū ġȳt dyde!'
     Bēowulf maþelode,   bearn Ecþeowes:
'Wē þæt ellenweorc   ēstum miclum,
feohtan fremedon,   frēcne ġenēðdon
960   eafoð uncūþes.   Ūþe iċ swīþor
þæt ðū hine selfne   ġesēon mōste,
fēond on frætewum   fylwēriġne.
Iċ hine hrædlīċe   heardan clammum
on wælbedde   wrīþan þōhte,
þæt hē for mundgripe   mīnum scolde
licgean līfbysiġ,   būton his līċ swice;
iċ hine ne mihte,   þā metod nolde,
ganges ġetwǣman,   nō iċ him þæs ġeorne ætfealh,
feorhġenīðlan;   wæs tō foremihtiġ
970   fēond on fēþe.   Hwæþere hē his folme forlēt
tō līfwraþe   lāst weardian,
earm ond eaxle.   Nō þǣr æniġe swā þēah
fēasceaft guma   frōfre ġebohte:
nō þȳ leng leofað   lāðġetēona

may well say, if she still is alive,
that God was abundantly gracious to her. 900
And now, Beowulf, best of men,
I will love you sincerely as my own son.
Nourish yourself in this new kinship,
and you shall lack nothing that you may long for
of any worldly goods I can give.
Many times I have rewarded men
for smaller achievements, given choice gifts
to less noble warriors. Now, by yourself,
you have done such deeds that your fame will endure
forever. May the Almighty always 910
grant you good things, as He has today."
    Then Beowulf, son of Ecgtheow, spoke:
"We Geats, my lord, gladly fulfilled
your dearest wish when we dared to face
that unknown evil. I would have preferred
to show you the fiend's corpse after the combat.
I wanted to kill him here in this hall,
to have him gasp out his life in my grip,
but I could not keep him from pulling away,
however tight I held on to him. 920
He pulled away with inhuman power—
it was the Lord's will—but wanting to save
his life, he left his torn arm behind.
Cold comfort it is for that wretched creature:
he must die soon, desperate, alone;

synnum ġeswenċed,   ac hyne sār hafað
in nīðgripe   nearwe befongen,
balwon bendum;   ðǣr ābīdan sceal
maga māne fāh   miclan dōmes,
hū him scīr metod   scrīfan wille.'

980   Ðā wæs swīġra secg,   sunu Eclāfes,
on ġylpsprǣċe   gūðġeweorca,
siþðan æþelingas   eorles cræfte
ofer hēanne hrōf   hand scēawedon,
fēondes fingras;   foran ǣġhwylċ wæs,
steda næġla ġehwylċ   stȳle ġelīcost,
hǣþenes handsporu,   hilderinċes,
eġl' unhēoru. Ǣġhwylċ ġecwæð
þæt him heardra nān   hrīnan wolde
īren ǣrgōd   þæt ðæs āhlǣċan
990   blōdġe beadufolme   onberan wolde.

Ðā wæs hāten hreþe   Heort innanweard
folmum ġefrætwod;   fela þǣra wæs,
wera ond wīfa   þe þæt wīnreċed,
ġestsele ġyredon.   Goldfāg scinon
web æfter wāgum,   wundorsīona fela
secga ġehwylcum   þāra þe on swylċ starað.
Wæs þæt beorhte bold   tōbrocen swīðe,
eal inneweard   īrenbendum fæst,
heorras tōhlidene;   hrōf āna ġenæs
1000   ealles ansund,   þē se āglǣċa
fyrendǣdum fāg   on flēam ġewand,
aldres orwēna.   Nō þæt ȳðe byð
tō befleonne   —fremme sē þe wille—
ac ġesēċan sceal   sāwlberendra
nȳde ġenȳdde,   niþða bearna,

pain has grasped him in its fierce grip,
and he cannot flee. Stained by his sins,
he will have to await the dreaded day
when the radiant Lord will render judgment."

    Unferth, the son of Ecglaf, was silent.   930
He spoke no insults after the nobles
saw the proof of Beowulf's prowess,
the hand and fingers that hung from the roof.
The deadly nail-tips were strong as steel;
together they formed a hideous hand-spike,
a cruel battle-claw. Everyone said
no iron on earth, however sharpened,
could have cut into the creature's flesh
or hacked through that blood-caked, murderous hand.

    Immediately the king commanded   940
that the hall be restored to its ancient splendor.
Many people, both men and women,
labored at it. Tapestries, gold-laced,
glowed from the walls with wondrous sights
to gladden the heart of any onlooker.
That bright room had almost been wrecked,
benches and tables damaged, the door
brutally wrenched from its iron braces.
Only the high roof remained unharmed
when that fierce ravager turned to flee,   950
in dread for his life. But death is not easy
to run away from (try, if you wish);
every soul-bearer dwelling on earth

grundbūendra   ġearwe stōwe,
þǣr his līċhoma   leġerbedde fæst
swefeþ æfter symle.
                              Þā wæs sǣl ond mǣl
þæt tō healle gang   Healfdenes sunu;
1010   wolde self cyning   symbel þicgan.
Ne ġefræġen iċ þā mǣġþe   māran weorode
ymb hyra sinċġyfan   sēl ġebǣran.
Bugon þā tō benċe   blǣdāgande,
fylle ġefǣgon;   fæġere ġeþǣgon
medoful maniġ   māgas þāra
swīðhicgende   on sele þām hēan,
Hrōðgār ond Hrōþulf.   Heorot innan wæs
frēondum āfylled;   nalles fācenstafas
Þēod-Scyldingas   þenden fremedon.
1020   Forġeaf þā Bēowulfe   brand Healfdenes,
seġen gyldenne   sigores tō lēane,
hroden hildecumbor,   helm ond byrnan.
Mǣre māðþumsweord   maniġe ġesāwon
beforan beorn beran.   Bēowulf ġeþāh
ful on flette;   nō hē þǣre feohġyfte
for sc[ē]oten[d]um   scamiġan ðorfte.
Ne ġefræġn iċ frēondlicor   fēower mādmas
golde ġeġyrede   gummanna fela
in ealobenċe   ōðrum ġesellan.
1030   Ymb þæs helmes hrōf   hēafodbeorge
wīrum bewunden   walu ūtan hēold,
þæt him fē[o]la lāf   frēcne ne meahte
scūrheard sceþðan,   þonne scyldfreca
onġean gramum   gangan scolde.
Heht ðā eorla hlēo   eahta mēaras
fætedhlēore   on flet teon,

must enter the place appointed for him
where the fallen body finally comes
to rest in its earth-bed after life's feast.
    At the proper time, as the princes waited,
the son of Healfdene went to the hall
and sat down in the royal seat.
I have never heard of a greater number   960
of liegemen gathered around their lord
conducting themselves with such dignity.
Many brave men were on those benches,
enjoying the meal. Hrothgar and Hrothulf,
their stalwart kinsmen, in courtesy drank
many mead-cups under that roof,
and Heorot filled with friends' talk and laughter.
(At that time, disloyalty and betrayal
were things unknown to the Danish nation.)
    The king gave Beowulf Healfdene's blade   970
as a gift, and also a golden banner,
helmet, and mail-shirt. Many admired
the jeweled sword that was set before him.
Beowulf drank with all the others,
pleased with the priceless rewards that Hrothgar
had conferred in front of so many men.
I have never heard of another king
giving in a more generous manner
four such majestic golden gifts.
Around the crown of the helmet a crest,   980
wound with golden wires, protected
the skull from the blows of sharp-filed swords
hardened in war; it would turn away harm
when a warrior went up against his foes.
The agèd chief then ordered his servants

(in) under eoderas;   þāra ānum stōd
sadol searwum fāh,   sinċe ġewurþad;
þæt wæs hildesetl   hēahcyninges
1040   ðonne sweorda ġelāc   sunu Healfdenes
efnan wolde—   næfre on ōre læġ
wīdcūþes wīġ   ðonne walu fēollon.
Ond ðā Bēowulfe   bēġa ġehwæþres
eodor Ingwina   onweald ġetēah,
wicga ond wǣpna;   hēt hine wēl brūcan.
Swā manlīċe   mǣre þēoden,
hordweard hæleþa,   heaþorǣsas ġeald
mēarum ond mādmum,   swā hȳ næfre man lyhð,
sē þe secgan wile   sōð æfter rihte.

1050   Ðā ġȳt ǣġhwylcum   eorla drihten
þāra þe mid Bēowulfe   brimlāde tēah
on þǣre medubenċe   māþðum ġesealde,
yrfelāfe,   ond þone ǣnne heht
golde forġyldan,   þone ðe Grendel ǣr
māne ācwealde—   swā hē hyra mā wolde,
nefne him wītiġ God   wyrd forstōde
ond ðæs mannes mōd.   Metod eallum wēold
gumena cynnes,   swā hē nū ġit deð.
Forþan bið andġit   ǣġhwǣr sēlest,
1060   ferhðes foreþanc: fela sceal ġebīdan
lēofes ond lāþes   sē þe longe hēr
on ðyssum windagum   worolde brūceð.
     Þǣr wæs sang ond swēġ   samod ætgædere
fore Healfdenes   hildewīsan,
gomenwudu grēted,   ġid oft wrecen,
ðonne healgamen,   Hrōþgāres scop

to lead eight horses into the hall
bearing gold-plated bits and bridles.
The first had a saddle studded with gems;
it had been the king's war-seat, on which he rode
to combat; his courage had never failed   990
in the front lines as warriors fell around him.
And that gracious lord then gave possession
of both to Beowulf—horses and weapons—
urging the young man to use them well.
So nobly did the renowned prince,
the royal keeper of rings, reward him
with those splendid steeds and golden treasures;
no one could say that he had been stingy.
Moreover, to each of Beowulf's men
who had sailed to the Danes' land over the sea   1000
the king presented a costly heirloom.
He also ordered that compensation
be paid in gold for the man whom Grendel
had murdered—he would have murdered more
if the wisdom of God and Beowulf's boldness
had not prevented that violent fate.
God ruled the earth then, as He does now,
and to understand this is always best.
Much bitter, much sweet must we endure
if we live long in these strife-filled times.   1010
    Song arose and the sound of music.
The harp was plucked. Hrothgar rejoiced.
Then the king's poet, from his place on the bench,

æfter medobenċe   mænan scolde
Finnes eaferan;   ðā hīe se fær beġeat,
hæleð Healf-Dena,   Hnæf Scyldinga
1070   in Frēswæle   feallan scolde.

    Nē hūru Hildeburh   herian þorfte
Ēotena trēowe;   unsynnum wearð
beloren lēofum   æt þām lindplegan
bearnum ond brōðrum;   hīe on ġebyrd hruron
gāre wunde;   þæt wæs ġeōmuru ides!
Nalles hōlinga   Hōces dohtor
meotodsceaft bemearn   syþðan morgen cōm,
ðā hēo under sweġle   ġesēon meahte
morþorbealo māga,   þær hē[o] ær mæste hēold
1080   worolde wynne.   Wīġ ealle fornam
Finnes þeġnas   nemne fēaum ānum,
þæt hē ne mehte   on þæm meðelstede
wīġ Henġeste   wiht ġefeohtan,
nē þā wēalāfe   wīġe forþringan,
þēodnes ðeġne;   ac hiġ him ġeþinġo budon,
þæt hīe him ōðer flet   eal ġerȳmdon,
healle ond hēahsetl,   þæt hīe healfre ġeweald
wið Ēotena bearn   āgan mōston,
ond æt feohġyftum   Folcwaldan sunu
1090   dōgra ġehwylċe   Dene weorþode,
Henġestes hēap   hringum wenede
efne swā swīðe   sinċġestrēonum
fættan goldes   swā hē Frēsena cyn
on bēorsele   byldan wolde.
Ðā hīe ġetruwedon   on twā healfa
fæste frioðuwǣre.   Fin Henġeste
elne unflitme   āðum benemde
þæt hē þā wēalāfe   weotena dōme

sang of Finn's sons:

              When the Danish force
was overwhelmed by a sudden onslaught,
Hnaef met his fate in the Frisian slaughter.
Hildeburh had no reason to praise
the Jutes' good faith; guiltless herself,
she lost her belovèd son and brother
in that fierce fight; they were doomed to fall,   1020
slain by spears. Prostrate with grief,
she lamented her lot when in the morning
she saw the corpses of her two kinsmen
slaughtered under the skies where once
she had tasted every earthly delight.
The battle had carried off all Finn's court
except for a few, so he could not
continue to fight Hengest's troops
or force those men to abandon the fortress.
He offered the terms of a truce then: first   1030
he would hand over a hall to the Danes,
for them to have control of one half
and the Jutes the other; and in addition
he agreed to honor the Danes whenever
gifts were given, to offer them
as much gold and as many treasures
as he gave the Frisians, to gladden their hearts.
    Then, on both sides, they bound themselves
to maintain the peace. Taking an oath,
Finn declared that he would defend   1040
and support the Danes; he would deal with them fairly,

ārum hēolde,   þæt ðǣr ǣniġ mon
1100 wordum nē worcum   wǣre ne brǣce,
nē þurh inwitsearo   ǣfre ġemǣnden,
ðēah hīe hira bēagġyfan   banan folgedon
ðēodenlēase,   þā him swā ġeþearfod wæs;
ġyf þonne Frȳsna hwylċ   frēcnen sprǣċe
ðæs morþorhetes   myndgiend wǣre,
þonne hit sweordes ecg   syððan scēde.
Ād wæs ġeæfned   ond icge gold
āhæfen of horde;   Here-Scyldinga
betst beadorinca   wæs on bǣl ġearu.
1110 Æt þǣm āde wæs   ēþġesȳne
swātfāh syrċe,   swȳn eal gylden,
eofer īrenheard,   æþeling maniġ
wundum āwyrded;   sume on wæle crungon.
Hēt ðā Hildeburh   æt Hnæfes āde
hire selfre sunu   sweoloðe befæstan,
bānfatu bærnan,   ond on bǣl don
ēame on eaxle.   Ides gnornode,
ġēomrode ġiddum.   Gūðrēċ āstāh,
wand tō wolcnum;   wælfȳra mǣst
1120 hlynode for hlāwe.   Hafelan multon,
benġeato burston   ðonne blōd ætspranc,
lāðbite līċes;   līġ ealle forswealg,
gǣsta ġīfrost,   þāra ðe þǣr gūð fornam
bēġa folces.   Wæs hira blǣd scacen.

Ġewiton him ðā wīġend   wīca neosian
frēondum befeallen,   Frȳsland ġesēon,
hāmas ond hēaburh.   Henġest ðā ġȳt
wælfāgne winter   wunode mid Finne;
h[ē] unhlitme   eard ġemunde,

as his nobles advised, and no one ever
would undo the pact by word or by deed
or taunt them with malicious intent,
though now there was no other choice
but to serve the man who had slain their prince;
and if in the future any Frisian
should have the gall to doubt their good faith
by reminding them of the murderous battle,
he would answer that man with the sword's edge.   1050

    A high funeral pyre was prepared,
and they heaped it with gold from Finn's great hoard.
The Danes' brave chief, their champion,
awaited the fire with blood-caked war-shirts,
gilt boar-images made of iron,
warriors with their wounds gaping
who lay beside him, sprawled on the pyre.
Hildeburh ordered that her own son
be placed upon it, his flesh and bones
to be burned alongside his uncle's body.   1060
She sang the funeral dirges, sobbing.
Smoke rose up and spiraled to heaven,
the flames in front of the burial mound
roared, wounds burst, heads melted, blood
bubbled and gushed. That greedy spirit,
fire, consumed the slain of both tribes,
and their glory was gone from the earth forever.

    Then Finn's warriors left the land,
returning to Frisia, bereft of their friends,
to their forts and houses. But Hengest stayed   1070
at Finn's place during that death-stained winter;
he deeply longed for his native land,

1130 þēah þe ne meahte   on mere drīfan
hrinġedstefnan   —holm storme wēol,
won wið winde,   winter ȳþe belēac
īsġebinde—   oþ ðæt ōþer cōm
ġēar in ġeardas,   swā nū ġȳt deð,
þā ðe syngāles   sēle bewitiað,
wuldortorhtan weder.   Ðā wæs winter scacen,
fæġer foldan bearm.   Fundode wreċċa,
ġist of ġeardum;   hē tō gyrnwræce
swīðor þōhte   þonne tō sǣlāde,
1140 ġif hē tornġemōt   þurhtēon mihte,
þæt hē Ēotena bearn   inne ġemunde—
swā hē ne forwyrnde   woroldrǣdenne—
þonne him Hūnlāfing   hildelēoman,
billa sēlest   on bearm dyde,
þæs wǣron mid Ēotenum   ecge cūðe.
Swylċe ferhðfrecan   Fin eft beġeat
sweordbealo slīðen   æt his selfes hām,
siþðan grimne gripe   Gūðlāf ond Ōslāf
æfter sǣsīðe   sorge mǣndon,
1150 ætwiton wēana dǣl;   ne meahte wǣfre mōd
forhabban in hreþre.   Ðā wæs heal roden
fēonda fēorum,   swilċe Fin slæġen,
cyning on corþre,   ond sēo cwēn numen.
Scēotend Scyldinga   tō scypon feredon
eal inġesteald   eorðcyninges,
swylċe hīe æt Finnes hām   findan meahton
siġla searoġimma.   Hīe on sǣlāde
drihtliċe wīf   tō Denum feredon,
lǣddon tō lēodum.
                    Lēoð wæs āsungen,
1160 glēomannes ġyd.   Gamen eft āstāh,

but he could not sail across the cold sea;
it raged with storms, was roiled by the wind,
and the waves lay locked in layers of ice
till spring arrived, as it still does,
with the wonder of light, one more year
with its seasons in their endless succession.
Winter left, and the land was lovely.
Hengest, though eager to sail back home,   1080
thought more of vengeance than of a voyage,
wondering how he could force a fight
to make the memory of his sword
stay with the sons of the Jutes forever.
So he was swift to swear his allegiance
when the son of Hunlaf set on his lap
the brilliant blade, finest of weapons,
whose edges were not unknown to the Jutes.
Thus, in turn, sword-fury caught Finn
at the hands of his enemies, in his own hall,   1090
once Guthlaf and Oslaf had voiced their grief
at the brutal onslaught after the voyage
and blamed that bitter sorrow on Finn.
Their rage burst out, and the hall was red
with even more slaughter. Finn was slain,
his courtiers too, and the queen was taken.
The Scyldings carried off to their ship
all the treasures they found in Finn's hall,
the golden brooches and brilliant gems,
then sailed with that lady to the Danes' land,   1100
bringing her back to her own people.

When the bard had finished his song, the sound
of talk and laughter began again,

beorhtode benċswēġ;   byrelas sealdon
wīn of wunderfatum.   Þā cwōm Wealhþēo forð
gān under gyldnum bēage   þǣr þā gōdan twēġen
sǣton suhterġefæderan;   þā ġȳt wæs hiera sib ætgædere,
ǣġhwylċ ōðrum trȳwe.   Swylċe þǣr Ūnferþ þyle
æt fōtum sæt frēan Scyldinga;   ġehwylċ hiora his ferhþe trēowde,
þæt hē hæfde mōd miċel,   þēah þe hē his māgum nǣre
ārfæst æt ecga ġelācum.   Spræc ðā ides Scyldinga:
'Onfōh þissum fulle,   frēodrihten mīn,
1170   sinċes brytta.   Þū on sǣlum wes,
goldwine gumena,   ond tō Ġeatum spræc
mildum wordum,   swā sceal man don.
Bēo wið Ġēatas glæd,   ġeofena ġemyndiġ,
nēan ond feorran   [þā] þū nū hafast.
Mē man sæġde   þæt þū ðē for sunu wolde
hereri[n]ċ habban.   Heorot is ġefǣlsod,
bēahsele beorhta;   brūc þenden þū mōte
maniġra mēdo,   ond þīnum māgum lǣf
folc ond rīċe   þonne ðū forð scyle,
1180   metodsceaft seon.   Iċ mīnne can
glædne Hrōþulf,   þæt hē þā ġeogoðe wile
ārum healdan   ġyf þū ǣr þonne hē,
wine Scildinga,   worold oflǣtest;
wēne iċ þæt hē mid gōde   ġyldan wille
uncran eaferan   ġif hē þæt eal ġemon,
hwæt wit tō willan   ond tō worðmyndum
umborwesendum ǣr   ārna ġefremedon.'
Hwearf þā bī benċe,   þǣr hyre byre wǣron,
Hrēðrīċ ond Hrōðmund,   ond hæleþa bearn,
1190   ġiogoð ætgædere;   þǣr se gōda sæt,
Bēowulf Ġēata   be þǣm ġebrōðrum twǣm.

revelry rang out, cupbearers poured
wine from rich vessels. Then Wealhtheow
came, in her golden crown, to the place
where Hrothgar and Hrothulf, those two proud men,
sat together, their trust still strong
and their bond unbroken. Unferth as well,
the spokesman, sat at his lord's feet; 1110
everyone knew his steadfast spirit
and admired his courage, though he had killed
his brothers, to his enduring blame.
Then the queen spoke: "Receive this cup,
my belovèd lord; drink deep and be merry.
Speak graciously to the Geats, as is proper;
be lavish with them when you allot
the gifts you have gathered from near and far.
I have been told that you mean to make
this hero your son. Heorot is cleansed 1120
and splendid again; therefore, bestow
many rewards while you still may,
but leave the kingdom to your own kin
when you must go forth to face God's judgment.
I trust that your noble nephew, Hrothulf,
will act with prudence toward all our people
if you, my lord, should leave before he does.
I am certain that he will help our sons
and treat them with kindness when he recalls
everything that we did to honor 1130
and cherish him when he was a child."
She turned to the bench where her boys were sitting,
Hrethric and Hrothmund, and all the young nobles.
There, among them, between the two,
sat that great man, Beowulf the Geat.

Him wæs ful boren,   ond frēondlaþu
wordum bewæġned,   ond wunden gold
ēstum ġeēawed,   earmrēade twā,
hræġl ond hringas,   healsbēaga mǣst
þāra þe iċ on foldan   ġefræġen hæbbe.
Nǣniġne iċ under sweġle   sēlran hȳrde
hordmāððum hæleþa   syþðan Hāma ætwæġ
tō þǣre byrhtan byriġ   Brōsinga mene,
1200   siġle ond sinċfæt—   searonīðas flēah
Eormenrīċes,   ġeċēas ēcne rǣd.
Þone hring hæfde   Hiġelāc Ġeata,
nefa Swertinges   nȳhstan sīðe,
siðþan hē under seġne   sinċ ealgode,
wælrēaf werede;   hyne wyrd fornam
syþðan hē for wlenċo   wēan āhsode,
fǣhðe tō Frȳsum.   Hē þā frætwe wæġ,
eorclanstānas   ofer ȳða ful,
rīċe þēoden;   hē under rande ġecranc.
1210   Ġehwearf þā in Francna fæþm   feorh cyninges,
brēostġewǣdu,   ond se bēah somod.
Wyrsan wīġfrecan   wæl rēafeden
æfter gūðsceare;   Ġeata lēode
hrēawīċ hēoldon.   Heal swēġe onfēng.
Wealhðēo maþelode;   hēo fore þǣm werede spræc:
'Brūc ðisses bēages,   Bēowulf lēofa,
hyse, mid hæle,   ond þisses hræġles nēot,
þēo[d]ġestrēona,   ond ġeþēoh tela,

The cup was brought, a cordial welcome
given to him, and the priceless presents
graciously offered: a pair of armbands,
a mail-shirt, rings, and the richest gold collar
I have ever heard of on all the earth.   1140
Never has a hero possessed
such a treasure since Hama stole
the Brosings' necklace, with its bright gems
set in wrought gold, and then sailed back
to his splendid fortress. He fled from the hate
of Eormanric, wishing eternal reward.
This collar hung on Hygelac's breast,
lord of the Geats, on his last voyage
as he fought to defend what he had plundered,
the spoils of war. Death snatched him away   1150
when, in his arrogance, he set out
to launch that fatal raid on the Frisians.
Fighting under his shield he fell,
wearing the gemstones and well-wrought gold
he had worn when he crossed the surging currents.
So Hygelac came into Frankish hands,
with his war gear and the great gold collar.
Low-born soldiers looted the dead
when the carnage stopped; the field was covered
with the corpses of Geats.
                              As the gifts were offered,   1160
the mead-hall echoed with much applause.
Once more Wealhtheow spoke:
"May this collar please you, belovèd prince;
may it bring you good luck, and may this mail-shirt
support you so that you prosper long.

79

cen þec mid cræfte,   ond þyssum cnyhtum wes
1220 lāra līðe.   Ic þē þæs lēan ġeman.
Hafast þū ġefēred   þæt ðē feor ond nēah
ealne wīdeferhþ   weras ehtiġað,
efne swā sīde   swā sǣ bebūgeð,
windġeard, weallas.   Wes þenden þū lifiġe,
æþeling, ēadiġ.   Ic þē an tela
sinċġestrēona.   Bēo þū suna mīnum
dǣdum ġedēfe,   drēamhealdende.
Hēr is ǣġhwylc eorl   ōþrum ġetrȳwe,
mōdes milde,   mandrihtne hol[d];
1230 þeġnas syndon ġeþwǣre,   þēod eal ġearo;
druncne dryhtguman   dōð swā ic bidde.'
    Ēode þā tō setle.   Þǣr wæs symbla cyst,
druncon wīn weras.   Wyrd ne cūþon,
ġeōsceaft grimme,   swā hit āgangen wearð
eorla manegum,   syþðan ǣfen cwōm,
ond him Hrōþgār ġewāt   tō hofe sīnum,
rīċe tō ræste.   Reċed weardode
unrīm eorla,   swā hīe oft ǣr dydon.
Benċþelu beredon;   hit ġeondbrǣded wearð
1240 beddum ond bolstrum.   Bēorscealca sum
fūs ond fǣġe   fletræste ġebēag.
Setton him tō hēafdon   hilderandas,
bordwudu beorhtan;   þǣr on benċe wæs
ofer æþelinge   ȳþġesēne
heaþostēapa helm,   hrinġed byrne,
þrecwudu þrymlic.   Wæs þēaw hyra
þæt hīe oft wǣron   anwīġġearwe,
ġē æt hām ġē on herġe,   ġē ġehwæþer þāra
efne swylċe mǣla   swylċe hira mandryhtne
1250 þearf ġesǣlde;   wæs sēo þēod tilu.

Make your strength known, and be to these boys
a gentle guide. I will be most grateful.
Because of your brave deeds men will admire you
near and far, now and forever,
for your fame is as wide as the wind's home: 1170
the sea that encircles all earth's shores.
Be happy, prince, as long as you live;
I wish you honor and endless wealth.
Treat my sons kindly; act in their interest.
Each man here is true to the other,
and each is loyal to his liege lord;
the princes are poised, the nation ready
to follow his will, and the warriors
mellow with drink. Now do as I ask."

    She returned to her seat. The banquet continued;   1180
the men drank their wine. They did not know
the destiny, ordained from of old,
that would come upon them when evening arrived
and Hrothgar had retired from the table.
A host of warriors guarded the hall;
when the king left they cleared the benches
and put beds and bolsters across the floor.
One of those drinkers, fated to die
before the sun rose, lay down to rest.
Near their heads battle-shields hovered,   1190
and above each warrior on his bench
lay his intricate iron-linked mail-shirt,
spear, and war-helmet. This was their way:
their weapons were with them at every moment,
always prepared for a sudden onslaught
at home or camp, whenever their king
called for them. They were competent soldiers.

Sigon þā tō slǣpe.   Sum sāre anġeald
æfenræste,   swā him ful oft ġelamp
siþðan goldsele   Grendel warode,
unriht æfnde,   oþ þæt ende becwōm,
swylt æfter synnum.   Þæt ġesȳne wearþ,
wīdcūþ werum,   þætte wrecend þā ġȳt
lifde æfter lāþum,   lange þrāge,
æfter gūðċeare;   Grendles mōdor,
ides āglǣċwīf   yrmþe ġemunde,
sē þe wætereġesan   wunian scolde,
ċealde strēamas,   siþðan Cāin wearð
tō ecgbanan   āngan brēþer,
fæderenmǣge;   hē þā fāg ġewāt,
morþre ġemearcod   mandrēam fleon,
wēsten warode.   Þanon wōc fela
ġeōsceaftgāsta;   wæs þǣra Grendel sum,
heorowearh heteliċ,   sē æt Heorote fand
wæċċendne wer   wīġes bīdan.
Þǣr him āglǣċa   ætgrǣpe wearð;
hwæþre hē ġemunde   mæġenes strenġe,
ġimfæste ġife   ðe him God sealde,
ond him tō anwaldan   āre ġelȳfde,
frōfre ond fultum;   ðȳ hē þone fēond ofercwōm,
ġehnǣġde helle gāst.   Þā hē hēan ġewāt,
drēame bedǣled   dēaþwīċ seon,
mancynnes fēond,   ond his mōdor þā ġȳt
ġīfre ond galgmōd   ġegān wolde
sorhfulne sīð,   sunu dēoð wrecan.
Cōm þā tō Heorote,   ðǣr Hring-Dene
ġeond þæt sæld swǣfun.   Þā ðǣr sōna wearð
edhwyrft eorlum,   siþðan inne fealh
Grendles mōdor.   Wæs se gryre lǣssa

THEY WENT TO SLEEP THEN, and one paid dearly
for his evening's rest, as had so often
happened when Grendel possessed the hall   1200
and committed his horrors, until the moment
when he was killed. But it was soon clear
that he had an avenger, vicious, deadly,
biding her time in bitter hatred:
Grendel's mother, a gruesome hag,
an ogress raging in her bereavement.
She had to dwell in the terrible depths
of ice-cold waters after Cain slew
his brother and was banished by God;
marked for the murder, he fled man's joys   1210
to live in the wilderness. From his loins
a race of fiends sprang, cursed like their father—
Grendel among them, a brutal beast
who did not know as he left his den
that a bold warrior waited for him.
When the hero was seized by this grim assailant,
he trusted the strength that God had lent him
and had faith in the Almighty's favor,
and so he was able to strike down,
single-handed, that creature from hell.   1220
Mankind's foe had fled to his doom,
and now his mother, desolate, mourning,
and ravenous, set out in her rage
to seek revenge for her son's death.
      She came to Heorot. Across the floor
Danes were sleeping beside the benches.
For all the warriors in that wide house
she marked a return to the reign of terror,

efne swā micle   swā bið mæġþa cræft,
wīġgryre wīfes   be wǣpnedmen,
þonne heoru bunden,   hamere ġeþrūen,
sweord swāte fāh   swīn ofer helme
ecgum dhyttiġ   andweard scireð.
Þā wæs on healle   heardecg togen
sweord ofer setlum,   sīdrand maniġ
1290   hafen handa fæst;   helm ne ġemunde,
byrnan sīde,   þā hine se brōga anġeat.
Hēo wæs on ofste,   wolde ūt þanon,
fēore beorgan,   þā hēo onfunden wæs;
hraðe hēo æþelinga   ānne hæfde
fæste befangen,   þā hēo tō fenne gang.
Sē wæs Hrōþgāre   hæleþa lēofost
on ġesīðes hād   be sǣm twēonum,
rīċe randwiga,   þone ðe hēo on ræste ābrēat,
blǣdfastne beorn.   Næs Bēowulf ðǣr,
1300   ac wæs ōþer in   ǣr ġeteohhod
æfter māþðumġife   mǣrum Ġeate.
Hrēam wearð on Heorote;   hēo under heolfre ġenam
cūþe folme;   cearu wæs ġenīwod,
ġeworden in wīcun.   Ne wæs þæt ġewrixle til,
þæt hīe on bā healfa   bicgan scoldon
frēonda fēorum.

                Þā wæs frōd cyning,
hār hilderinċ   on hrēon mōde
syðþan hē aldorþeġn   unlyfiġendne,
þone dēorestan   dēadne wisse.
1310   Hraþe wæs tō būre   Bēowulf fetod,
sigorēadiġ secg.   Samod ǣrdæġe
ēode eorla sum,   æþele cempa
self mid ġesīðum   þǣr se snotera bād

which was only less since a female's force
cannot be like a man's in combat   1230
when the keen, hammer-forged, blood-wet blade
splits the skull in an enemy's helmet.
At the grim onslaught, they grabbed their swords,
gripped their shields and sheltered behind them,
though none remembered helmets or mail-shirts
as they woke in horror. She hurried in,
meaning to leave immediately,
before the men could gather against her.
Quickly then, in her cruel grip,
she snatched up one of the warriors   1240
and ran out clutching him in her claws.
This man, loved by Hrothgar more
than any other between the two seas,
was a famous fighter, now horribly ripped
and wrenched from his bed in Beowulf's absence.
(The staunch Geat hero had been assigned
another building to sleep in, that night.)
Clamor arose; the famous claw
on the blood-caked arm of Grendel was gone;
she had taken it with her, and all their woe   1250
had begun again. An evil barter,
when the two parties pay with the lives
of their most belovèd kinsman. The king
was sick at heart on hearing the news
that his chief counselor and close friend
had been slain. He summoned Beowulf
to his chamber at dawn, and that dauntless fighter
came at once with his comrades. Hrothgar

hwæþer him alwalda   æfre wille
æfter wēaspelle   wyrpe ġefremman.
Gang ðā æfter flōre   fyrdwyrðe man
mid his handscale   —healwudu dynede—
þæt hē þone wīsan   wordum næġde
frēan Ingwina,   fræġn ġif him wære
æfter nēodlaðu[m]   niht ġetǣse.

Hrōðgār maþelode,   helm Scyldinga:
'Ne frīn þū æfter sǣlum!   Sorh is ġenīwod
Deniġea lēodum: dēad is Æschere,
Yrmenlāfes   yldra brōþor,
mīn rūnwita   ond mīn rǣdbora,
eaxlġestealla   ðonne wē on orleġe
hafelan weredon,   þonne hniton fēþan,
eoferas cnysedan.   Swy(lċ) scolde eorl wesan,
[æþeling] ǣrgōd,   swylċ Æschere wæs.
Wearð him on Heorote   tō handbanan
wælgǣst wǣfre;   iċ ne wāt hwæder
atol ǣse wlanc   eftsīðas tēah,
fylle ġefrēcnod.   Hēo þā fǣhðe wræc
þē þū ġystran niht   Grendel cwealdest
þurh hǣstne hād   heardum clammum,
forþan hē tō lange   lēode mīne
wanode ond wyrde.   Hē æt wīġe ġecrang
ealdres scyldiġ,   ond nū ōþer cwōm
mihtiġ mānscaða,   wolde hyre mǣġ wrecan,
ġē feor hafað   fǣhðe ġestǣled—
þæs þe þinċean mæġ   þeġne monegum,
sē þe æfter sinċġyfan   on sefan grēoteþ—
hreþerbealo hearde;   nū sēo hand liġeð,
sē þe ēow wēlhwylcra   wilna dohte.

86

was wondering whether Almighty God
would ever favor him after this sorrow.   1260
The mighty hero marched through the hall
with his band of men—the floorboards boomed—
then paid the old king his courtesies
and asked him if his night had been pleasant.

    Then Hrothgar, the Scyldings' sovereign, spoke:
"Do not ask about pleasure. Grief
has returned to the Danes. Aeschere is dead,
the elder brother of Yrmenlaf,
my counselor and my closest friend,
who stood by my side in every battle   1270
when the fighting was fiercest and the swords clanged
against the boar-helmets. He was the bravest
and noblest man I have ever known.
Now a death-spirit has come and killed him,
and no one knows where the ghoul went
to devour his body and gnaw his bones.
She avenged what happened in Heorot last night
when you killed Grendel in your strong grip.
For far too long he had terrorized us
with his foul murders; he fell in battle   1280
and paid with his life. And now another
dark ravager has come here to wreak
havoc and do irreversible harm
to each of us. Every warrior here
is aching with grief for this great man,
the treasure-winner, who served us well.

Iċ þæt londbūend,   lēode mīne,
selerǣdende   secgan hȳrde
þæt hīe ġesāwon   swylċe twēġen
micle mearcstapan   mōras healdan,
ellorgǣstas.   Ðǣra ōðer wæs,
1350   þæs þe hīe ġewislicost   ġewitan meahton,
idese onlīcnæs;   ōðer earmsceapen
on weres wæstmum   wræclāstas træd,
næfne hē wæs māra   þonne ǣniġ man ōðer;
þone on ġeārdagum   Grendel nemdo(n)
foldbūende;   nō hīe fæder cunnon,
hwæþer him ǣniġ wæs   ǣr ācenned
dyrnra gāsta.   Hīe dȳġel lond
wariġeað, wulfhleoþu,   windiġe næssas,
frēcne fenġelād,   ðǣr fyrġenstrēam
1360   under næssa ġenipu   niþer ġewīteð,
flōd under foldan.   Nis þæt feor heonon
mīlġemearces   þæt se mere standeð;
ofer þǣm hongiað   hrinda bearwas,
wudu wyrtum fæst   wæter oferhelmað.
Þǣr mæġ nihta ġehwǣm   nīðwundor sēon,
fȳr on flōde.   Nō þæs frōd leofað
gumena bearna   þæt þone grund wite.
Ðēah þe hǣðstapa   hundum ġeswenċed,
heorot hornum trum   holtwudu sēċe,
1370   feorran ġeflȳmed,   ǣr hē feorh seleð,
aldor on ōfre,   ǣr hē in wille,
hafelan [beorgan];   nis þæt hēoru stōw.
Þonon ȳðġeblond   up āstīgeð
won tō wolcnum   þonne wind styreþ
lāð ġewidru,   oð þæt lyft ðrysmaþ,
roderas rēotað.   Nū is se rǣd ġelang

"I have heard it said by some of my people,
counselors, capable men,
that they have seen two savage creatures
prowling the moors, misshapen, massive,   1290
from some wicked place. One of them seems
like a woman in form, so people say,
the other monstrous thing like a male,
though bigger than any human could be.
The country folk have been calling him Grendel
since the old days; nobody knows
of a father, or if, before he was born,
other appalling siblings were spawned.
They live in the hidden land, high country
where the wolf hunts on windy headlands,   1300
treacherous marsh-paths where mountain torrents
plunge down cloud-covered cliffs to form
an underground river. That lake lies
not many miles from this mead-hall; boughs
heavy with frost hang all around it,
and a root-thick wood looms over the water.
Each night something uncanny occurs:
the water burns. Not even the wisest
man alive knows the lake's bottom.
The strong-horned stag who is pursued   1310
by a pack of hounds, though he seeks safety
desperately, would much rather die
on the shore of that lake than save his life
by plunging in. It is a foul place.
Enormous waves surge from the waters
to the dark heavens, and storm-winds heave
till the air strangles and the sky weeps.
You are our hero, our only hope.

eft æt þē ānum.   Eard ġīt ne const,
frēcne stōwe,   ðǣr þū findan miht
sinniġne secg;   sēċ ġif þū dyrre!
1380   Iċ þē þā fǣhðe   fēo lēaniġe,
ealdġestrēonum,   swā iċ ǣr dyde,
wundnan golde,   ġyf þū on weġ cymest.'

   Bēowulf maþelode,   bearn Ecgþeowes:
'Ne sorga, snotor guma.   Sēlre bið ǣġhwǣm
þæt hē his frēond wrece   þonne hē fela murne.
Ūre ǣġhwylċ sceal   ende ġebīdan
worolde līfes;   wyrċe sē þe mōte
dōmes ǣr dēaþe;   þæt bið drihtguman
unlifġendum   æfter sēlest.
1390   Ārīs, rīċes weard,   uton hraþe fēran,
Grendles māgan   gang scēawiġan.
Iċ hit þē ġehāte,   nō hē on helm losaþ,
nē on foldan fæþm   nē on fyrġenholt
nē on ġyfenes grund,   gā þǣr hē wille.
Ðȳs dōgor þū   ġeþyld hafa
wēana ġehwylċes,   swā iċ þē wēne tō.'
Āhlēop ðā se gomela,   Gode þancode,
mihtigan drihtne,   þæs se man ġespræc.
   Þā wæs Hrōðgāre   hors ġebǣted,
1400   wicg wundenfeax.   Wīsa fenġel
ġeatoliċ gende;   gumfēþa stōp
lindhæbbendra.   Lāstas wǣron
æfter waldswaþum   wīde ġesȳne,
gang over grundas,   [þǣr] ġeġnum fōr
ofer myrċan mōr,   magoþeġna bær
þone sēlestan   sāwollēasne

You do not yet know the dreadful region
where the demon lurks. Go, if you dare. 1320
For this great work I will richly reward you
with ancient treasures of twisted gold
as I did last time, if you live to return."

   Dauntless, Beowulf said, "Do not
give in to grief, my lord. It is good
to avenge a friend's murder, rather than mourn
excessively. For sooner or later
each man's life will come to an end;
so let him who may, gain worldly glory
for his brave deeds. That is the best 1330
reward for a warrior once he is gone.
Arise, great king. Let us go quickly
and follow the footprints of Grendel's kin.
I promise you this: she will have no haven
in the bowels of the earth or on the sea's bottom
or in mountain forests—wherever she flees.
Be patient now amid your great pain
and endure these woes, as I know you will."

   The old king rose and gave thanks to God
for the strength and wisdom of Beowulf's words. 1340

THEN A HORSE was bridled for Hrothgar,
with braided mane and brilliant trappings,
and he rode in splendor. Soldiers marched
before and beside him, bearing their spears.
Everyone could easily see
the beast's tracks on the forest trail,
marked in the loam as she had lumbered
toward the dark moor, dragging the body
of that fine nobleman, Hrothgar's friend,

þāra þe mid Hrōðgāre   hām eahtode.
Oferēode þā   æþelinga bearn
stēap stānhliðo,   stīge nearwe,
1410 enge ānpaðas,   uncūð gelād,
neowle næssas,   nicorhūsa fela;
hē fēara sum   beforan gengde
wīsra monna   wong scēawian,
oþ þæt hē fǣringa   fyrgenbēamas
ofer hārne stān   hleonian funde,
wynlēasne wudu;   wæter under stōd
drēorig ond gedrēfed.   Denum eallum wæs,
winum Scyldinga,   weorce on mōde
tō geþolianne,   ðegne monegum,
1420 oncȳð eorla gehwǣm,   syðþan Æscheres
on þām holmclife   hafelan mētton.
Flōd blōde wēol   —folc tō sǣgon—
hātan heolfre.   Horn stundum song
fūslic (fyrd)lēoð.   Fēþa eal gesæt.
Gesāwon ðā æfter wætere   wyrmcynnes fela,
sellice sǣdracan   sund cunnian,
swylce on næshleoðum   nicras licgean,
ðā on undernmǣl   oft bewitigað
sorhfulne sīð   on seglrāde,
1430 wyrmas ond wildēor.   Hīe on weg hruron,
bitere ond gebolgne;   bearhtm ongēaton,
gūðhorn galan.   Sumne Gēata lēod
of flānbogan   fēores getwǣfde,
ȳðgewinnes,   þæt him on aldre stōd
herestrǣl hearda;   hē on holme wæs
sundes þē sǣnra   ðē hyne swylt fornam.
Hræþe wearð on ȳðum   mid eofersprēotum
heorohōcyhtum   hearde genearwod,

who had counseled him as he ruled the country.   1350
Hrothgar climbed into the headlands,
up perilous cliffs, on narrow paths
that forced the troop to a single file
past waters where dreadful sea-monsters swam.
He rode ahead with a few horsemen
to scout out the land, when suddenly
he came upon cramped, stunted trees
drooped over rocks: a dismal wood.
Above the roiled and reddened waters
the bravest men were chilled to the bone;   1360
it broke their hearts when they found the bloody
head of Aeschere at the cliff's edge.
The waves welled up with still-hot gore.
Again and again the battle-horn blared
its urgent war-call. The soldiers sat down.
As they looked at the dismal lake, they saw
deadly serpents, dragon-like shapes
that swam beneath them, and on the slopes
gigantic monsters like those that move
at daybreak to capsize ships, and cause   1370
misery to the sons of men.
Away they slithered, enraged, at the sound
of the battle-horn. A Geatish bowman
with a long arrow cut off the life
of one sea-demon; the point drove
into its flesh and pierced its organs;
it was slower at swimming once death seized it.
Immediately men gaffed it with boar-pikes

nīða ġenǣġed,   ond on næs togen,
1440 wundorliċ wǣgbora;   weras scēawedon
gryrelicne ġist.

        Ġyrede hine Bēowulf
eorlġewǣdum,   nalles for ealdre mearn;
scolde herebyrne   hondum ġebrōden,
sīd ond searofāh,   sund cunnian,
sēo ðe bāncofan   beorgan cūþe,
þæt him hildegrāp   hreþre ne mihte,
eorres inwitfenġ,   aldre ġesceþðan;
ac se hwīta helm   hafelan werede,
sē þe meregrundas   menġan scolde,
1450 sēċan sundġebland   sinċe ġeweorðad,
befongen frēawrāsnum,   swā hine fyrndagum
worhte wǣpna smið,   wundrum tēode,
besette swīnlīcum,   þæt hine syðþan nō
brond ne beadomēċas   bītan ne meahton.
Næs þæt þonne mǣtost   mæġenfultuma
þæt him on ðearfe lāh   ðyle Hrōðgāres;
wæs þǣm hæftmēċe   Hrunting nama;
þæt wæs ān foran   ealdġestrēona;
ecg wæs īren,   ātertānum fāh,
1460 āhyrded heaþoswāte;   nǣfre hit æt hilde ne swāc
manna ǣngum   þāra þe hit mid mundum bewand,
sē ðe gryresīðas   ġegān dorste,
folcstede fāra;   næs þæt forma sīð
þæt hit ellenweorc   æfnan scolde.
Hūru ne ġemunde   mago Ecglāfes,
eafoþes cræftiġ,   þæt hē ǣr ġespræc
wīne druncen,   þā hē þæs wǣpnes onlāh
sēlran sweordfrecan;   selfa ne dorste
under ȳða ġewin   aldre ġenēþan,

and dragged it to shore. They gazed with dread
at the hideous beast from the lake's bottom.   1380
    Then Beowulf put on his battle gear,
indifferent to death. His iron mail-shirt,
woven by hand with wondrous skill,
had covered him and kept him safe
so that sword-thrusts and the hurtling spears
of enemies had not injured his flesh.
His shining helmet guarded his head;
soon it would plunge down, plumbing the depths,
and stir the lake's bottom, its iron band
jewel-adorned, with dangling chain-mail,   1390
bright as a master smith had made it
in ancient times, with a circle of silver
around it, emblazoned with golden boars;
no axe or blade could ever bite through it.
The last of his arms was lent by Unferth:
a sword named Hrunting, hilted with gold,
preeminent among ancient treasures;
its iron blade, etched with a pattern
of rippling waves, was hardened in war-blood.
Never in fights had it failed a man   1400
who knew how to swing it as he strode forth
onto the field. Not for the first time
would it have to perform a hero's deed.
    When he gave that blade to the better swordsman,
Unferth had utterly disremembered
the drunken words he had once said.
He did not dare to risk his own life

1470 drihtscype drēogan;   þǣr hē dōme forlēas,
ellenmǣrðum.   Ne wæs þǣm ōðrum swā
syðþan hē hine tō gūðe   ġeġyred hæfde.

Bēowulf maðelode,   bearn Ecgþeowes:
'Ġeþenċ nū, se mǣra   maga Healfdenes,
snottra fenġel,   nū iċ eom sīðes fūs,
goldwine gumena,   hwæt wit ġeō sprǣcon,
ġif iċ æt þearfe   þīnre scolde
aldre linnan,   þæt ðū mē ā wǣre
forðġewitenum   on fæder stæle.
1480 Wes þū mundbora   mīnum magoþeġnum,
hondġesellum,   ġif meċ hild nime;
swylċe þū ðā mādmas   þe þū mē sealdest,
Hrōðgār lēofa,   Hiġelāce onsend.
Mæġ þonne on þǣm golde onġitan   Ġeata dryhten,
ġesēon sunu Hrǣdles,   þonne hē on þæt sinċ starað,
þæt iċ gumcystum   gōdne funde
bēaga bryttan,   brēac þonne mōste.
Ond þū Ūnferð lǣt   ealde lāfe,
wrǣtliċ wǣġsweord   wīdcūðne man
1490 heardecg habban;   iċ mē mid Hruntinge
dōm ġewyrċe,   oþðe meċ dēað nimeð.'
Æfter þǣm wordum   Weder-Ġēata lēod
efste mid elne,   nalas andsware
bīdan wolde;   brimwylm onfēng
hilderinċe.   Ðā wæs hwīl dæġes
ǣr hē þone grundwong   onġytan mehte.
Sōna þæt onfunde   sē ðe flōda begong
heoroġīfre behēold   hund missera,
grim ond grǣdiġ,   þæt þǣr gumena sum
1500 ælwihta eard   ufan cunnode.

96

under the waves. So he lost honor
and a chance for glory. Not so the Geat,
who had put on his gear and prepared for battle.   1410
    Then Beowulf, son of Ecgtheow, spoke:
"Since I am ready, son of Healfdene,
wisest of kings, remember well
what we spoke of before: that if in your service
I lose my life, you will always be
like a father to me when I have gone forth.
Take good care of my young comrades,
and treat them kindly if I am killed.
The priceless gifts you have granted to me,
Hrothgar—send them to Hygelac,   1420
lord of the Geats. When he sees such gold,
he will know I found a powerful friend,
a great and generous giver of rings,
and earned your gratitude while I was able.
To Unferth I leave my splendid sword,
its blade wave-patterned and battle-hard,
a treasured ancient heirloom. With Hrunting
I will gain glory, or else I will die."
    After these words, he did not wait
for a reply but plunged right in,   1430
and the heaving waves closed over his head.
(It was many hours—much of the day—
before he would look on dry land again.)
Right away, the ravenous monster
who had held that expanse for a hundred years
knew that some alien being from above
was coming to her in her hidden realm.

Grāp þā tōġēanes,   gūðrinċ ġefēng
atolan clommum;   nō þȳ ǣr in ġescōd
hālan līċe;   hring ūtan ymbbearh,
þæt hēo þone fyrdhom   ðurhfōn ne mihte,
locene leoðosyrċan   lāþan fingrum.
Bær þā sēo brimwyl[f],   þā hēo tō botme cōm,
hringa þenġel   tō hofe sīnum,
swā hē ne mihte   —nō hē þæs mōdiġ wæs—
wǣpna ġewealdan,   ac hine wundra þæs fela
swe[n]cte on sunde,   sǣdēor moniġ
hildetūxum   heresyrċan bræc,
ēhton āglǣċan.   Ðā se eorl onġeat
þæt hē [in] nīðsele   nāthwylcum wæs,
þǣr him nǣniġ wæter   wihte ne sceþede,
nē him for hrōfsele   hrīnan ne mehte
fǣrgripe flōdes;   fȳrlēoht ġeseah,
blācne lēoman   beorhte scīnan.
    Onġeat þā se gōda   grundwyrġenne,
merewīf mihtiġ;   mæġenrǣs forġeaf
hildebille,   hond swenġ ne oftēah,
þæt hire on hafelan   hrinġmǣl āgōl
grǣdiġ gūðlēoð.   (Ð)ā se ġist onfand
þæt se beadolēoma   bītan nolde,
aldre sceþðan,   ac sēo ecg ġeswāc
ðēodne æt þearfe;   ðolode ǣr fela
hondġemōta,   helm oft ġescær,
fǣġes fyrdhræġl;   ðā wæs forma sīð
dēorum māðme   þæt his dōm ālæġ.
    Eft wæs ānrǣd,   nalas elnes læt,
mǣrða ġemyndiġ   mæġ Hȳlāces:

1510

1520

1530

98

She swam up and seized him, but his strong body
remained unharmed in her murderous grip;
the mail-shirt saved him, and her sharp claws   1440
could find no way to tear through his flesh.
That savage thing swam to the bottom,
clasping him so close to her breast
that despite his strength he was unable
to draw his sword. Strange sea-monsters
came to attack him with pointed tusks,
trying to pierce his armor. The prince
saw that he was in some kind of hall;
no water could reach him, because its roof
kept the current from entering. Firelight   1450
burned inside; he could see the flames.

    Then he saw that accursèd creature,
the hulking ogress. With all his might
he swung the sword, bringing it down
upon her head, and as it hurtled
the iron screamed out its battle song.
But Beowulf found that the famous weapon
could not bite into her; its sharp blade
failed the man when he needed it most.
Before, in many hand-to-hand fights,   1460
it had slashed through the heavy helmets and mail
of brave warriors doomed to die.
This was the first time glory failed
for the mighty sword that had killed so many.

wearp ðā wundenmǣl　wrǣttum ġebunden
yrre ōretta,　þæt hit on eorðan lǣġ,
stīð ond stȳlecg;　strenġe ġetruwode,
mundgripe mæġenes.　Swā sceal man don
þonne hē æt gūðe　ġegān þenċeð
longsumne lof,　nā ymb his līf cearað.
Ġefēng þā be feaxe　—nalas for fǣhðe mearn—
Gūð-Ġēata lēod　Grendles mōdor;
bræġd þā beadwe heard,　þā hē ġebolgen wæs,
1540　feorhġenīðlan,　þæt hēo on flet ġebēah.
Hēo him eft hraþe　andlēan forġeald
grimman grāpum　ond him tōġēanes fēng;
oferwearp þā wēriġmōd　wigena strenġest,
fēþecempa,　þæt hē on fylle wearð.
Ofsæt þā þone seleġyst,　ond hyre seax ġetēah
brād [ond] brūnecg;　wolde hire bearn wrecan,
āngan eaferan.　Him on eaxle lǣġ
brēostnet brōden;　þæt ġebearh fēore
wið ord ond wið ecge,　ingang forstōd.
1550　Hæfde ðā forsīðod　sunu Ecgþeowes
under ġynne grund,　Ġēata cempa,
nemne him heaðobyrne　helpe ġefremede,
herenet hearde,　ond hāliġ God.
Ġewēold wīġsigor　wītiġ drihten,
rodera rǣdend;　hit on ryht ġescēd
ȳðelīċe,　syþðan hē eft āstōd.

Ġeseah ðā on searwum　siġeēadiġ bil,
ealdsweord eotenisc　ecgum þȳhtiġ,
wigena weorðmynd;　þæt [wæs] wǣpna cyst,—
1560　būton hit wæs māre　ðonne ǣniġ mon ōðer
tō beadulāce　ætberan meahte,

In a great fury he flung it away;
it lay on the ground with its golden hilt
and its bright steel-edged wave-patterned blade.
But the Geatish hero did not lose heart;
he trusted himself and his strong hands.
(Every man who wants to earn war-fame   1470
must, in combat, care nothing for life.)
Then, with a fierce joy, he vaulted forward,
seized that savage beast by the hair,
and hurled her face down onto the floor.
She quickly pushed up and paid him back
by pulling him close and crushing him
in her harsh embrace, until he could hardly
breathe. Fainting, he stumbled and fell.
She towered above the hall-intruder
and drew her dagger with its sharp blade,   1480
to tear his life out and take revenge
for her only child. But across his chest
lay the strong chain-mail; it saved his life,
protecting him as she slashed and stabbed.
Beowulf would have breathed his last
far down under the dark waves,
had not the armor come to his aid.
The heavenly Lord wished to help him
and ended the fight in the hero's favor.
Looking into her arsenal,   1490
he saw a victory sword; it was ancient,
fashioned by giants in former days,
an honor for any human to use—
the best of blades, but so long and heavy
that no other warrior would have been able

gōd and ġeatoliċ,   ġīganta ġeweorc.
Hē ġefēng þā fetelhilt,   freca Scyldinga
hrēoh ond heorogrim,   hrinġmǣl ġebræġd
aldres orwēna,   yrringa slōh,
þæt hire wið halse   heard grāpode,
bānhringas bræc;   bil eal ðurhwōd
fǣġne flǣschoman,   hēo on flet ġecrong;
sweord wæs swātiġ,   secg weorce ġefeh.

1570   Līxte se lēoma,   lēoht inne stōd,
efne swā of hefene   hādre scīneð
rodores candel.   Hē æfter reċede wlāt;
hwearf þā be wealle,   wǣpen hafenade
heard be hiltum   Hiġelāces ðeġn,
yrre ond ānrǣd.   Næs sēo ecg fracod
hilderinċe,   ac hē hraþe wolde
Grendle forġyldan   gūðrǣsa fela
ðāra þe hē ġeworhte   tō West-Denum
oftor micle   ðonne on ǣnne sīð,

1580   þonne hē Hrōðgāres   heorðġenēatas
slōh on sweofote,   slǣpende frǣt
folces Deniġea   fȳftȳne men
ond ōðer swylċ   ūt offerede,
lāðlicu lāc.   Hē him þæs lēan forġeald,
rēþe cempa,   ðæs þe hē on ræste ġeseah
gūðwēriġne   Grendel licgan,
aldorlēasne,   swā him ǣr ġescōd
hild æt Heorote   —hrā wīde sprong
syþðan hē æfter dēaðe   drepe þrōwade,

1590   heoroswenġ heardne—   ond hine þā hēafde beċearf.
    Sōna þæt ġesāwon   snottre ċeorlas,
þā ðe mid Hrōðgāre   on holm wliton,
þæt wæs ȳðġeblond   eal ġemenġed,

to wield it in battle. Beowulf seized
its hilt and, raging, swung it around;
the deadly blade bit through her neck,
sliced her spine, and cut off her head.
That huge body fell to the floor.   1500
The blade was bloody. The hero rejoiced.

   A light arose, and the room brightened
like the whole sky when heaven's candle
illumines the earth. He looked through the cave,
holding the hilt at shoulder level
as he watchfully moved along the wall,
enraged and resolute. Now the sword
would stand him in good stead, for he intended
to recompense Grendel for all his wrongs,
the many dire assaults on the Danes—   1510
not only on the first of his onslaughts
when he burst inside and killed in their beds
fifteen of Hrothgar's hearth-companions,
gobbled them up as they lay there groaning,
and dragged off another fifteen to his den:
a loathsome haul. The furious hero
paid him back when he saw his body
lying splayed and lifeless before him
because of the fatal wound from the fight.
The corpse bounced up as Beowulf sliced   1520
the neck-bone with one stupendous blow
that sheared off the monster's massive head.

   Soon the counselors keeping watch,
gazing with Hrothgar at the grim lake,

brim blōde fāh. Blondenfeaxe,
gomele ymb gōdne   onġeador spræcon
þæt hiġ þæs æðelinges   eft ne wēndon,
þæt hē siġehrēðiġ   sēċean cōme
mǣrne þēoden;   þā ðæs moniġe ġewearð
þæt hine sēo brimwylf   ābroten hæfde.

1600   Ðā cōm nōn dæġes.   Næs ofġeafon
hwate Scyldingas;   ġewāt him hām þonon
goldwine gumena.   Ġistas sētan
mōdes sēoce   ond on mere staredon;
wīston ond ne wēndon   þæt hīe heora winedrihten
selfne ġesāwon.

                Þā þæt sweord ongan
æfter heaþoswāte   hildeġiċelum,
wīġbil wanian;   þæt wæs wundra sum
þæt hit eal ġemealt   īse ġelīcost,
ðonne forstes bend   fæder onlǣteð,
1610   onwindeð wælrāpas,   sē ġeweald hafað
sǣla ond mǣla;   þæt is sōð metod.
Ne nōm hē in þǣm wīcum,   Weder-Ġeata lēod,
māðmǣhta mā,   þēh hē þǣr moniġe ġeseah,
būton þone hafelan   ond þā hilt somod
sinċe fāge;   sweord ǣr ġemealt,
forbarn brōdenmǣl;   wæs þæt blōd tō þæs hāt,
ǣttren ellorgǣst   sē þǣr inne swealt.
Sōna wæs on sunde   sē þe ǣr æt sæċċe ġebād
wīġhryre wrāðra,   wæter up þurhdēaf;
1620   wǣron ȳðġebland   eal ġefǣlsod,
ēacne eardas,   þā se ellorgāst
oflēt līfdagas   ond þās lǣnan ġesceaft.
    Cōm þā tō lande   lidmanna helm
swīðmōd swymman;   sǣlāca ġefeah

104

saw it stirred up and stained with blood.
They spoke about that brave man with grief
and regretted that he would never again
come to the king with another triumph;
many gray-haired elders agreed
that the vicious demon must have devoured him.   1530
The ninth hour came. The noble Scyldings
left the cliff, and the king went home.
The Geats stayed, heartsick, staring ahead
with the desperate hope that their hero and friend
might still return.
                        Meanwhile, the sword
quickly dissolved in the boiling blood
of the slain demon; it cracked into splinters
and melted away, wondrously,
like a slab of ice in spring, when the Father
loosens the bonds of frost, and frees   1540
the stiffened water, controlling the seasons
and times of year. (He is the true Lord.)
The noble hero took nothing at all
from the cave—though he saw countless treasures—
except that huge head and the inlaid hilt,
bright with jewels; the sword's blade
had wholly melted, so hot was the blood
of the poisonous ghoul who had just perished.
Soon he made his way to the surface;
the surging currents were now clear   1550
since the fiend had departed this fleeting world.
Then with powerful strokes he swam
to the lake's shore, much delighting

mæġenbyrþenne   þāra þe hē him mid hæfde.
Ēodon him þā tōġēanes,   Gode þancodon,
ðrȳðliċ þeġna hēap,   þēodnes ġefēgon,
þæs þe hī hyne ġesundne   ġesēon mōston.
Ðā wæs of þǣm hrōran   helm ond byrne

1630 lungre ālȳsed.   Lagu drūsade,
wæter under wolcnum,   wældrēore fāg.
Fērdon forð þonon   fēþelāstum
ferhþum fæġne,   foldweġ mǣton,
cūþe strǣte;   cyningbalde men
from þǣm holmclife   hafelan bǣron
earfoðlīċe   heora ǣġhwæþrum
felamōdiġra;   fēower scoldon
on þǣm wælstenġe   weorcum ġeferian
tō þǣm goldsele   Grendles hēafod,

1640 oþ ðæt semninga   tō sele cōmon
frome fyrdhwate   fēowertȳne
Ġēata gongan;   gumdryhten mid
modiġ on ġemonge   meodowongas træd.
Ðā cōm in gan   ealdor ðeġna,
dædcēne mon   dōme ġewurþad,
hæle hildedēor,   Hrōðgār grētan.
Þā wæs be feaxe   on flet boren
Grendles hēafod,   þǣr guman druncon,
eġesliċ for eorlum   ond þǣre idese mid,

1650 wliteseōn wrǣtliċ;   weras on sāwon.

Bēowulf maþelode,   bearn Ecgþeowes:
'Hwæt, wē þē þās sǣlāc,   sunu Healfdenes,
lēod Scyldinga,   lustum brōhton
tīres tō tācne,   þē þū hēr tō lōcast.
Iċ þæt unsōfte   ealdre ġedīġde

106

in the two weights he had brought from the water.
His men ran over to meet their prince,
gave thanks to God, shouting with joy
to see that he had come back to them safely,
and loosened the hero's helmet and mail-shirt.
Under the clouds the lake grew calm,
though still the waters were stained with gore.   1560

    They left that place by a narrow path,
happy at heart, and they soon came
to a path they knew well. As proud as kings,
they carried the huge head down from the cliff,
straining beneath the weight; four strong
warriors bore the battle-spear,
two at each end, and in the middle,
bound for the gold-hall, was Grendel's head.
Soon these fourteen stout-hearted Geats
came to Heorot, led by their captain,   1570
and passed superbly through the front door.
The returning hero entered the hall,
flushed with glory, and greeted the king.
Grendel's head was dragged by its hair
to the company drinking; then it was dropped
on the floor in front of the queen and nobles.
The men stared at the horrible sight.

THEN BEOWULF, SON of Ecgtheow, spoke:
"These splendid spoils are for you, my lord—
a proof of our glory! Gaze on them now.   1580
I barely survived that brutal combat

wiġġe under wætere,   weorc ġenēþde
earfoðlīċe;   ætrihte wæs
gūð ġetwǣfed,   nymðe meċ God scylde.
Ne meahte iċ æt hilde   mid Hruntinge
1660   wiht ġewyrċan,   þēah þæt wǣpen duge;
ac mē ġeūðe   ylda waldend
þæt iċ on wāge ġeseah   wlitiġ hangian
ealdsweord ēacen;   ofost wīsode
winiġea lēasum,   þæt iċ ðȳ wǣpne ġebrǣd.
Ofslōh ðā æt þǣre sæċċe,   þā mē sǣl āġeald,
hūses hyrdas.   Þā þæt hildebil
forbarn brogdenmǣl,   swā þæt blōd ġesprang,
hātost heaþoswāta.   Iċ þæt hilt þanan
fēondum ætferede,   fyrendǣda wræc,
1670   dēaðcwealm Deniġea,   swā hit ġedēfe wæs.
Iċ hit þē þonne ġehāte   þæt þū on Heorote mōst
sorhlēas swefan   mid þīnra secga ġedryht
ond þeġna ġehwylċ   þīnra lēoda,
duguðe ond iogoþe,   þæt þū him ondrǣdan ne þearft,
þēoden Scyldinga,   on þā healfe,
aldorbealu eorlum,   swā þū ǣr dydest.'
Ðā wæs gylden hilt   gamelum rinċe,
hārum hildfruman   on hand ġyfen,
enta ǣrġeweorc;   hit on ǣht ġehwearf
1680   æfter dēofla hryre   Deniġea frean,
wundorsmiþa ġeweorc;   ond þā þās worold ofġeaf
gromheort guma,   Godes andsaca,
morðres scyldiġ,   ond his mōdor ēac,
on ġeweald ġehwearf   woroldcyninga
ðǣm sēlestan   be sǣm twēonum
ðāra þe on Scedeniġġe   sceattas dǣlde.

under the waves. I almost died;
the fight would have been finished soon
if God had not graciously spared my life.
I could not use Hrunting, however able
that weapon may be, but the world's Ruler
let my eyes see a beautiful sword,
huge and ancient, that hung on the wall.
As soon as I could, I snatched it; quickly
I swung it over my head and struck   1590
the horrid brutes who lived in that hall.
The sword's blade melted in the hot blood
that gushed out of my enemies' wounds.
I took this hilt to avenge their horrors,
the Danes who have died. It was only fitting.
And now, my lord, I promise you peace
in Heorot; now you can sleep in safety,
free from care, with your company
and every retainer, both old and young.
You need not fear any further attacks   1600
or grisly deaths, as you did before."
    Then the gold hilt was handed to Hrothgar.
And so that exquisite ancient smithwork,
wondrously fired in the giants' forge,
had come into the king's possession
when the devils were dead—that heartless beast,
God's enemy, and his equally foul
murderous mother. It now belonged
to the noblest ruler between the two seas,
the most gracious lord in the northern lands.   1610

Hrōðgār maðelode;   hylt scēawode,
ealde lāfe.   On ðǣm wæs ōr writen
fyrnġewinnes;   syðþan flōd ofslōh,
1690   ġifen ġēotende   ġīganta cyn,
frēcne ġefērdon;   þæt wæs fremde þēod
ēċean dryhtne;   him þæs endelēan
þurh wæteres wylm   waldend sealde.
Swā wæs on ðǣm scennum   scīran goldes
þurh rūnstafas   rihte ġemearcod,
ġeseted ond ġesǣd,   hwām þæt sweord ġeworht,
īrena cyst   ǣrest wǣre,
wreoþenhilt ond wyrmfāh.   Ðā se wīsa spræc
sunu Healfdenes;   swīgedon ealle:
1700   'Þæt, lā, mæġ secgan   sē þe sōð ond riht
fremeð on folce,   feor eal ġemon,
eald ēþelweard,   þæt ðes eorl wǣre
ġeboren betera.   Blǣd is ārǣred
ġeond wīdwegas,   wine mīn Bēowulf,
ðīn ofer þēoda ġehwylċe.   Eal þū hit ġeþyldum healdest,
mæġen mid mōdes snyttrum.   Iċ þē sceal mīne ġelǣstan
frēode, swā wit furðum sprǣcon.   Ðū scealt tō frōfre weorþan
eal langtwīdiġ   lēodum þīnum,
hæleðum tō helpe.
                 Ne wearð Heremōd swā
1710   eaforum Ecgwelan,   Ār-Scyldingum;
ne ġewēox hē him tō willan   ac tō wælfealle
ond tō dēaðcwalum   Deniġa lēodum;
brēat bolgenmōd   bēodġenēatas,
eaxlġesteallan,   oþ þæt hē āna hwearf,
mǣre þēoden   mondrēamum from.
Ðēah þe hine mihtiġ God   mæġenes wynnum,
eafeþum stēpte   ofer ealle men,

Hrothgar closely examined the hilt.
It was engraved with the beginning
of human conflict, before the Flood
came down, dooming the giants' race—
a brutal end. But they had brought it
upon themselves by their proud estrangement
from God Almighty; He made the waters
rise, and He drowned them for their misdeeds.
Upon the elaborate golden blade-guard
with its fine scrollwork and serpentine patterns,   1620
in runic letters carefully written
there was also the name of the ancient hero
for whom this mighty sword had been made.
　　All were silent. Then the king spoke:
"As someone pledged to defend the people,
promote justice, remember our past,
and safeguard this land, I may truly say
that Beowulf is a better man
than anyone else. You have tempered your strength
with your mind's wisdom. The words I spoke   1630
to you before, when I promised you friendship
I reaffirm now. I know you will live
as your people's pride and their protector,
a bulwark in battle to all your men.
　　"Remember Heremod, who as king
brought evil to everyone in the land;
his legacy to the Danes was death.
In his rage he would kill his steadfast servants,
his closest friends and comrades-in-arms,
until at last he was left alone,   1640
hopeless, deprived of all human joys.
Though God had given him strength of body
and power exceeding all his peers,

forð ġefremede,   hwæþere him on ferhþe grēow
brēosthord blōdrēow,   nallas bēagas ġeaf
1720   Denum æfter dōme;   drēamlēas ġebād
þæt hē þæs ġewinnes   weorc þrōwade,
lēodbealo longsum.   Ðū þē lǣr be þon,
gumcyste onġit;   iċ þis ġid be þē
āwræc wintrum frōd.
                  Wundor is tō secganne
hū mihtiġ God   manna cynne
þurh sīdne sefan   snyttru bryttað,
eard ond eorlscipe;   hē āh ealra ġeweald.
Hwīlum hē on lufan   lǣteð hworfan
monnes mōdġeþonc   mǣran cynnes,
1730   seleð him on ēþle   eorþan wynne,
tō healdanne   hlēoburh wera,
ġedēð him swā ġewealdene   worolde dǣlas,
sīde rīċe,   þæt hē his selfa ne mæġ
for his unsnyttrum   ende ġeþenċean.
Wuna(ð) hē on wiste;   nō hine wiht dweleð
ādl nē yldo,   nē him inwitsorh
on sefa(n) sweorceð,   nē ġesacu ōhwǣr,
ecghete eoweð,   ac him eal worold
wendeð on willan;   hē þæt wyrse ne con—

1740   oð þæt him on innan   oferhyġda dǣl
weaxe(ð) ond wrīdað;   þonne se weard swefeð,
sāwele hyrde;   bið se slǣp tō fæst,
bisgum ġebunden,   bona swīðe nēah,
sē þe of flānbogan   fyrenum scēoteð.
Þonne bið on hreþre   under helm drepen
biteran strǣle   —him bebeorgan ne con—
wōm wunderbebodum   werġan gāstes;

his mind grew harsh, his heart bloodthirsty;
he gave no rings to secure his glory;
wretched he lived, and he suffered long
for the great pain that he caused his people.
Learn from his life to be openhanded;
this I tell you as a true friend
who has grown wise through many winters. 1650

"I have often marveled how God Almighty
gives wisdom to some and to others grants
riches and rank. It is all in His power.
He will lavish upon a lord of high birth
everything any human could want:
enormous wealth, all worldly pleasures,
men to rule over, many lands
subject to him, such wide kingdoms
that a man in his blindness cannot imagine
that this will ever come to an end. 1660
He dwells in abundance and does not think
of illness or old age; no cares or worries
darken his mind; nowhere does malice
hone its blade for him, and the whole world
aligns with his will. He expects no worse.

"But then inside him arrogance starts
to flourish. The guardian falls asleep:
conscience, the soul's protector. Too sound
is that sleep; he is crushed by cares, and the killer
approaches, drawing his deadly bow. 1670
The bitter arrow rips through his armor
and pierces his heart; he is helpless against
the dark commands of the menacing foe.

þinċeð him tō lȳtel   þæt hē lange hēold,
ġȳtsað gromhȳdiġ,   nallas on ġylp seleð
1750   fætte bēagas,   ond hē þā forðġesceaft
forġyteð ond forġȳmeð,   þæs þe him ǣr God sealde,
wuldres waldend,   weorðmynda dǣl.
Hit on endestæf   eft ġelimpeð
þæt se līċhoma   lǣne ġedrēoseð,
fǣġe ġefealleð;   fēhð ōþer tō,
sē þe unmurnlīċe   mādmas dǣleþ,
eorles ǣrġestrēon,   eġesan ne ġȳmeð.
Bebeorh þē ðone bealonīð,   Bēowulf lēofa,
secg bet[e]sta,   ond þē þæt sēlre ġeċēos,
1760   ēċe rǣdas;   oferhȳda ne ġȳm,
mǣre cempa.   Nū is þīnes mæġnes blǣd
āne hwīle;   eft sōna bið
þæt þeċ ādl oððe ecg   eafoþes ġetwǣfeð,
oððe fȳres fenġ,   oððe flōdes wylm,
oððe gripe mēċes,   oððe gāres fliht,
oððe atol yldo;   oððe ēagena bearhtm
forsiteð ond forsworceð;   semninga bið
þæt ðeċ, dryhtguma,   dēað oferswȳðeð.
    Swā iċ Hrinġ-Dena   hund missera
1770   wēold under wolcnum   ond hiġ wiġġe belēac
manigum mǣġþa   ġeond þysne middanġeard,
æscum ond ecgum,   þæt iċ mē ǣniġne
under sweġles begong   ġesacan ne tealde.
Hwæt, mē þæs on ēþle   edwenden cwōm,
gyrn æfter gomene,   seoþðan Grendel wearð,
ealdġewinna,   ingenġa mīn;
iċ þǣre sōcne   singāles wæġ
mōdċeare micle.   Þæs siġ metode þanc,
ēċean dryhtne,   þæs ðe iċ on aldre ġebād

What he has long held, seems too little;
he is always angry; he covets, he hoards,
he gives no gold rings to honor his men,
he forgets his future state, and he feels
no gratitude for all God's bounty
or the portion of honor he has been paid.
At last his body, which was on loan,   1680
weakens, falls, and goes to its fate.
Another man takes his ancestral treasures
and hands them out with a generous heart.

    "Guard against that pernicious evil,
dear Beowulf. Choose the better way:
eternal rewards. Turn from all pride,
for your strength will last just a little while.
A sudden outbreak of sickness or war
will enfeeble it, or the grip of fire,
surging waves, the thrust of a sword,   1690
a hurtling spear, or horrid old age.
Your eyes will darken, and all at once,
O warrior, death will sweep you away.

    "For fifty years I ruled the Ring-Danes
as a good king; with my spear and sword
I turned back many tribes, and I thought
I was safe from all enemies on the earth.
But what a reversal I underwent,
from joy to grief, when Grendel began
breaking my heart with his hellish onslaughts!   1700
I always suffered the deepest sorrow
from those grim visits. Thanks be to God,
the eternal Lord, that I lived to see

1780   þæt iċ on þone hafelan   heorodrēoriġne
ofer eald ġewin   ēagum stariġe.
Gā nū tō setle,   symbelwynne drēoh
wiġġeweorþad;   unc sceal worn fela
māþma ġemǣnra   siþðan morgen bið.'
    Ġēat wæs glædmōd,   ġēong sōna tō,
setles nēosan,   swā se snottra heht.
Þā wæs eft swā ǣr   ellenrōfum,
fletsittendum   fæġere ġereorded
nīowan stefne.   Nihthelm ġeswearc
1790   deorc ofer dryhtgumum.   Duguð eal ārās;
wolde blondenfeax   beddes nēosan,
gamela Scylding.   Ġēat uniġmetes wēl,
rōfne randwigan,   restan lyste;
sōna him seleþeġn   sīðes wērgum,
feorrancundum   forð wīsade,
sē for andrysnum   ealle beweotede
þeġnes þearfe,   swylċe þȳ dōgor
heaþolīðende   habban scoldon.
    Reste hine þā rūmheort;   reċed hlīuade
1800   ġēap ond goldfāh;   gæst inne swæf,
oþ þæt hrefn blaca   heofones wynne
blīðheort bodode.   Ðā cōm beorht [lēoma]
[ofer sceadwa] scacan;   scaþan ōnetton,
wǣron æþelingas   eft tō lēodum
fūse tō farenne;   wolde feor þanon
cuma collenferhð,   ċēoles nēosan.
    Heht þā se hearda   Hrunting beran
sunu Ecglāfes,   heht his sweord niman,
lēofliċ īren;   sæġde him þæs lēanes þanc,
1810   cwæð, hē þone gūðwine   gōdne tealde,

with my own eyes his horrible head
lying before me after your fight.
As you go to your seat, be glad of your triumph.
Eat and drink now. I will deal out
many treasures when morning comes."

    Joyful, the great warrior went
to sit back down as the king had requested,   1710
and then a second banquet was served
to the brave heroes who sat in the hall.

    Night came down and darkened the world.
The courtiers rose. The old king was ready
to go to his bed. The Geatish hero
wanted nothing but a night's rest;
he was infinitely tired from his exploit.
A hall-chamberlain came to help him
and led him out; with all reverence
he attended to the nobleman's needs,   1720
taking care of him with such comforts
as travelers could expect in those times.

THE GREAT-HEARTED HERO rested. The hall
towered, gold-splendid. The guest slept
till the black raven, happy at heart,
announced the joy of heaven; just then
daylight poured down over the shadows.
The Geatish warriors got up quickly,
longing to sail to their distant land
and to their comrades across the sea.   1730

    Then Beowulf had Hrunting brought out;
he told Unferth to take back his sword,
thanking him for the thoughtful loan.
He said he had found it a friend in battle,

wīġcræftiġne,　nales wordum lōg
mēċes ecge;　þæt wæs mōdiġ secg.
　　Ond þā sīðfrome,　searwum ġearwe
wīġend wǣron;　ēode weorð Denum
æþeling tō yppan,　þǣr se ōþer wæs,
hæle hildedēor　Hrōðgār grētte.

Bēowulf maþelode,　bearn Ecgþeowes:
'Nū wē sǣlīðend　secgan wyllað
feorran cumene　þæt wē fundiaþ
1820　Hiġelāc sēċan.　Wǣron hēr tela,
willum bewenede;　þū ūs wēl dohtest.
Ġif iċ þonne on eorþan　ōwihte mæġ
þīnre mōdlufan　māran tilian,
gumena dryhten,　ðonne iċ ġȳt dyde,
gūðġeweorca,　iċ bēo ġearo sōna.
Ġif iċ þæt ġefricge　ofer flōda begang
þæt þeċ ymbsittend　eġesan þȳwað,
swā þeċ hetende　hwīlum dydon,
iċ ðē þūsenda　þeġna bringe,
1830　hæleþa tō helpe.　Iċ on Hiġelāc wāt,
Ġēata dryhten,　þēah ðe hē ġeong sy,
folces hyrde,　þæt hē meċ fremman wile
wordum ond worcum,　þæt iċ þē wēl heriġe
ond þē tō ġēoce　gārholt bere,
mæġenes fultum,　þǣr ðē bið manna þearf.
Ġif him þonne Hrēþrīċ　tō hofum Ġēata
ġeþinġeð þēodnes bearn,　hē mæġ þǣr fela
frēonda findan;　feorcȳþðe bēoð
sēlran ġesōhte　þǣm þe him selfa dēah.'
1840　　Hrōðgār maþelode　him on andsware:
'Þē þā wordcwydas　wiġtiġ drihten

and he did not blame that excellent blade
for not performing. His mind was noble.
    When the men were ready, wearing their mail-shirts,
their honored prince walked up to the place
where Hrothgar sat, and wished him good health.
Then Beowulf, son of Ecgtheow, spoke: 1740
"We seafarers, who have sailed from afar,
long to go home to Hygelac's land.
You have entertained us in splendid style,
treated us with true kindness, given
us every comfort that we might crave.
If I can ever do anything else
to gain your enduring love, my lord,
beyond the deeds I have done already,
tell me; I will be eager to do it.
And if ever over the sea's expanse   1750
I hear that you have been harmed or threatened
by neighboring nations, as enemies
have sometimes done in the past, I promise
to sail back here with a thousand thanes.
Though Hygelac, the lord of the Geats,
is young, he is a man of much sense,
and I know that he will strongly support
my coming to aid you with a large army,
a forest of spears to fight for your honor.
And if your son Hrethric should have a reason   1760
to come to the Geats' court, I can assure you
that he will find friends there. Seeing far lands
can be helpful to one who wants to prevail."
    Then Hrothgar, the Scyldings' sovereign, spoke:
"It must be God who has put these gracious

on sefan sende;   ne hȳrde iċ snotorlicor
on swā ġeongum feore   guman þingian.
Þū eart mæġenes strang   ond on mōde frōd,
wīs wordcwida.   Wēn iċ taliġe,
ġif þæt ġegangeð   þæt ðe gār nymeð,
hild heorugrimme   Hrēþles eaferan,
ādl oþðe īren   ealdor ðīnne,
folces hyrde,   ond þū þīn feorh hafast,
1850   þæt þe Sǣ-Ġēatas   sēlran næbben
tō ġeċēosenne   cyning ǣniġne,
hordweard hæleþa,   ġyf þū healdan wylt
māga rīċe.   Mē þīn mōdsefa
līcað lenġ swā wēl,   lēofa Bēowulf.
Hafast þū ġefēred   þæt þām folcum sceal,
Ġēata lēodum   ond Gār-Denum
sib ġemǣnu,   ond sacu restan,
inwitnīþas   þe hīe ǣr drugon,
wesan, þenden iċ wealde   wīdan rīċes,
1860   māþmas ġemǣne,   maniġ ōþerne
gōdum ġegrētan   ofer ganotes bæð;
sceal hrinġnaca   ofer heafu bringan
lāc ond luftācen.   Iċ þā lēode wāt
ġē wið fēond ġē wið frēond   fæste ġeworhte,
ǣġhwæs untǣle   ealde wīsan.'
        Ðā ġīt him eorla hlēo   inne ġesealde,
mago Healfdenes,   māþmas twelfe;
hēt [h]ine mid þǣm lācum   lēode swǣse
sēċean on ġesyntum,   snūde eft cuman.
1870   Ġecyste þā   cyning æþelum gōd,
þēoden Scyldinga   ðeġn bet[e]stan
ond be healse ġenam;   hruron him tēaras
blondenfeaxum.   Him wæs bēġa wēn

120

words in your heart. I have never heard
such a young man so astute in statecraft.
You are strong in body, mature in mind,
and judicious in speech. If the son of Hrethel,
your king, should ever be killed in battle   1770
or yield to illness and you should survive,
the Geats could not wish for a worthier choice
as their guardian and giver of rings—
if it ever pleased you to rule your people.
The longer I know you, the more I like
your integrity, my trusted friend.
You have brought it about that our two peoples,
the Geats and the Danes, will dwell in friendship;
the strife that was once between them has ceased—
the fierce attacks they suffered before.   1780
As long as I rule this spacious land,
we will share our gold, and many ships
laden with splendid treasures will sail
between the two coasts of our countries, over
the broad sea where the gannet bathes.
I know our nations are firm in spirit
toward friend and foe, and in all things
both are blameless in the old ways."

    There in the hall the son of Healfdene
gave him a dozen precious gifts,   1790
bade him now sail back to his homeland,
and invited him to visit again.
Then the noble, kindhearted king
embraced the champion and kissed his cheek.
Tears ran down from the old man's eyes.

ealdum infrōdum,   ōþres swīðor,
þæt h[ī]e seoðða(n nō)   ġesēon mōston,
mōdiġe on meþle.   (W)æs him se man tō þon lēof
þæt hē þone brēostwylm   forberan ne mehte,
ac him on hreþre   hyġebendum fæst
æfter dēorum men   dyrne langað
1880 born wið blōde.   Him Bēowulf þanan,
gūðrinċ goldwlanc   græsmoldan træd
sinċe hrēmiġ;   sægenġa bād
āge[n]dfrean,   sē þe on ancre rād.
Þā wæs on gange   ġifu Hrōðgāres
oft ġeæhted;   þæt wæs ān cyning
æġhwæs orleahtre,   oþ þæt hine yldo benam
mæġenes wynnum,   sē þe oft manegum scōd.
    Cwōm þā tō flōde   felamōdiġra,
hæġstealdra [hēap],   hrinġnet bǣron,
1890 locene leoðosyrċan.   Landweard onfand
eftsīð eorla,   swā hē ǣr dyde;
nō hē mid hearme   of hliðes nōsan
gæs(tas) grētte,   ac him tōġēanes rād,
cwæð þæt wilcuman   Wedera lēodum
scaþan scīrhame   tō scipe fōron.
Þā wæs on sande   sǣġēap naca
hladen herewǣdum,   hrinġedstefna
mēarum ond māðmum;   mæst hlīfade
ofer Hrōðgāres   hordġestrēonum.
1900 Hē þǣm bātwearde   bunden golde
swurd ġesealde,   þæt hē syðþan wæs
on meodubenċe   māþme þȳ weorþra,
yrfelāfe.   Ġewāt him on naca
drēfan dēop wæter,   Dena land ofġeaf.
Þā wæs be mæste   merehræġla sum,

He knew that never again would they meet.
So strong was the sentiment that he could not
hold back the welling-up in his heart;
a deep affection for the dear man
burned in his blood.

                     Beowulf left him,   1800
proud of his prizes, and walked, exultant,
over the green earth. The ship awaited,
riding at anchor, ready to sail.
As they were going, Hrothgar's gifts
were praised many times. That proud king
was blameless in all things, though now old age,
which harms so many, had sapped him of strength.
    Then Beowulf's soldiers came to the sea,
wearing their war-shirts of close-linked iron.
The king's watchman saw them coming,   1810
but on this occasion he greeted the guests
courteously as he stood on the cliff,
without insults, then rode to meet them
and wished the seafarers a safe voyage
and a warm welcome when they sailed home.
The broad ship was beached on the sand
and loaded with armor, heirlooms, and horses.
The mast stood high over Hrothgar's treasures.
Beowulf gave a gold-trimmed sword
to the ship-sentinel. (Ever after   1820
he was greatly honored by other men
because of that gift, when he came to the mead-hall.)
    The ship set sail, stirred up deep waters,
and left land behind. Her high sea-cloth,
rigged with its strong ropes, bellied out,

seġl sāle fæst;   sundwudu þunede;
nō þǣr wēġflotan   wind ofer ȳðum
sīðes ġetwǣfde;   sǣgenġa fōr,
flēat fāmiġheals   forð ofer ȳðe,
1910   bundenstefna   ofer brimstrēamas,
þæt hīe Ġēata clifu   onġitan meahton,
cūþe næssas;   ċēol up ġeþrang,
lyftġeswenċed   on lande stōd.
Hreþe wæs æt holme   hȳðweard ġeara,
sē þe ǣr lange tīd   lēofra manna
fūs æt faroðe   feor wlātode;
sǣlde tō sande   sīdfæþme scip
oncerbendum fæst,   þȳ lǣs hym ȳþa ðrym
wudu wynsuman   forwrecan meahte.
1920   Hēt þā up beran   æþelinga ġestrēon,
frætwe ond fǣtgold;   næs him feor þanon
tō ġesēċanne   sinċes bryttan,
Hiġelāc Hrēþling,   þǣr æt hām wunað
selfa mid ġesīðum   sǣwealle nēah.

Bold wæs betliċ,   bregorōf cyning,
hēa[h on] healle,   Hyġd swīðe ġeong,
wīs wēlþungen,   þēah ðe wintra lȳt
under burhlocan   ġebiden hæbbe,
Hǣreþes dohtor;   næs hīo hnāh swā þēah,
1930   nē tō gnēað ġifa   Ġēata lēodum,
māþmġestrēona.   Mōdþrȳðo wæġ
fremu folces cwēn,   firen' ondrysne;
nǣniġ þæt dorste   dēor ġenēþan
swǣsra ġesīða,   nefne sinfrea,
þæt hire an dæġes   ēagum starede,
ac him wælbende   weotode tealde
handġewriþene;   hraþe seoþðan wæs

and her planks creaked as the breeze blew.
She flew forward, with foam on her prow,
skimming over the quick sea-currents,
until they came to the cliffs of Geatland,
which they knew well. Thrust by the wind,   1830
the ship ran far up onto the shingle.

    The harbor-guard saw them and hurried down;
for a long time he had scanned the sea-roads,
eager for his old friends' return.
He moored the broad-beamed ship to the beach
by her anchor ropes, to keep the rough waves
from driving her back into deep water.
Then he commanded that the men take
the treasures ashore, the gold and the war-gear.
It was a short distance from where they were   1840
to the house of Hygelac, son of Hrethel,
who lived with his courtiers close by the seawall.

    The building was splendid, the king brave
and confident. The very young queen,
Hygd, daughter of Haereth, was wise,
an accomplished woman, free in her wealth
and generous with gifts to the Geats—
unlike Offa's arrogant lady,
who carried out dreadful crimes in her youth.
Not even the boldest among her men   1850
dared to set eyes on her openly;
if anyone did, he was swiftly seized,
thrown into prison and put in chains,

æfter mundgripe   mēċe ġeþinġed,
þæt hit sceādenmǣl   scȳran mōste,
1940   cwealmbealu cȳðan.   Ne bið swylċ cwēnliċ þēaw
idese tō efnanne,   þēah ðe hīo ǣnlicu sȳ,
þætte freoðuwebbe   fēores onsǣċe
æfter liġetorne   lēofne mannan.
Hūru þæt onhōhsnod[e]   Hemminges mǣġ:
ealodrincende   ōðer sǣdan,
þæt hīo lēodbealewa   lǣs ġefremede,
inwitnīða,   (s)yððan ǣrest wearð
ġyfen goldhroden   ġeongum cempan,
æðelum dīore,   syððan hīo Offan flet
1950   ofer fealone flōd   be fæder lāre
sīðe ġesōhte;   ðǣr hīo syððan well
in gumstōle,   gōde mǣre,
līfġesceafta   lifiġende brēac,
hīold hēahlufan   wið hæleþa brego,
ealles moncynnes   mīne ġefrǣġe
þone sēlestan   bī sǣm twēonum,
eormencynnes;   forðām Offa wæs
ġeofum ond gūðum,   gārcēne man,
wīde ġeweorðod,   wīsdōme hēold
1960   ēðel sīnne;   þonon Ēomēr wōc
hæleðum tō helpe,   Hem[m]inges mǣġ,
nefa Gārmundes,   nīða cræftiġ.

Ġewāt him ðā se hearda   mid his hondscole
sylf æfter sande   sǣwong tredan,
wīde waroðas.   Woruldcandel scān,
siġel sūðan fūs.   Hī sīð drugon,
elne ġeēoden,   tō ðæs ðe eorla hlēo,
bonan Ongenþeoes   burgum in innan,

and the sword's sharp edge would sever his life
with a painful stroke. That is no proper
custom for a great queen to practice,
however distinguished in birth and beauty;
a woman should be a weaver of peace,
not execute men for imagined insults.
But Offa put an end to all that.   1860
This was another side to the story;
ale-drinkers said that after her marriage
she no longer caused pain to the people,
once she was given, gold-adorned,
to that young warrior when she sailed
at her father's behest to Offa's hall
in a voyage over the sparkling sea.
She was later lauded for her good deeds;
she pledged herself to the people's welfare
and had a deep love for the man she married,   1870
who was the kindest and best of kings—
so I have heard—from sea to sea.
Since Offa was a brave man in battle
and generous as a giver of gold,
he was honored far and wide, and in wisdom
he ruled the land. From his loins sprang Eomer,
Hemming's kinsman and grandson of Garmund,
who was a bulwark to his bold men.

    Then Beowulf turned and strode with his troop
over the sand of the broad beach.   1880
Hastening from the south, the sun,
the world's candle, shone on their war-gear
as they eagerly made their way to where
they had heard that Hygelac, patron of heroes,

ġeongne gūðcyning   gōdne ġefrūnon
1970 hringas dǣlan.   Hiġelāce wæs
sīð Bēowulfes   snūde ġecȳðed,
þæt ðǣr on worðiġ   wīġendra hlēo,
lindġestealla   lifiġende cwōm,
heaðolāces hāl   tō hofe gongan.
Hraðe wæs ġerȳmed,   swā se rīċa bebēad,
fēðeġestum   flet innanweard.
   Ġesæt þā wið sylfne   sē ðā sæċċe ġenæs,
mǣġ wið mǣġe,   syððan mandryhten
þurh hlēoðorcwyde   holdne ġegrētte,
1980 mēaglum wordum.   Meoduscenċum hwearf
ġeond þæt [heal]reċed   Hæreðes dohtor,
lufode ðā lēode,   liðwǣġe bær
hæleðum tō handa.   Hiġelāc ongan
sīnne ġeseldan   in sele þām hēan
fæġre fricgcean;   hyne fyrwet bræc,
hwylċe Sǣ-Ġeata   sīðas wǣron:
'Hū lomp ēow on lāde,   lēofa Bīowulf,
þā ðū fǣringa   feorr ġehogodest
sæċċe sēċean   ofer sealt wæter,
1990 hilde tō Hiorote?   Ac ðū Hrōðgāre
wīdcūðne wēan   wihte ġebēttest,
mǣrum ðēodne?   Iċ ðæs mōdċeare
sorhwylmum sēað,   sīðe ne truwode
lēofes mannes;   iċ ðē lange bæd
þæt ðū þone wælgǣst   wihte ne grētte,

their young sovereign, Ongentheow's slayer,
was giving out golden rings in his hall.
The news was soon announced to the king
that Beowulf, his battle-companion,
protector of heroes, had, unharmed,
just returned from his perilous journey   1890
and was coming, even now, to the court.
It was quickly cleared on Hygelac's orders,
and in their triumph the troop marched in.

    Then Beowulf sat down beside the king,
kinsman with kinsman, having expressed
his fealty to his belovèd lord
with courteous words that came from the heart.
Hygd, the queen, daughter of Haereth,
moved about with the mead pitcher,
caring for everyone, filling cups.   1900
Then Hygelac questioned his old comrade,
and a great eagerness rose up within him
to find out how they had fared on their journey:
"My dear Beowulf, what did you do
after you decided to seek
that distant combat across the salt water,
the fight at Heorot? Was there in fact
anything you achieved that could end
the horror that had descended on Hrothgar
or ease that king of his agony?   1910
I have felt a constant fear for your life;
worries have overwhelmed my heart.
I dreaded your expedition's outcome;
I begged you not to attack that beast,

lēte Sūð-Dene   sylfe ġeweorðan
gūðe wið Grendel.   Gode iċ þanc secge
þæs ðe iċ ðē ġesundne   ġesēon mōste.'
      Bīowulf maðelode,   bearn Ecgðioes:
2000 'Þæt is undyrne,   dryhten Hiġe(lāc),
miċel ġemēting   monegum fira,
hwyl(ċ) or(leġ)hwīl   uncer Grendles
wearð on ðām wange,   þǣr hē worna fela
Siġe-Scyldingum   sorge ġefremede,
yrmðe tō aldre;   iċ ðæt eall ġewræc,
swā beġylpan [ne] þearf   Grendeles māga
(ǣ)n(iġ) ofer eorðan   ūhthlem þone,
sē (ð)e lenġest leofað   lāðan cynnes,
fǣr(e) bifongen.   Iċ ðǣr furðum cwōm
2010 tō ðām hrinġsele   Hrōðgār grētan;
sōna mē se mǣra   mago Healfdenes,
syððan hē mōdsefan   mīnne cūðe,
wið his sylfes sunu   setl ġetǣhte.
Weorod wæs on wynne;   ne seah iċ wīdan feorh
under heofones hwealf   healsittendra
medudrēam māran.   Hwīlum mǣru cwēn,
friðusibb folca   flet eall ġeondhwearf,
bǣdde byre ġeonge;   oft hīo bēahwriðan
secge (sealde)   ǣr hīe tō setle ġēong.
2020 Hwīlum for (d)uguðe   dohtor Hrōðgāres
eorlum on ende   ealuwǣġe bær,
þā iċ Frēaware   fletsittende
nemnan hȳrde,   þǣr hīo (næ)ġled sinċ
hæleðum sealde.   Sīo ġehāten (is),
ġeong goldhroden,   gladum suna Frōdan;
(h)afað þæs ġeworden   wine Scyldinga,
rīċes hyrde,   ond þæt rǣd talað,

and many times told you to let the Danes
themselves settle their war with Grendel.
But God be thanked: you are once again
back in your homeland, safe and sound."
　　Then Beowulf, son of Ecgtheow, spoke:
"To many men it is not a secret,　　　　　　　　　1920
my honored lord, how I met that monster
Grendel, and seized him in the great hall
where he had been devastating the Danes
and had made a horror of many lives.
I took my revenge on the vicious beast,
and none of that despicable spawn
will want to boast of our night battle.
Once I had landed, right away
I went to the great hall and greeted Hrothgar.
When I had told him of my intention,　　　　　　1930
he sat me down beside his own sons.
They were all happy; in my whole life
I have never known such heartfelt rejoicing.
Their renowned queen, the peace-pledge of nations,
walked among us, telling the men
to enjoy the feast, and generously
gave out many golden bracelets
before she finally went to her seat.
I saw their daughter carry the ale-cup
to each one of the oldest retainers,　　　　　　　1940
and the company called her Freawaru
when she passed it, precious, studded with gems.
She is promised—a beautiful, gold-clad bride—
to Ingeld, heir to the Heathobards' throne.
The Scyldings' ruler was keen to arrange this;
he considered it wise that with this young woman

þæt hē mid ðȳ wīfe   wælfæhða dǣl,
sæċċa ġesette.   Oft seldan hwǣr
2030 æfter lēodhryre   lȳtle hwīle
bongār būgeð,   þēah sēo brȳd duge.
Mæġ þæs þonne ofþynċan   ðēoden Heaðo-Beardna
ond þeġna ġehwām   þāra lēoda
þonne hē mid fǣmnan   on flett gǣð,
dryhtbearn Dena,   duguða biwenede.
On him gladiað   gomelra lāfe,
heard ond hrinġmǣl   Heaða-Bear[d]na ġestrēon,
þenden hīe ðām wǣpnum   wealdan mōston—

oð ðæt hīe forlǣddan   tō ðām lindplegan
2040 swǣse ġesīðas   ond hyra sylfra feorh.
    Þonne cwið æt bēore   sē ðe bēah ġesyhð,
eald æscwiga,   sē ðe eall ġe(man),
gārcwealm gumena   —him bið grim (se)fa—
onġinneð ġēomormōd   ġeong(um) cempan
þurh hreðra ġehyġd   hiġes cunnian,
wīġbealu weċċean,   ond þæt word ācwyð:
"Meaht ðū, mīn wine,   mēċe ġecnāwan,
þone þīn fæder   tō ġefeohte bær
under heregrīman   hindeman sīðe,
2050 dȳre īren,   þǣr hyne Dene slōgon,
wēoldon wælstōwe,   syððan Wiðerġyld lǣġ,
æfter hæleþa hryre,   hwate Scyldungas?
Nū hēr þāra banena   byre nāthwylċes
frætwum hrēmiġ   on flet gǣð,
morðres ġylpe(ð),   ond þone māðþum byreð,
þone þe ðū mid rihte   rǣdan sceoldest."
Manað swā ond myndgað   mǣla ġehwylċe
sārum wordum,   oð ðæt sǣl cymeð

132

he could settle his share of the savage feud.
Yet after a king's fall, in any land,
the murderous spear does not stay idle,
however perfect a bride may be.   1950
It may not please the Heathobards' prince
or every one of his warriors
when the Danish escort enters their hall
with the bride and her brilliant entourage,
upon whom hang the Heathobards' heirlooms,
ancestral swords that are inlaid with gold,
which their own fathers had wielded once,
until they came to that fatal combat
and lost those treasures along with their lives.
Then at the feast some grizzled fighter   1960
sees those swords and remembers it all,
the death of his dear battle-companions,
and bitter rage boils up in his heart;
he tries to tempt a young man beside him
to stir up resentment, and speaks these words:
'Look, friend: that is the sword your father
bore into battle for the last time
when the Danes killed him and won the day
on that blood-drenched field where Withergyld fell
and many of our brave men were slaughtered.   1970
Now a son of your father's slayer
in his Danish arrogance dares to appear;
he boasts of the murder, and from his belt
hangs the rare blade that is rightfully yours.'
He taunts the young man at every turn
with cruel words, till the day comes

þæt se fǣmnan þeġn   fore fæder dǣdum
æfter billes bite   blōdfāg swefeð,
ealdres scyldiġ;   him se ōðer þonan
losað (li)fiġende,   con him land ġeare.
Þonne bīoð (āb)rocene   on bā healfe
āðsweord eorla;   (syð)ðan Inġelde
weallað wælnīðas,   ond him wīflufan
æfter ċearwælmum   cōlran weorðað.
Þȳ iċ Heaðo-Bear[d]na   hyldo ne telġe,
dryhtsibbe dǣl   Denum unfǣcne,
frēondscipe fæstne.

                           Iċ sceal forð sprecan
ġēn ymbe Grendel,   þæt ðū ġeare cunne,
sinċes brytta,   tō hwan syððan wearð
hondrǣs hæleða.   Syððan heofones ġim
glād ofer grundas,   gǣst yrre cwōm,
eatol ǣfengrom   ūser nēosan,
ðǣr wē ġesunde   sæl weardodon.
Þǣr wæs Hondsciō   hild onsǣġe,
feorhbealu fǣġum;   hē fyrmest læġ,
gyrded cempa;   him Grendel wearð,
mǣrum maguþeġne   tō mūðbonan,
lēofes mannes   līċ eall forswealg.
Nō ðȳ ǣr ūt ðā ġēn   īdelhende
bona blōdiġtōð,   bealewa ġemyndiġ,
of ðām goldsele   gongan wolde,
ac hē mæġnes rōf   mīn costode,
grāpode ġearofolm.   Glōf hangode
sīd ond sylliċ,   searobendum fæst;
sīo wæs orðoncum   eall ġeġyrwed
dēofles cræftum   ond dracan fellum.
Hē meċ þǣr on innan   unsynniġne,

2060
2070
2080

when the lady's attendant lies there dead,
blood-smeared from the bite of a sword
for his father's sake. The assailant knows
the country well and escapes with his life.   1980
Then on both sides the oath is broken
that was sworn in the hall; violent hatred
wells up in Ingeld, and once it does,
his love for his wife becomes much cooler.
So I have no faith in the Heathobards' firmness
or their loyalty to this Danish alliance.
   "And now, my lord, I would like to tell you
further about my fight with Grendel.
As soon as heaven's bright gem had sunk
below the horizon, that raging beast   1990
came to attack us and bring his terror
where we kept guard in the great hall.
There the fight was fatal to Handscioh.
Our dear comrade was killed that night
when the cruel fiend tore into his flesh
and devoured the victim's entire body.
And this was not all: the evil marauder,
with bloody teeth, was bent on more crimes
and did not mean to depart from the mead-hall
empty-handed. With his huge claw   2000
he seized me, standing over my bed
in the dim light. His belly hung down,
immense, magical, armored with many
seams and clasps, cunningly wrought
with devil's devices and dragons' skins.
The foul brute wished to stuff me inside,

2090 dīor dǣdfruma   ġedōn wolde
maniġra sumne;   hyt ne mihte swā,
syððan iċ on yrre   upprihte āstōd.
Tō lang ys tō reċċenne   hū i(ċ ð)ām lēodsceaðan
yfla ġehwylċes   ondlēan forġeald;
þǣr iċ, þēoden mīn,   þīne lēode
weorðode weorcum.   Hē on weġ losade,
lȳtle hwīle   līfwynna brē(a)c;
hwæþre him sīo swīðre   swaðe weardade
hand on Hiorte,   ond hē hēan ðonan,
2100 mōdes ġeōmor   meregrund ġefēoll.
Mē þone wælrǣs   wine Scildunga
fǣttan golde   fela lēanode,
manegum māðmum,   syððan merġen cōm,
ond wē tō symble   ġeseten hæfdon.
Þǣr wæs ġidd ond glēo;   gomela Scilding,
felafricgende   feorran rehte;
hwīlum hildedēor   hearpan wynne,
gome(n)wudu grētte,   hwīlum ġyd āwræc
sōð ond sārliċ,   hwīlum sylliċ spell
2110 rehte æfter rihte   rūmheort cyning;
hwīlum eft ongan   eldo ġebunden,
gomel gūðwiga   ġioguðe cwīðan,
hildestrenġo;   hreðer (in)ne wēoll
þonne hē wintrum frōd   worn ġemunde.
Swā wē þǣr inne   andlangne dæġ
nīode nāman,   oð ðæt niht becwōm
ōðer tō yldum.   Þā wæs eft hraðe
ġearo gyrnwræce   Grendeles mōdor,
sīðode sorhfull;   sunu dēað fornam,

along with my comrades' blood-smeared bodies;
but the deed was not so easy to do
after I rose to my feet, enraged.
It would take too long to tell you of what   2010
I did to pay back that pestilent demon
for the horrors he brought to Heorot, my lord,
but I earned much honor for you and your people.
He slipped from my grasp and stayed alive
for a little longer, but his right arm
stayed behind when he fled from the hall,
lurching, and sank to the lake's bottom.
　　"For that fierce combat the king of the Danes
rewarded me with gem-studded weapons
and with much gold when morning came   2020
and everyone gathered in the great hall.
There was song and laughter; the Scylding lord
recited stories from distant days.
When he who had once been bold in battle
touched the harp-strings, they trembled with joy,
and then he began to sing a story
that was true and mournful, or he would tell
a wonder-tale in just the right way.
Or the great king, now cramped with age,
lamented the loss of his manly powers;   2030
his heart ached when he remembered what
he used to be in the time of his youth.
And so, in Heorot, that whole day
we feasted and laughed, till another night
came to the world. Then all at once
Grendel's mother left her dark lair
on a violent journey to take revenge
for the death that through us had seized her son.

2120 wīġhete Wedra.   Wīf unhȳre

hyre bearn ġewræc,   beorn ācwealde

ellenlīċe;   þǣr wæs Æschere,

frōdan fyrnwitan   feorh ūðġenġe.

Nōðer hȳ hine ne mōston,   syððan merġen cwōm,

dēaðwēriġne   Denia lēode

bronde forbærnan,   nē on bēl hladan

lēofne mannan;   hīo þæt līċ ætbær

fēondes fæð(mum   un)der firġenstrēam.

Þæt wæs Hrōðgār(e)   hrēowa tornost

2130 þāra þe lēodfruman   lange beġēate.

Þā se ðēoden meċ   ðīne līfe

healsode hrēohmōd   þæt iċ on holma ġeþrinġ

eorlscipe efnde,   ealdre ġenēðde,

mærðo fremede;   hē mē mēde ġehēt.

Iċ ðā ðæs wælmes,   þē is wīde cūð,

grimne gryrelicne   grundhyrde fond;

þǣr unc hwīle wæs   hand ġemǣne;

holm heolfre wēoll,   ond iċ hēafde beċearf

in ðām [gūð]sele   Grendeles mōdor

2140 ēacnum ecgum;   unsōfte þonan

feorh oðferede;   næs iċ fǣġe þā ġȳt,

ac mē eorla hlēo   eft ġesealde

māðma meniġeo,   maga Healfdenes.

    Swā se ðēodkyning   þēawum lyfde;

nealles iċ ðām lēanum   forloren hæfde,

mæġnes mēde,   ac hē mē (māðma)s ġeaf,

sunu Healfdenes   on (mīn)ne sylfes dōm;

ðā iċ ðē, beorncyning,   bringan wylle,

ēstum ġeȳwan.   Ġēn is eall æt ðē

2150 lissa ġelong;   iċ lȳt hafo

hēafodmāga   nefne, Hyġelāc, ðeċ.'

That monstrous female fiercely avenged
her child by killing a counselor there— 2040
Aeschere, an old friend of the king's.
When morning arrived, the men of Denmark
discovered that they could not burn
the body of the brave counselor
on a funeral pyre, because the fiend
had carried it off in her cold embrace
and taken it under the mountain torrents.
This was a horrible grief for Hrothgar,
the bitterest he had ever borne.
Sick at heart, the old king beseeched me, 2050
in your name, to do a heroic deed
and risk my life in the lake's tumult;
he promised to grant me a great reward.
Far and wide men tell how I found
the dreadful guardian of the deep waters
and killed her in hand-to-hand combat. The waves
seethed with blood; then I sliced off
her gigantic head in that battle-hall
with her own blade. I barely managed
to leave with my life, but I was not yet 2060
fated to die. The Danes' protector
again gave me a noble reward.
    "Thus the king respected old customs
and recompensed me with priceless gifts
for my service to him—whatever I wanted
out of his storehouse of splendid treasures.
All this is yours now. I give it to you
as a gesture of gratitude; all my joys
depend on your favor, and I have few
kinsmen except for you, great king." 2070

Hēt ðā in beran   eaforhēafodseġn,
heaðostēapne helm,   hāre byrnan,
gūðsweord ġeatoliċ,   ġyd æfter wræc:
'Mē ðis hildesceorp   Hrōðgār sealde,
snotra fenġel;   sume worde hēt
þæt iċ his ǣrest ðē   ēst ġesǣġde:
cwæð þæt hyt hæfde   Hiorogār cyning,
lēod Scyldunga   lange hwīle;
2160   nō ðȳ ǣr suna sīnum   syllan wolde,
hwatum Heorowearde,   þēah hē him hold wǣre,
brēostġewǣdu.   Brūc ealles well!'
Hȳrde iċ þæt þām frætwum   fēower mēaras
lungre, ġelīċe   lāst weardode,
æppelfealuwe;   hē him ēst ġetēah
mēara ond māðma.   Swā sceal mǣġ don,
nealles inwitnet   ōðrum breġdon
dyrnum cræfte,   dēað rēn(ian)
hondġesteallan.   Hyġelāce wæs
2170   nīða heardum   nefa swȳðe hold,
ond ġehwæðer ōðrum   hrōþra ġemyndiġ.
Hȳrde iċ þæt hē ðone healsbēah   Hyġde ġesealde,
wrǣtlicne wundurmāððum,   ðone þe him Wealhðēo ġeaf,
ðēod(nes) dohtor,   þrīo wicg somod
swancor ond sadolbeorht;   hyre syððan wæs
æfter bēahðeġe   br[ē]ost ġeweorðod.
Swā b(eal)dode   bearn Ecgðeowes,
guma gūð(um) cūð,   gōdum dǣdum,
drēah æfter dōme;   nealles druncne slōg
2180   heorðġenēatas;   næs him hrēoh sefa,
ac hē mancynnes   mǣste cræfte
ġinfæstan ġife   þe him God sealde
hēold hildedēor.   Hēan wæs lange,

Then Beowulf ordered his men to bring in
the boar's-head banner, the battle-helmet,
the mail-shirt and jeweled sword, and he said:
"All this war-gear Hrothgar gave me.
He commanded me to explain how much
the gifts are a measure of his good will.
They had been owned by his elder brother,
Heorogar, who had not bequeathed them
to the stalwart Heoroweard, his own son,
loyal as he was. Enjoy them well."   2080
    Then, I have heard, four swift horses,
sleek, bay-colored, and of the same size,
were bestowed on the king. (A kinsman should always
act in this way, and never weave
nets of malice for his own men
or plot the death of his close companions.
He kept faith with the king, his uncle,
and each one worked for the other's welfare.)
I have also heard that he gave Queen Hygd
three graceful steeds with gold-fitted saddles   2090
and the awe-inspiring, gem-studded collar
that Wealhtheow had presented him with;
beautifully it had adorned her breast.
    Thus Beowulf proved himself a brave man,
renowned for his fighting and noble deeds;
he acted with honor and never killed
his dear companions when they were drinking;
his heart was not savage; he held the gift
that God had graciously given him—
the mightiest body a man ever had—   2100
humbly, as a great hero should.
Yet in his youth he had been despised;

swā hyne Ġēata bearn   gōdne ne tealdon,
nē hyne on medobenċe   micles wyrðne
(dry)hten Wedera   ġedōn wolde;
swȳðe (wēn)don   þæt hē slēac wǣre,
æðeling unfrom.   Edwenden cwōm
tīrēadigum menn   torna ġehwylċes.

2190   Hēt ðā eorla hlēo   in ġefetian,
heaðorōf cyning   Hrēðles lāfe
golde ġeġyrede;   næs mid Ġēatum ðā
sinċmāðþum sēlra   on sweordes hād;
þæt hē on Bīowulfes   bearm āleġde,
ond him ġesealde   seofan þūsendo,
bold ond bregostōl.   Him wæs (b)ām samod
on ðām lēodscipe   lond ġecynde,
eard ēðelriht,   ōðrum swīðor
sīde rīċe   þām ðǣr sēlra wæs.

2200   Eft þæt ġeīode   ufaran dōgrum
hildehlæmmum,   syððan Hyġelāc læġ,
ond Hear[dr]ēde   hildemēċeas
under bordhrēoðan   tō bonan wurdon,
ðā hyne ġesōhtan   on siġeþēode
hearde hildefrecan,   Heaðo-Scilfingas,
nīða ġenǣġdan   nefan Hererīċes:
syððan Bēowulfe   br(ā)de rīċe
on hand ġehwearf;   hē ġehēold tela
fīftiġ wintr(a)   —wæs ðā frōd cyning,
2210   eald ēþel(w)eard—   oð ðæt (ā)n ongan
deorcum nihtum   draca rīċs[i]an,
sē ðe on hēa(um) h(of)e   hord beweotode,
stānbeorh stēar(c)ne;   stīġ under læġ
eldum uncūð.   Þǣr on innan ġīong

none of the noblemen thought him brave,
and the Geats' king was reluctant to grant
golden gifts to him at the mead-bench.
They firmly believed that he was lazy,
a feeble young prince. But good fortune came
and changed his troubles into great triumphs.

    Then Hygelac had them bring in a sword
handed down by his father, Hrethel;   2110
it was gold-adorned, and among the Geats
there was no greater treasure than this.
He laid the sword in Beowulf's lap
and rewarded him with wondrous gifts:
a large mead-hall, a thousand square miles
of the richest land, and a regal throne.
(Both men held inherited land
by ancestral right, but the realm belonged
to Hygelac, whose rank was higher.)

YEARS WENT BY. In the crash of battles   2120
Hygelac fell, then Heardred was killed,
his last son, behind the shelter of shields
when the fierce Swedes had sought him out
and attacked him in a terrible onslaught.
The kingdom came into Beowulf's hands.
He ruled it well for fifty winters,
until in his old age an evil beast,
a dragon, began to rule the dark nights—
the guardian of a treasure trove
in the steep vault of a stone barrow.   2130
The entrance to it was hidden from humans,

nið[ð]a nāthwyl(ċ,   sē ðe nē)h ġ(eþ[r]on)g
hǣðnum horde;   hond (ēðe ġefēng)
(searo) sinċe fāh.   Nē hē þæt syððan (bemāð),
þ(ēah) ð(e hē) slǣpende   besyre(d wur)de
þēofes cræfte: þæt sīe ðīod (onfand),
2220   b(ū)folc b(i)orn(a),   þæt hē ġebolge(n) wæs.

Nealles (met ġe)wēaldum   wyrmhorda cræft,
sylfes willum,   sē ðe him sāre ġesceōd,
ac for þrēanēdlan   þē(o) nāthwylċes
hæleða bearna   heteswenġeas flē(a)h,
ærnes þearf(a),   ond ðǣr inne (f)eal(h)
secg syn(by)siġ   sōna (in þ)ā tīde,
þæt (þǣr) ðām ġyst(e)   g(r)yrebr(ō)g(a) stōd;
hwæðr(e earm)sceapen   (ealdre nēþd)e,
2230   forh(t on ferhðe)   þā hyne se fǣ(r) beġeat,*
sinċfæt (sōhte).   Þǣr wæs swylcra fela
in ðām eorðse(le)   ǣrġestrēona,
swā hȳ on ġeārdagum   gumena nāthwylċ,
eormenlāfe   æþelan cynnes,
þanchycgende   þǣr ġehȳdde,
dēore māðmas.   Ealle hīe dēað fornam
ǣrran mǣlum,   ond s(ē) ān ðā ġēn
lēoda duguðe,   sē ðǣr lenġest hwearf,
weard wineġeōmor,   (wēn)de þæs yl(c)an,
2240   þæt hē lȳtel fæc   longġestrēona
brūcan mōste.   Beorh eall ġearo
wunode on wonge   wæterȳðum nēah,
nīwe be næsse,   nearocræftum fæst;
þǣr on inn(a)n bær   eorlġestrēona
hringa hyrde   h(o)rdwyrðne dǣl,

*Because it has eliminated a dittograph from the text, the Klaeber fourth edition lacks a line 2229.

but some man managed to make his way
into the treasure cave; he took
a gold cup, and the dragon discovered
that someone had stolen it while he slept.
Soon the people all around suffered
the effects of that dragon's fiery rage.
    The man was not trying to penetrate
a heathen hoard or to harm the beast.
He was a slave; in a state of panic   2140
he had just fled from his master's flogging.
Wandering into the wilderness,
he found the barrow and slipped inside,
and his heart grew chill with a great horror.
But the wretched fugitive risked his life;
though his spirit quailed and dread clutched him,
he took the treasure. Many rare things,
heaps of gold and gems, had been hidden
inside the earth-hall in ancient days;
some unknown person had thought to place them   2150
carefully there in that deep cave,
the rich bequest of a noble race
whom death had consumed in that distant age.
The last of them who was still alive,
as he guarded the gold and mourned his people,
knew that his time to enjoy the treasure
would be brief before he must share their fate.
A barrow stood waiting, high on the headland,
overlooking the ocean waves,
new-built, its narrow entrance concealed.   2160
The ring-guardian hid what riches

fǣttan goldes,   fē(a) worda cwæð:
'Heald þū nū, hrūse,   nū hæleð ne m(ō)stan,
eorla ǣhte.   Hwæt, hyt ǣr on ðē
gōde beġēaton;   gūðdēað fornam,
2250   (f)eorhbeal(o) frēcne   fȳra ġe(h)wylcne
lēoda mīnra,   þ(o)n(e) ðe þis [līf] ofġeaf;
ġesāwon seledrēam(as).   Nāh hwā sweord weġe
oððe f(orð bere)   fǣted wǣġe,
dryncfæt dēore;   dug(uð) ellor s[c]eōc.
Sceal se hearda helm   (hyr)stedgolde,
fǣtum befeallen;   feormynd swefað,
þā ðe beadogrīman   bȳwan sceoldon;
ġē swylċe sēo herepād,   sīo æt hilde ġebād
ofer borda ġebræc   bite īrena,
2260   brosnað æfter beorne.   Ne mæġ byrnan hrinġ
æfter wīġfruman   wīde fēran,
hæleðum be healfe.   Næs hearpan wyn,
gomen glēobēames,   nē gōd hafoc
ġeond sæl swingeð,   nē se swifta mearh
burhstede bēateð.   Bealocwealm hafað
fela feorhcynna   forð onsended.'
Swā ġiōmormōd   giohðo mǣnde
ān æfter eallum,   unblīðe hwear(f)
dæġes ond nihtes,   oð ðæt dēaðes wylm
2270   hrān æt heortan.   Hordwynne fond
eald ūhtsceaða   opene standan,
sē ðe byrnende   biorgas sēċeð,
nacod nīðdraca,   nihtes flēogeð
fȳre befangen;   hyne foldbūend
(swīðe ondrǣ)da(ð).   Hē ġesēċean sceall
hord on hrūsan,   þǣr hē hǣðen gold
warað wintrum frōd;   ne byð him wihte ðȳ sēl.

were worth saving and spoke these words:
    "Hold this treasure within you, O earth,
now that I cannot hold it here.
Death claimed all my kinfolk in battle;
every last one has left this world,
never again to know its pleasures.
Now there is not even one remaining
to carry the sword or bear the cup;
all those warriors—hurried away.   2170
The hardened helmet must lose the gold trim
that now adorns it; the stewards sleep
who used to burnish the battle-masks;
so too the mail-shirt that marched to war,
a shelter behind the thick shields crashing
as the blades bit; it decays like the body,
and the linked chains cannot travel along
with the commander beside his men;
no longer is there delight from the harp,
surges of joy from the singing wood;   2180
no well-trained hawk now flies through the hall,
and the swift horse does not stamp in the courtyard.
Savage death has silenced them all."
Desolate, grieving both day and night,
he mourned for his friends until death's flood
covered his spirit.
               The ancient serpent
happened to find that hidden hoard—
the smooth ravager, wrapped in flames,
who flies through the night, pernicious, searching
for treasure under the earth, and guards   2190
heathen gold-heaps for many winters,
though it gains nothing from what it guards.

Swā se ðēodsceaða   þrēohund wintra
hēold on hrūsan   hordærna sum
2280 ēacencræftiġ,   oð ðæt hyne ān ābealch
mon on mōde;   mandryhtne bær
fæted wǣġe,   frioðowǣre bæd
hlāford sīnne.   Ðā wæs hord rāsod,
onboren bēaga hord,   bēne ġetīðad
fēasceaftum men;   frēa scēawode
fīra fyrnġeweorc   forman sīðe.
Þā se wyrm onwōc,   wrōht wæs ġenīwad;
stonc ðā æfter stāne,   stearcheort onfand
fēondes fōtlāst;   hē tō forð ġestōp
2290 dyrnan cræfte   dracan hēafde nēah.
Swā mæġ unfǣġe   ēaðe ġedīġan
wēan ond wræcsīð,   sē ðe waldendes
hyldo ġehealdeþ.   Hordweard sōhte
ġeorne æfter grunde,   wolde guman findan,
þone þe him on sweofote   sāre ġetēode;
hāt ond hrēohmōd   hlǣw oft ymbehwearf
ealne ūtanweardne;   nē ðǣr æniġ mon
on þ(ām) wēstenne—   hwæðre wīġes ġefeh,
bea(dwe) weorces;   hwīlum on beorh æthwearf,
2300 sinċfæt sōhte;   hē þæt sōna onfand,
ðæt hæfde gumena sum   goldes ġefandod,
hēahġestrēona.   Hordweard onbād
earfoðlīċe   oð ðæt ǣfen cwōm;
wæs ðā ġebolgen   beorges hyrde,
wolde se lāða   līġe forġyldan
drinċfæt dŷre.   Þā wæs dæġ sceacen
wyrme on willan;   nō on wealle læ[n]ġ
bīdan wolde,   ac mid bǣle fōr,
fŷre ġefŷsed.   Wæs se fruma eġeslīċ

For three hundred years this scaly scourge
sat in the treasure-hall under the earth,
until one human enraged its heart.
The intruder took the cup to his lord
and begged his pardon. The barrow was robbed,
the treasure diminished, the wretched man
forgiven the fault; for the first time his lord
gazed upon the gold of the ancients.   2200
When the dragon awoke, a time of trouble
began for the Geats. Furiously
it slithered along the stones, until
it found a footprint; the reckless thief
had stepped too close to its head. (When someone
is unfated to die, he can endure
grief and hardship, by the Lord's grace.)
The dragon tried to find the intruder
who had harmed it so while it was asleep.
Sick at heart, it circled the cave,   2210
searched outside it in every corner,
but no one appeared in that wild place.
It imagined how it would punish that man;
sometimes it went back into the barrow
and searched again for the golden cup.
When it was clear that someone had stolen
part of its wealth, the fire-beast waited
restlessly till evening arrived.
By then its fury was even fiercer;
it violently wanted revenge   2220
on that man for taking its treasured cup.
So it was happy when daylight dimmed
and it could come forth out of its cavern.
It flew up into the heavens, flaming.

2310 lēodum on lande, swā hyt lungre wearð
on hyra sinċġifan sāre ġeendod.

 Ðā se gæst ongan glēdum spīwan,
beorht hofu bærnan— brynelēoma stōd
eldum on andan; nō ðǽr āht cwices
lāð lyftfloga lǽfan wolde.
Wæs þæs wyrmes wīġ wīde ġesȳne,
nearofāges nīð nēan ond feorran,
hū se gūðsceaða Ġēata lēode
hatode ond hȳnde; hord eft ġescēat,
2320 dryhtsele dyrnne, ǽr dæġes hwīle.
Hæfde landwara līġe befangen,
bǽle ond bronde; beorges ġetruwode,
wīġes ond wealles; him sēo wēn ġelēah.

 Þā wæs Bīowulfe brōga ġecȳðed
snūde tō sōðe, þæt his sylfes hām,
bolda sēlest, brynewylmum mealt,
ġifstōl Ġēata. Þæt ðām gōdan wæs
hrēow on hreðre, hyġesorga mǽst;
wēnde se wīsa þæt hē wealdende
2330 ofer ealde riht, ēċean dryhtne
bitre ġebulge; brēost innan wēoll
þēostrum ġeþoncum, swā him ġeþȳwe ne wæs.
Hæfde līġdraca lēoda fæsten,
ēalond ūtan, eorðweard ðone
glēdum forgrunden; him ðæs gūðkyning,
Wedera þīoden wræce leornode.
Heht him þā ġewyrċean wīġendra hlēo
eall īrenne, eorla dryhten,
wīġbord wrǽtliċ; wisse hē ġearwe
2340 þæt him holtwudu he(lpan) ne meahte,
lind wið līġe. Sceolde lǽn daga,

This onset was grim for all the people,
as the end was grievous for their good king.

    The creature started to spew out fire
and burn down buildings; the blaze rose high
and terrified men; that heartless monster
left nothing alive beneath its wings.   2230
The dragon's onslaught was seen all over;
it was known everywhere, near and far,
how that sky-ravager hurled down rage
on the country people and then crawled back
to its hidden hoard just before dawn.
It had scorched the countryside with its fire;
now it retreated, trusting the barrow
and its own strength, though its trust deceived it.

    To Beowulf then the terror was told,
that his own house, that majestic hall,   2240
the Geats' throne-room, had gone up in flames.
This caused the good man untold anguish,
a bitter sorrow that seared his heart.
He feared that he had somehow offended
the eternal Lord, had broken His law
in some horrible way; dark thoughts heaved
in his troubled spirit and took it over.
The fire-dragon had devastated
the coastal land, along with a fortress,
the people's stronghold; and so the king   2250
planned vengeance on him. The valiant hero
commanded then that a marvelous shield,
all of iron, be forged by the smiths,
for well he knew that mere linden wood
could not defend him against those flames.

æþeling ǣrgōd   ende ġebīdan,
worulde līfes,   ond se wyrm somod,
þēah ðe hordwelan   hēolde lange.
Oferhogode ðā   hringa fenġel
þæt hē þone wīdflogan   weorode ġesōhte,
sīdan herġe;   nō hē him þā sǽċċe ondrēd,
nē him þæs wyrmes wīg   for wiht dyde,
eafoð ond ellen,   forðon hē ǣr fela

2350 nearo nēðende   nīða ġedīġde,
hildehlemma,   syððan hē Hrōðgāres,
sigorēadiġ secg,   sele fǣlsode,
ond æt gūðe forgrāp   Grendeles mǣgum
lāðan cynnes.   Nō þæt lǣsest wæs
hondġemōt(a)   þǣr mon Hyġelāc slōh,
syððan Ġēata cyning   gūðe rǣsum,
frēawine folca   Frēslondum on,
Hrēðles eafora   hiorodrynċum swealt,
bille ġebēaten.   Þonan Bīowulf cōm

2360 sylfes cræfte,   sundnytte drēah;
hæfde him on earme   (ealra) þrītiġ
hildeġeatwa   þā hē tō holme (þron)g.
Nealles Hetware   hrēmġe þorf(t)on
fēðewīġes,   þē him foran onġēan
linde bǣron;   lȳt eft becwōm
fram þām hildfrecan   hāmes nīosan.
Oferswam ðā sioleða bigong   sunu Ecgðeowes,
earm ānhaga   eft tō lēodum;
þǣr him Hyġd ġebēad   hord ond rīċe,

2370 bēagas ond bregostōl;   bearne ne truwode,
þæt hē wið ælfylċum   ēþelstōlas
healdan cūðe,   ðā wæs Hyġelāc dēad.

But soon he was going to see the end
of his earthly days; the dragon was too,
after long guarding the golden hoard.

    Beowulf scorned to pursue that beast
with a troop of fighters; he did not fear   2260
single combat with the huge creature.
He had fought many battles before
and had taken great risks amid the tumult
when he had purged Hrothgar's hall,
putting an end to the power of Grendel
and his hideous mother. One of his hardest
hand-to-hand fights took place in Frisia,
when Hygelac, son of Hrethel, was killed
in the crush of battle; the king of the Geats
died when a sword's edge drank his blood.   2270
The hero escaped by his strength and courage,
and in his arms he carried the war-gear
of thirty thanes whom he had cut down
as he pressed toward the sea. The proud Hetware
had nothing to boast of about the battle;
few of those who had fought against him
could get up and go home again.
Then Beowulf swam across the vast sea
alone, back to the land of the Geats.
Afterward Queen Hygd offered him   2280
the royal throne, for she did not think
that her son could safeguard the Geats' country
from foreigners, now that his father was dead.

Nō ðȳ ǣr fēasceafte   findan meahton
æt ðām æðelinge   ǣniġe ðinga
þæt hē Heardrēde   hlāford wǣre,
oððe þone cynedōm   ċīosan wolde;
hwæðre hē him on folce   frēondlārum hēold,
ēstum mid āre,   oð ðæt hē yldra wearð,
Weder-Ġēatum wēold.

                    Hyne wræcmæcgas
2380   ofer sǣ sōhtan,   suna Ōhteres;
hæfdon hȳ forhealden   helm Scylfinga,
þone sēlestan   sǣcyninga
þāra ðe in Swīorīċe   sinċ brytnade,
mǣrne þēoden.   Him þæt tō mearce wearð:
hē þǣr [f]or feorme   feorhwunde hlēat,
sweordes swenġum,   sunu Hyġelāces,
ond him eft ġewāt   Ongenðioes bearn
hāmes nīosan   syððan Heardrēd læġ,
lēt ðone bregostōl   Bīowulf healdan,
2390   Ġēatum wealdan;   þæt wæs gōd cyning.

Sē ðæs lēodhryres   lēan ġemunde
uferan dōgrum,   Ēadġilse wearð
fēasceaftum frēond;   folce ġestēpte
ofer sǣ sīde   sunu Ōhteres,
wigum ond wǣpnum;   hē ġewræc syððan
ċealdum ċearsīðum,   cyning ealdre binēat.
    Swā hē nīða ġehwane   ġenesen hæfde,
slīðra ġeslyhta,   sunu Ecgðiowes,
ellenweorca,   oð ðone ānne dæġ
2400   þe hē wið þām wyrme   ġewegan sceolde.
Ġewāt þā twelfa sum   torne ġebolgen
dryhten Ġēata   dracan scēawian;

But the grieving nobles could not persuade
that loyal man to be Heardred's lord;
he declined their offer to make him king.
He supported the young prince with his advice
and honored him till he came of age
and could rule his people. Then exiles arrived,
seeking Heardred—Ohthere's sons,   2290
who were rebels against the Scylfings' ruler,
the best of the sea-kings who gave out gold
in the Swedes' land. This led to the killing
of Heardred, whose hospitality cost him
a fatal slash from a Swedish blade.
After the battle, Onela went
back to his own land, leaving the hero
to rule the Geats; he was a good king.
In later days, he repaid his lord's death
by supporting Eadgils when he was impoverished;   2300
he sent him help across the sea-currents—
weapons and warriors. Eadgils took
his revenge by raids that ravaged the land,
and he killed Onela in a fierce combat.

    And so the son of Ecgtheow survived
through all these struggles and savage onslaughts
with heroic deeds, until the day came
when he had to fight with the fire-dragon.
The king of the Geats, with eleven comrades,
furious, went to look for the lair.   2310

hæfde þā ġefrūnen   hwanan sīo fæhð ārās,
bealonīð biorna;   him tō bearme cwōm
mā(ð)þumfæt mære   þurh ðæs meldan hond.
Sē wæs on ðām ðrēate   þreottēoða secg,
sē ðæs orleġes   ōr onstealde,
hæft hyġeġiōmor,   sceolde hēan ðonon
wong wīsian.   Hē ofer willan ġīong
2410   tō ðæs ðe hē eorðsele   ānne wisse,
hlǣw under hrūsan   holmwylme nēh,
ȳðġewinne;   sē wæs innan full
wrǣtta ond wīra.   Weard unhīore,
ġearo gūðfreca   goldmāðmas hēold
eald under eorðan;   næs þæt ȳðe ċēap
tō ġegangenne   gumena ǣnigum.
Ġesæt ðā on næsse   nīðheard cyning
þenden hǣlo ābēad   heorðġenēatum,
goldwine Ġēata.   Him wæs ġeōmor sefa,
2420   wǣfre ond wælfūs,   wyrd unġemete nēah,
sē ðone gomelan   grētan sceolde,
sēċean sāwle hord,   sundur ġedǣlan
līf wið līċe;   nō þon lange wæs
feorh aþelinges   flǣsce bewunden.
Bīowulf maþelade,   bearn Ecgðeowes:
'Fela iċ on ġiogoðe   gūðrǣsa ġenæs,
orleġhwīla;   iċ þæt eall ġemon.
Iċ wæs syfanwintre   þā meċ sin(c)a baldor,
frēawine folca   æt mīnum fæder ġenam;
2430   hēold meċ ond hæfde   Hrēðel cyning,
ġeaf mē sinċ ond symbel,   sibbe ġemunde;
næs iċ him tō līfe   lāðra ōwihte,
beorn in burgum,   þonne his bearna hwylċ,
Herebeald ond Hæðcyn   oððe Hyġelāc mīn.

He had found out by then the cause of the creature's
bitter hatred and malice toward men;
the precious cup had been placed in his hands
by the thief himself, who was the thirteenth
in their company; he was now a captive,
abject, despised as the origin
of so much sorrow. Against his will
he led them to the underground lair,
the barrow close to the surging sea,
hidden from men, heaped with treasures   2320
of filigreed gold and jeweled war-gear.
The monstrous beast was ready for battle
as it guarded those treasures. Obtaining them
would not be easy for any man.

 The king sat down on the cliff-top then
and wished good health to his hearth-companions.
His heart was sorrowful, restless, ready
for death, as his fate edged infinitely
closer, seeking to separate
the old man's life from his body. Not long   2330
would his spirit be enfolded in flesh.

 Then Beowulf, son of Ecgtheow, spoke:
"In the days of my youth I endured much fighting,
many wars; I remember them all.
I was seven years old when my father sent me
to live with Hrethel, lord of the Geats.
The king could not have been kinder to me;
he sheltered me as a kinsman should,
feasted me, gave me generous gifts.
Never did he in the banquet hall   2340
love me less than he loved his sons,
Herebeald, Haethcyn, or Hygelac, my lord.

157

Wæs þām yldestan unġedēfelīċe
mǣġes dǣdum morþorbed stred,
syððan hyne Hæðcyn of hornbogan,
his frēawine flāne ġeswencte,
miste merċelses ond his mǣġ ofscēt,
2440 brōðor ōðerne blōdigan gāre.
Þæt wæs feohlēas ġefeoht, fyrenum ġesyngad,
hreðre hyġemēðe; sceolde hwæðre swā þēah
æðeling unwrecen ealdres linnan.
    Swā bið ġeōmorlīċ gomelum ċeorle
tō ġebīdanne, þæt his byre rīde
ġiong on galgan. Þonne hē ġyd wrece,
sāriġne sang, þonne his sunu hangað
hrefne tō hrōðre, ond hē him helpe ne mæġ
eald ond infrōd ǣniġe ġefremman,
2450 symble bið ġemyndgad morna ġehwylċe
eaforan ellorsīð; ōðres ne ġȳmeð
tō ġebīdanne burgum in innan
yrfeweardas, þonne se ān hafað
þurh dēaðes nȳd dǣda ġefondad.
Ġesyhð sorhċeariġ on his suna būre
wīnsele wēstne, windġe reste,
rēot[ġ]e berofene; rīdend swefað,
hæleð in hoðman; nis þǣr hearpan swēġ,
gomen in ġeardum, swylċe ðǣr iū wǣron.

2460 Ġewīteð þonne on sealman, sorhlēoð gǣleð
ān æfter ānum; þūhte him eall tō rūm,
wongas ond wīċstede.
                            Swā Wedra helm
æfter Herebealde heortan sorge
weallinde wæġ; wihte ne meahte

158

The eldest was accidentally
killed by his own kinsman's mistake
when Haethcyn, with his horn-tipped bow,
shot his dear friend and future lord;
he had missed the mark, and the arrow hit
his brother, piercing the prince's heart.
Irreparable, that terrible wrong,
for who could avenge Herebeald's death   2350
or pay blood-money? The king was baffled.
His misery was like an old man's
who sees his only son on the gallows;
he weeps and wails as his dear child
swings from the rope, to the ravens' joy,
and he cannot offer him any help.
Every morning he is reminded
of his boy's death, and he does not wish
to have a second son, when the first
died in such a desperate way.   2360
He looks at the son's house and sees, heartbroken,
the abandoned beer-hall, the windswept rooms
that are desolate now; the nobles sleep
under the earth; there is no harp music,
no joy in the homestead, as once there was.
He goes to the bedroom, utters his grief,
one groan after another, and now
it seems to him there is too much space
in his fields and household.
                              Thus Hrethel felt
a sickening grief for his eldest son.   2370

on ðām feorhbonan   fǣghðe ġebētan;
nō ðȳ ǣr hē þone heaðorinċ   hatian ne meahte
lāðum dǣdum,   þēah him lēof ne wæs.
Hē ðā mid þǣre sorhge,   þē him sīo sār belamp,
gumdrēam ofġeaf,   Godes lēoht ġeċēas;
2470   eaferum lǣfde,   swā dēð ēadiġ mon,
lond ond lēodbyriġ,   þā hē of līfe ġewāt.
   Þā wæs synn ond sacu   Swēona ond Ġeata
ofer (w)īd wæter   wrōht ġemǣne,
herenīð hearda,   syððan Hrēðel swealt,
oð ðe him Ongenðeowes   eaferan wǣran
frome fyrdhwate,   frēode ne woldon
ofer heafo healdan,   ac ymb Hrēosna Beorh
eatolne inwitscear   oft ġefremedon.
   Þæt mǣġwine   mīne ġewrǣcan,
2480   fǣhðe ond fyrene,   swā hyt ġefrǣġe wæs,
þēah ðe ōðer his   ealdre ġebohte,
heardan ċēape;   Hæðcynne wearð,
Ġeata dryhtne   gūð onsǣġe.
   Þā iċ on morgne ġefræġn   mǣġ ōðerne
billes ecgum   on bonan stǣlan,
þǣr Ongenþēow   Eofores nīosað;
gūðhelm tōglād,   gomela Scylfing
hrēas [hilde]blāc;   hond ġemunde
fǣhðo ġenōge,   feorhswenġ ne oftēah.
2490   Iċ him þā māðmas   þe hē mē sealde
ġeald æt gūðe,   swā me ġifeðe wæs
lēohtan sweorde;   hē mē lond forġeaf,
eard ēðelwyn.   Næs him ǣniġ þearf
þæt hē tō Ġifðum   oððe tō Gār-Denum
oððe in Swīorīċe   sēċean þurfe
wyrsan wīġfrecan,   weorðe ġeċȳpan;

He could not remedy the great wrong
by punishing Haethcyn or hating the boy
for his heedless act, though he held it against him.
Because of this bitter grief, he gave up
all life's joys, and he chose God's light,
leaving his land and goods to his sons,
as the prosperous do when they depart.

"Then hatred grew between Swedes and Geats,
and war broke out across the wide water.
Ongentheow's sons were bold and combative   2380
and did not want peace between the peoples;
in terrible, falsehearted attacks
they slaughtered Geats at the Hill of Sorrows.
My two kinsmen avenged that crime,
as is well known, though the elder one,
Haethcyn, fell in that fierce combat
and paid with his life—a painful bargain.
But then Prince Hygelac, so we all heard,
had his revenge the very next morning
in battle, when Ongentheow sought out Eofor,   2390
whose sword cut the king's helmet in two;
with fury he dealt him that fatal blow,
and, death-pale, Ongentheow dropped to the ground.

"The treasures that Hygelac heaped upon me
I earned—as fate let me—whenever I fought
with my gleaming sword. He gave me land
and a noble estate, so there was no need
for him to go out and search for Gifthas
or Swedes or Danes to hire as soldiers,
to choose some lesser champion among them.   2400

symle iċ him on fēðan   beforan wolde,
āna on orde,   ond swā tō aldre sceall
sæċċe fremman,   þenden þis sweord þolað
2500   þæt meċ ǣr ond sīð   oft ġelǣste,
syððan iċ for dugeðum   Dæġhrefne wearð
tō handbonan,   Hūga cempan—
nalles hē ðā frætwe   Frēscyning[e],
brēostweorðunge   bringan mōste,
ac in campe ġecrong   cumbles hyrde,
æþeling on elne;   ne wæs ecg bona,
ac him hildegrāp   heortan wylmas,
bānhūs ġebræc.   Nū sceall billes ecg,
hond ond heard sweord   ymb hord wīgan.'
2510   Bēowulf maðelode,   bēotwordum spræc
nīehstan sīðe: 'Iċ ġenēðde fela
gūða on ġeogoðe;   ġȳt iċ wylle,
frōd folces weard   fǣhðe sēċan,
mǣrðu fremman,   ġif meċ se mānsceaða
of eorðsele   ūt ġesēċeð.'
Ġegrētte ðā   gumena ġehwylcne,
hwate helmberend   hindeman sīðe,
swǣse ġesīðas: 'Nolde iċ sweord beran,
wǣpen tō wyrme,   ġif iċ wiste hū
2520   wið ðām āglǣċean   elles meahte
ġylpe wiðgrīpan,   swā iċ giō wið Grendle dyde;
ac iċ ðǣr heaðufȳres   hātes wēne,
[o]reðes ond āttres;   forðon iċ mē on hafu

I would always go before him on foot,
alone in the front line; and all my life
I will fight, as long as this sword lasts,
which has served me so well in battle since
I killed Daeghrefn, the Hugas' hero,
as the two armies faced each other.
He could not bring back the looted collar
to the Frisian king, since he fell in the fight,
their standard-bearer, a strong, brave man.
No blade killed him: I crushed out his life   2410
with my bare hands; I cracked his bones
till his heartbeat stopped. Now the sword's edge
and its hard blade will fight for the treasure."

THEN BEOWULF MADE a battle vow
for the last time: "I was often tested
in fierce fighting when I was young.
Now I am old, but I am still eager
to take on this task for the people's good
and do a great deed if the evil creature
dares to come out of his earthen hall."   2420
    Then he addressed his dear companions,
those loyal young men, for the last time:
"I would not carry a sword to this combat
if I knew another way I could grapple
honorably with this great beast
as I did with Grendel, long ago;
but in this fight I expect to feel
the blazing, poisoned fire of its breath,
and so I have put on my shield and mail-shirt.

bord ond byrnan.   Nelle iċ beorges weard
oferflēon fōtes trem,   ac unc [feohte] sceal
weorðan æt wealle,   swā unc wyrd ġetēoð
metod manna ġehwæs.   Iċ eom on mōde from,
þæt iċ wið þone gūðflogan   ġylp ofersitte.
Ġebīde ġē on beorge   byrnum werede,
2530   secgas on searwum,   hwæðer sēl mæġe
æfter wælræse   wunde ġedȳġan
uncer twēġa.   Nis þæt ēower sīð,
nē ġemet mannes   nef(ne) mīn ānes,
þæt hē wið āglæċean   eofoðo dæle,
eorlscype efne.   Iċ mid elne sceall
gold ġegangan,   oððe gūð nimeð,
feorhbealu frēcne   frēan ēowerne.'
     Ārās ðā bī ronde   rōf ōretta,
heard under helme,   hioroserċean bær
2540   under stāncleofu,   strenġo ġetruwode
ānes mannes;   ne bið swylċ earges sīð!
Ġeseah ðā be wealle   sē ðe worna fela
gumcystum gōd   gūða ġedīġde,
hildehlemma,   þonne hnitan fēðan,
sto[n]dan stānbogan,   strēam ūt þonan
brecan of beorge;   wæs þǣre burnan wælm
heaðofȳrum hāt,   ne meahte horde nēah
unbyrnende   ǣniġe hwīle
dēop ġedȳġan   for dracan lēġe.
2550   Lēt ðā of brēostum,   ðā hē ġebolgen wæs,
Weder-Ġēata lēod   word ūt faran,
stearcheort styrmde;   stefn in becōm
heaðotorht hlynnan   under hārne stān.
Hete wæs onhrēred,   hordweard oncnīow
mannes reorde;   næs ðǣr māra fyrst

Not one footstep will I fall back   2430
from the huge creature; here, at the wall,
the conflict will surely turn out according
to the fate the Lord has allotted to us.
I am resolute now; there is no need
for a vow against this vicious destroyer.
Do not go with me. Wait for me here,
safe, to see which one of us two
is better able to bear his wounds
from this fight to the death. It is not fitting
for anybody except myself   2440
to match strength with this monstrous being
and thus win gold and a hero's glory.
I will kill the beast, or else in the battle
a fatal wound will bear me away."
    The hero stood up beside his shield,
wearing a helmet and iron war-shirt,
and strode under the stony cliffs,
trusting entirely in his strength.
(Cowards do not have courage like this.)
Then he who had braved so many battles   2450
where foot-troops clash in the frenzy of war
saw a stone arch and a blazing stream
that burst from the barrow; it had flowed past
the dazzling hoard in the barrow's depths
and caught fire from the dragon's flames.
Beowulf bellowed; out of his breast
came a fierce shout, a cry of fury;
he roared with battle-rage under gray stone.
Hatred arose; the dragon heard
the sound of a man and was stirred to combat;   2460

frēode tō friclan.   From ǣrest cwōm
oruð āglǣċean   ūt of stāne,
hāt hildeswāt;   hrūse dynede.
Biorn under beorge   bordrand onswāf
2560   wið ðām gryreġieste,   Ġēata dryhten;
ðā wæs hrinġbogan   heorte ġefȳsed
sæċċe tō sēċeanne.   Sweord ǣr ġebrǣd
gōd gūðcyning,   gomele lāfe,
ecgum unslāw;   ǣġhwæðrum wæs
bealohycgendra   brōga fram ōðrum.
Stīðmōd ġestōd   wi(ð) stēapne rond
winia bealdor,   ðā se wyrm ġebēah
snūde tōsomne;   hē on searwum bād.
Ġewāt ðā byrnende   ġebogen scrīðan,
2570   tō ġescipe scyndan.   Scyld wēl ġebearg
līfe ond līċe   lǣssan hwīle
mǣrum þēodne   þonne his myne sōhte,
ðǣr hē þȳ fyrste   forman dōgore
wealdan mōste   swā him wyrd ne ġescrāf
hrēð æt hilde.   Hond up ābrǣd
Ġēata dryhten,   gryrefāhne slōh
inċġelāfe,   þæt sīo ecg ġewāc
brūn on bāne,   bāt unswīðor
þonne his ðīodcyning   þearfe hæfde
2580   bysigum ġebǣded.   Þā wæs beorges weard
æfter heaðuswenġe   on hrēoum mōde,
wearp wælfȳre;   wīde sprungon
hildelēoman.   Hrēðsigora ne ġealp
goldwine Ġēata;   gūðbill ġeswāc
nacod æt nīðe,   swā hyt nō sceolde,
īren ǣrgōd.   Ne wæs þæt ēðe sīð,
þæt se mǣra   maga Ecgðēowes

its hot breath issued out of the rock
in a rush of steam, and the ground rumbled.
Down in the barrow, Beowulf turned
toward the hideous coiled creature
that wanted to wreak its rage upon him.
He had drawn his sword, an ancient heirloom
with a keen edge. Each attacker
was terrified as his enemy faced him.
But the hero stood firm behind his shield
as the beast quickly uncoiled itself   2470
and, swathed in fire, came slithering forth
toward its fate. The thick shield sheltered
the agèd leader's body and life
for a shorter while than he could have wished;
that terrible day was the only time
fate had ever refused to grant him
a battle-triumph. Beowulf lifted
his ancient sword and slashed the creature
on its shimmering back, but the sharp edge
could not bite through the bony scales;   2480
it failed him in the battle's first
moment, just when he needed it most.
After this, the beast grew bolder
and spat out fire; war-flames leaped
all over the cave. As they burned, the king
did not boast of his battle triumphs.
His good sword, which had always served him,
miscarried at the most crucial time.
It was not easy for Ecgtheow's son

grundwong þone   ofġyfan wolde;
sceolde [ofer] willan   wīċ eardian
2590   elles hwerġen,   swā sceal ǣġhwylċ mon
ālǣtan lǣndagas.
              Næs ðā long tō ðon
þæt ðā āglǣċean   hȳ eft ġemētton.
Hyrte hyne hordweard,   hreðer ǣðme wēoll,
nīwan stefne;   nearo ðrōwode
fȳre befongen   sē ðe ǣr folce wēold.
Nealles him on hēape   handġesteallan,
æðelinga bearn   ymbe ġestōdon
hildecystum,   ac hȳ on holt bugon,
ealdre burgan.   Hiora in ānum wēoll
2600   sefa wið sorgum;   sibb' ǣfre ne mæġ
wiht onwendan   þām ðe wēl þenċeð.

Wīġlāf wæs hāten,   Wēoxstānes sunu,
lēoflīċ lindwiga,   lēod Scylfinga,
mǣġ Ælfheres;   ġeseah his mondryhten
under heregrīman   hāt þrōwian.
Ġemunde ðā ðā āre   þe hē him ǣr forġeaf,
wīċstede weliġne   Wǣġmundinga,
folcrihta ġehwylċ,   swā his fæder āhte;
ne mihte ðā forhabban,   hond rond ġefēng,
2610   ġeolwe linde,   gomel swyrd ġetēah;
þæt wæs mid eldum   Ēanmundes lāf,
suna Ōhtere[s];   þām æt sæċċe wearð,
wrǣċċa(n) winelēasum   Wēohstān bana
mēċes ecgum,   ond his māgum ætbær
brūnfāgne helm,   hringde byrnan,
ealdsweord etonisc;   þæt him Onela forġeaf,
his gædelinges   gūðġewǣdu,

to leave the present world and, unwilling,   2490
make a home elsewhere, but every man
must surrender this life that is lent to him.
Soon after this the two assailants
came together again. The dragon
took heart, and again its hot breast heaved
with withering flames. Wrapped in fire,
the hero suffered a searing pain.
His comrades in that perilous combat
could not match up to his manly courage;
they fled to the forest to save their lives.   2500

    One of them, though, welled up with sorrow.
(In a decent man the claims of kinship
will always ward off a wavering heart.)
His name was Wiglaf, Weohstan's son,
a staunch warrior, prince of the Swedes,
Aelfhere's kinsman. He saw the king
tormented by heat beneath his helmet.
He remembered his many kindnesses,
the wealthy estate of the Waegmunding clan,
the freehold that his father had owned,   2510
and he could not hold back; his hand seized
his strong shield, and he drew his sword,
which was known to men as the heirloom of Eanmund,
son of Ohthere. Weohstan had slain
that friendless exile with his blade's edge
and had brought to the uncle, Onela,
the nephew's shining helmet, his mail-shirt,
and the famous sword, fashioned by giants.
Onela gave him all these things

fyrdsearo fūsliċ— nō ymbe ðā fǣhðe spræc,
þēah ðe hē his brōðor bearn ābredwade.

2620 Hē frætwe ġehēold fela missera,
bill ond byrnan, oð ðæt his byre mihte
eorlscipe efnan swā his ǣrfæder;
ġeaf him ðā mid Ġēatum gūðġewǣda
ǣġhwæs unrīm þā hē of ealdre ġewāt
frōd on forðweġ. Þā wæs forma sīð
ġeongan cempan þæt hē gūðe rǣs
mid his frēodryhtne fremman sceolde.
Ne ġemealt him se mōdsefa, nē his mǣġes lāf
ġewāc æt wīġe; þæt se wyrm onfand,

2630 syððan hīe tōgædre ġegān hæfdon.

    Wīġlāf maðelode, wordrihta fela
sǣġde ġesīðum— him wæs sefa ġeōmor:
'Iċ ðæt mǣl ġeman, þǣr wē medu þēgun,
þonne wē ġehēton ūssum hlāforde
in bīorsele, ðē ūs ðās bēagas ġeaf,
þæt wē him ðā gūðġetawa ġyldan woldon
ġif him þyslicu þearf ġelumpe,
helmas ond heard sweord. Ðē hē ūsiċ on herġe ġeċēas
tō ðyssum sīðfate sylfes willum,

2640 onmunde ūsiċ mǣrða, ond mē þās māðmas ġeaf,
þē hē ūsiċ gārwīġend gōde tealde,
hwate helmberend— þēah ðe hlāford ūs
þis ellenweorc āna āðōhte
tō ġefremmanne, folces hyrde,
forðām hē manna mǣst mǣrða ġefremede,
dǣda dollicra. Nū is se dæġ cumen
þæt ūre mandryhten mæġenes behōfað
gōdra gūðrinca; wutun gongan tō,
helpan hildfruman þenden hyt sy,

and never mentioned the blood-money debt, 2520
though Weohstan had slain his brother's son.
The warrior used them for many years—
the mail-shirt and sword—till his son was ready
to do such deeds as the father had done;
they were living among the Geats, and he left him
his war-gear when he went from the world.
For the first time the young man would be tested
in the storm of battle beside his king.
His will did not wane, nor his father's gift
fail him, as the dragon found out 2530
after they came together in combat.

    Wiglaf spoke these words to his comrades
as his heart brimmed with bitter grief:
"I remember that moment in the great hall,
during a feast, when we pledged our faith
to the gracious lord who had given us rings.
We promised him that we would repay
his gifts of helmets and hard-forged blades
if he should ever require our help.
He chose us himself from all his soldiers 2540
because he had confidence in our strength;
he believed that we would be brave in battle,
and so he gave us these splendid gifts,
though he intended to do the great deed
by himself, alone, as the people's leader,
since of all men he has done the most
by his courage and daring. The day has come
when our liege lord is in desperate need
of valiant fighters. So let us go forth
and help him now through the terrible heat 2550

2650   glēdeġesa grim.   God wāt on meċ
       þæt mē is micle lēofre   þæt mīnne līċhaman
       mid mīnne goldġyfan   glēd fæðmie.
       Ne þynċeð mē ġerysne   þæt wē rondas beren
       eft tō earde,   nemne wē ǣror mæġen
       fāne ġefyllan,   feorh ealgian
       Wedra ðēodnes.   Iċ wāt ġeare,
       þæt nǣron ealdġewyrht   þæt hē āna scyle
       Ġēata duguðe   gnorn þrōwian,
       ġesīgan æt sæċċe;   ūrum sceal sweord ond helm,
2660   byrne ond beaduscrūd   bām ġemǣne.'
       Wōd þā þurh þone wælrēċ,   wīġheafolan bær
       frēan on fultum,   fēa worda cwæð:
       'Lēofa Bīowulf,   lǣst eall tela,
       swā ðū on ġeoguðfēore   ġeāra ġecwǣde
       þæt ðū ne ālǣte   be ðē lifiġendum
       dōm ġedrēosan;   scealt nū dǣdum rōf,
       æðeling ānhȳdiġ,   ealle mæġene
       feorh ealgian;   iċ ðē fullǣstu.'
       Æfter ðām wordum   wyrm yrre cwōm,
2670   atol inwitgæst   ōðre sīðe
       fȳrwylmum fāh   fīonda nīos(i)an,
       lāðra manna.   Līġ ȳðum fōr;
       born bord wið rond.   Byrne ne meahte
       ġeongum gārwigan   ġēoce ġefremman,
       ac se maga ġeonga   under his mǣġes scyld
       elne ġeēode,   þā his āgen (wæs)
       glēdum forgrunden.   Þā ġēn gūðcyning
       m(ō)d ġemunde,   mæġenstrenġo slōh
       hildebille,   þæt hyt on heafolan stōd
2680   nīþe ġenȳded;   Næġling forbærst,
       ġeswāc æt sæċċe   sweord Bīowulfes

and ghastly fire. As God is my witness,
I would rather that flames enfold my body
than leave my belovèd lord down there.
It is not right to depart from this place
and return to our homes unless we try
to kill the serpent and save the life
of our noble king. For I know well
that after all he has done for us
he does not deserve to die like this.
And so I will go with sword and helmet   2560
to fight beside him and share his fate."

    Then he strode through the deadly smoke
to his king's aid, saying only:
"My lord Beowulf, try to bear up.
In the days of your youth you used to say
that your glory in fighting would never fail
as long as you lived. Defend yourself now
with all your strength. I am here beside you."

    After these words, a savage anger
arose in the serpent; shimmering, surging   2570
in fiery coils, it sprang for the kill.
The flames swept forward in waves, destroying
Wiglaf's shield. His mail-shirt was useless.
He sheltered under Beowulf's shield
when his own burned. The old commander
called up his courage; with all his strength
he swung his war-blade down on the dragon
with such force that it stuck in its skull.
But Naegling, Beowulf's noble sword,
snapped; it failed in the midst of the fight.   2580

gomol ond grǣġmǣl.   Him þæt ġifeðe ne wæs
þæt him īrenna   ecge mihton
helpan æt hilde;   wæs sīo hond tō strong,
sē ðe mēċa ġehwane   mīne ġefrǣġe
swenġe ofersōhte   þonne hē tō sæċċe bær
wǣpen wundum heard;   næs him wihte ðē sēl.
    Þā wæs þēodsceaða   þriddan sīðe,
frēcne fȳrdraca   fǣhða ġemyndiġ,
2690   rǣsde on ðone rōfan,   þā him rūm āġeald,
hāt ond heaðogrim,   heals ealne ymbefēng
biteran bānum.   Hē ġeblōdegod wearð
sāwuldrīore;   swāt ȳðum wēoll.

    Ðā iċ æt þearfe [ġefræġn]   þēodcyninges
andlongne eorl   ellen cȳðan,
cræft ond cēnðu,   swā him ġecynde wæs.
Ne hēdde hē þæs heafolan,   ac sīo hand ġebarn
mōdiġes mannes   þǣr hē his mǣġes healp,
þæt hē þone nīðgæst   nioðor hwēne slōh,
2700   secg on searwum,   þæt ðæt sweord ġedēaf
fāh ond fǣted,   þæt ðæt fȳr ongon
sweðrian syððan.   Þā ġēn sylf cyning
ġewēold his ġewitte,   wællseaxe ġebrǣd
biter ond beaduscearp,   þæt hē on byrnan wæġ;
forwrāt Wedra helm   wyrm on middan.
Fēond ġefyldan   —ferh ellen wræc—
ond hī hyne þā bēġen   ābroten hæfdon,
sibæðelingas;   swylċ sceolde secg wesan,
þeġn æt ðearfe!   Þæt ðām þēodne wæs
2710   sīðas[t] siġehwīla   sylfes dǣdum,
worlde ġeweorces.
                    Ðā sīo wund ongon,

(Iron edges were not ordained
to help him; his hand was too mighty for them—
it broke each weapon he carried in combat.
So he was no better for bearing a sword.)
Then the dragon, the fierce destroyer,
attacked a third time. It lunged at the king;
streaming with fire, it seized his neck
with bitter fangs. Beowulf fell.
Blood and gore gushed from his wound.

    Then, I have heard, as the hero lay there,   2590
Wiglaf, stouthearted, stood at his side
and showed the bravery he had been born with.
His hand had been burned as he helped his king,
but he did not draw back; he aimed his sword
not at the fire-spewing serpent's head
but a little lower, so that his blade
plunged through the beast's soft flesh, and the flames
immediately began to diminish.
The king, having recovered his senses,
drew the dagger that hung from his belt   2600
and drove it into the dragon's belly,
ripping it open. The enemy
was dead because of their skill and daring;
together they had brought down the beast.
(Thus should a thane act in times of trouble.)
But this was the hero's final fight,
the last of his illustrious triumphs.
The deep wound that the dragon had made

þē him se eorðdraca   ǣr ġeworhte,
swelan ond swellan;   hē þæt sōna onfand,
þæt him on brēostum   bealonīð(e) wēoll
āttor on innan.   Ðā se æðeling ġīong,
þæt hē bī wealle   wīshycgende
ġesæt on sesse;   seah on enta ġeweorc,
hū ðā stānbogan   stapulum fæste
ēċe eorðreċed   innan healde.

2720   Hyne þā mid handa   heorodrēoriġne,
þēoden mǣrne,   þeġn unġemete till,
winedryhten his   wætere ġelafede
hilde sædne   ond his hel(m) onspēon.

       Bīowulf maþelode—   hē ofer benne spræc,
wunde wælblēate;   wisse hē ġearwe
þat hē dæġhwīla   ġedrogen hæfde,
eorðan wyn(ne);   ðā wæs eall sceacen
dōgorġerīmes,   dēað unġemete nēah:
'Nū iċ suna mīnum   syllan wolde

2730   gūðġewǣdu,   þǣr mē ġifeðe swā
ǣniġ yrfeweard   æfter wurde
līċe ġelenġe.   Iċ ðās lēode hēold
fīftiġ wintra;   næs sē folccyning,
ymbesittendra   ǣniġ ðāra
þe meċ gūðwinum   grētan dorste,
eġesan ðeon.   Iċ on earde bād
mǣlġesceafta,   hēold mīn tela,
ne sōhte searonīðas,   nē mē swōr fela
āða on unriht.   Iċ ðæs ealles mæġ

2740   feorhbennum sēoc   ġefēan habban;
forðām mē wītan ne ðearf   waldend fīra
morðorbealo māga,   þonne mīn sceaceð
līf of līċe.   Nū ðū lungre ġeong

now burned and swelled; Beowulf knew
that some great evil ached in his breast,   2610
a deadly poison that doomed his life.
So in his wisdom he went to sit
on a ledge near the wall; he looked at the barrow,
built by giants, and saw how the broad
age-old earth-hall was held up inside
by arches of stone and strong stone pillars.
The brave young man unbuckled the helmet
and washed the wounds of his dear lord,
bathing the battle-weary king
and wiping the blood off with both his hands.   2620
    Then Beowulf spoke, in spite of his wounds;
he knew that his stay on earth was over,
his hours numbered. Death was near.
"Now is the time that I would have wanted
to give this war-gear to my own son,
had it been granted that any heir
be born of my body. For fifty years
I ruled this country. Not one king
of any neighboring nation dared
to attack me with troops or even threaten   2630
war against me. I stood my ground,
took what fate brought, defended my people,
never stirred up a quarrel or swore
a false oath. I can still find joy
in this, although my wound is mortal.
Once the life-spirit has left my flesh,
the eternal Lord has no cause to condemn me
for the murder of kinsmen. Go now, quickly,

hord scēawian   under hārne stān,
Wīġlāf lēofa,   nū se wyrm liġeð,
swefeð sāre wund,   sinċe berēafod.
Bīo nū on ofoste,   þæt iċ ǣrwelan,
goldǣht onġite,   ġearo scēawiġe
sweġle searoġimmas,   þæt iċ ðȳ sēft mæġe
2750   æfter māððumwelan   mīn ālǣtan
līf ond lēodscipe,   þone iċ longe hēold.'

     Ðā iċ snūde ġefræġn   sunu Wīhstānes
æfter wordcwydum   wundum dryhtne
hȳran heaðosīocum,   hringnet beran,
brogdne beaduserċean   under beorges hrōf.
Ġeseah ðā siġehrēðiġ,   þā hē bī sesse ġēong,
magoþeġn mōdiġ   māððumsiġla fealo,
gold glitinian   grunde ġetenġe,
wundur on wealle,   ond þæs wyrmes denn,
2760   ealdes ūhtflogan,   orcas stondan,
fyrnmanna fatu,   feormendlēase,
hyrstum behrorene;   þǣr wæs helm moniġ
eald ond ōmiġ,   earmbēaga fela
searwum ġesǣled.   Sinċ ēaðe mæġ,
gold on grund(e),   gumcynnes ġehwone
oferhīgian,   hȳde sē ðe wylle.
Swylċe hē siomian ġeseah   seġn eall gylden
hēah ofer horde,   hondwundra mǣst,
ġelocen leoðocræftum;   of ðām lēoma stōd,
2770   þæt hē þone grundwong   onġitan meahte,
wrǣtte ġiondwlītan.   Næs ðæs wyrmes þǣr
onsȳn æniġ,   ac hyne ecg fornam.
Ðā iċ on hlǣwe ġefræġn   hord rēafian,
eald enta ġeweorc   ānne mannan,

look for the gold-hoard under gray stone,
dearest Wiglaf, now that the dragon   2640
lies there dead, bereft of its riches.
Go now, for I would like to gaze
on that fabulous wealth, the finely wrought gold
and splendid jewels. Seeing them here
would ease my heart as I leave this life
and the land that I have ruled for so long."
    Wiglaf hurried, as I have heard,
to obey the request of his wounded king
and set off, wearing his woven mail-shirt,
under the barrow's ancient roof.   2650
Thrilled at his victory, the young thane
saw piles of gold all over the ground,
brilliant jewels, wondrous wall-hangings;
the dragon's den was filled with such treasures,
the vessels of a long-vanished race,
dull, unpolished, deprived of their gems,
heaps of helmets, ancient, rusty,
and of golden armbands artfully made.
(How easily gold and gems in the ground
pass away from a powerful man,   2660
however carefully he may hide them!)
He also caught sight of a golden standard
hanging over the hoard; it was woven
with marvelous skill, and it sent out a light
that let him look at the barrow's floor
and examine the treasures. There was no trace
of the serpent anywhere he could see.
Then that brave man, deep in the barrow,
looted the hoard of the ancient lair;

him on bearm hladon   bunan ond discas
sylfes dōme;   seġn ēac ġenōm,
bēacna beorhtost.   Bill ǣr ġescōd
—ecg wæs īren—   ealdhlāfordes
þām ðāra māðma   mundbora wæs
2780 longe hwīle,   līġeġesan wǣġ
hātne for horde,   hioroweallende
middelnihtum,   oð þæt hē morðre swealt.
Ār wæs on ofoste,   eftsīðes ġeorn,
frætwum ġefyrðred;   hyne fyrwet bræc,
hwæðer collenferð   cwicne ġemētte
in ðām wongstede   Wedra þēoden
ellensīocne,   þǣr hē hine ǣr forlēt.
Hē ðā mid þām māðmum   mǣrne þīoden,
dryhten sīnne   drīoriġne fand
2790 ealdres æt ende;   hē hine eft ongon
wætere sweorfan,   oð þæt wordes ord
brēosthord þurhbræc.
                        [Biorncyning spræc]
gomel on giohðe,   gold scēawode:
'Iċ ðāra frætwa   frēan ealles ðanc,
wuldurcyninge   wordum secge,
ēcum dryhtne,   þē iċ hēr on starie,
þæs ðe iċ mōste   mīnum lēodum
ǣr swyltdæġe   swylċ ġestrȳnan.
Nū iċ on māðma hord   mīne bebohte
2800 frōde feorhleġe,   fremmað ġēna
lēoda þearfe;   ne mæġ iċ hēr lenġ wesan.
Hātað heaðomǣre   hlǣw ġewyrċean
beorhtne æfter bǣle   æt brimes nōsan;
sē scel tō ġemyndum   mīnum lēodum
hēah hlīfian   on Hrones Næsse,

he piled gold cups and plates in his arms— 2670
whatever he wanted—and also took
the standard, that most brilliant of banners.
(Already the old king's iron edge
had killed the creature who for so long
guarded the gold and in its defense
inflicted fire-terror upon the people,
rising up fiercely and spewing flames
down from the sky in the dead of night.)
    Wiglaf rushed to return with the riches
while his lord lived. Anxiety pressed 2680
down on his heart; he hoped the hero
would still be breathing when he got back.
As he came to that place, he found his king
quickly fading, covered with gore.
He began to wash his wounds, until
faint words fell from Beowulf's lips
as he gazed in sorrow upon the gold:
"For all these treasures I offer thanks
to the King of Glory, the gracious Lord,
who has allowed me to win such wealth 2690
for my people's sake on the day I die.
I have given my life for this hoard of gold,
which can be used to support the people.
Now I must leave; I can stay no longer.
Order my men to build a mighty
funeral mound beside the sea;
let it rise high on Whale's Rock
as a reminder among my people;
seafarers, ever after, shall call it
'Beowulf's Barrow,' as their ships sail 2700

þæt hit sǣlīðend   syððan hātan
Bīowulfes Biorh,   ðā ðe brentingas
ofer flōda ġenipu   feorran drīfað.'
Dyde him of healse   hrinġ gyldenne
2810 þīoden þrīsthȳdiġ,   þeġne ġesealde,
ġeongum gārwigan,   goldfāhne helm,
bēah ond byrnan,   hēt hyne brūcan well:
'Þū eart endelāf   ūsses cynnes,
Wǣġmundinga;   ealle wyrd forswēop
mīne māgas   tō metodsceafte,
eorlas on elne;   iċ him æfter sceal.'
Þæt wæs þām gomelan   ġinġæste word
brēostġehyġdum,   ǣr hē bǣl cure,
hāte heaðowylmas;   him of hræðre ġewāt
2820 sāwol sēċean   sōðfæstra dōm.

Ðā wæs ġegongen   guman unfrōdum
earfoðlīċe,   þæt hē on eorðan ġeseah
þone lēofestan   līfes æt ende
blēate ġebǣran.   Bona swylċe læġ,
eġesliċ eorðdraca   ealdre berēafod,
bealwe ġebǣded.   Bēahhordum lenġ
wyrm wōhbogen   wealdan ne mōste,
ac him īrenna   ecga fornāmon,
hearde heaðoscearpe   homera lāfe,
2830 þæt se wīdfloga   wundum stille
hrēas on hrūsan   hordærne nēah.
Nalles æfter lyfte   lācende hwearf
middelnihtum,   māðmǣhta wlonc
ansȳn ȳwde,   ac hē eorðan ġefēoll
for ðæs hildfruman   hondġeweorce.
Hūru þæt on lande   lȳt manna ðāh

upon the dark waters, from far away."
   Then the king unclasped from his neck
the golden collar and gave it to Wiglaf,
and also the gilded helmet, arm-ring,
and war-shirt, and told him to use them well.
"You are the last man left of our tribe,
the Waegmundings; fate has swept away
all our kin to a common doom—
those valiant nobles. Now I must follow."
This was the warrior's last word,   2710
his final thought before he was borne
to the searing flames of the funeral pyre.
Soon from his breast his soul departed
to seek the glory God holds for the just.

IT WAS BITTER THEN for the brave young hero
to see that most belovèd of men
lying there dead. The earth-dragon
who had furiously inflicted the wound
also lay there bereft of life.
Never again would the serpent guard   2720
its beautiful gold; the iron blades
beaten hard and sharpened by hammers
had destroyed it, so that it lay there stiff,
that killer, on the ground by the cave.
Never again would it glory in
its brilliant treasures and, blazing up,
fly through the midnight air; it fell
to earth by the warrior's powerful arm.
No other man, however mighty

mæġenāgendra   mīne ġefræġe,
þēah ðe hē dæda ġehwæs   dyrstiġ wære,
þæt hē wið āttorsceaðan   oreðe ġerǣsde,
2840   oððe hrinġsele   hondum styrede,
ġif hē wæċċende   weard onfunde
būon on beorge.   Bīowulfe wearð
dryhtmāðma dǣl   dēaðe forgolden;
hæfde ǣġhwæðer   ende ġefēred
lǣnan līfes.
        Næs ðā lang tō ðon
þæt ðā hildlatan   holt ofġēfan,
tȳdre trēowlogan   tȳne ætsomne,
ðā ne dorston ǣr   dareðum lācan
on hyra mandryhtnes   miclan þearfe;
2850   ac hȳ scamiende   scyldas bǣran,
gūðġewǣdu   þǣr se gomela læġ;
wlitan on Wīlāf.   Hē ġewērġad sæt,
fēðecempa   frēan eaxlum nēah,
wehte hyne wætre;   him wiht ne spēow.
Ne meahte hē on eorðan,   ðēah hē ūðe wēl,
on ðām frumgāre   feorh ġehealdan,
nē ðæs wealdendes   wiht onċirran;
wolde dōm Godes   dǣdum rǣdan
gumena ġehwylcum,   swā hē nū ġēn deð.
2860   Þā wæs æt ðām ġeongan   grim andswaru
ēðbeġēte   þām ðe ǣr his elne forlēas.
Wīġlāf maðelode,   Wēohstānes sunu;
sec sāriġferð   seah on unlēofe:
'Þæt, lā, mæġ secgan   sē ðe wyle sōð specan
þæt se mondryhten,   sē ēow ðā māðmas ġeaf,
ēoredġeatwe   þe ġē þǣr on standað,
þonne hē on ealubenċe   oft ġesealde,

or daring he was in every deed,   2730
so I have heard, could have succeeded
in braving the noxious breath of that foe
or disturbing the hoard in the treasure-hall
if he found the guardian wide awake there.
These brilliant riches had come to Beowulf
at the cost of his life. Both he and the creature
had finished their time in this fleeting world.

    Soon the men who had slunk from battle
left the forest—those ten faith-breaking
cowards who had fled from their king   2740
at the moment when he needed them most.
Ashamed of themselves, they carried their shields
and mail-shirts to where the old man lay,
and they watched Wiglaf. He sat, bone-weary,
close to the king's shoulder and tried
to wake him with water. It did no good.
Much as he wished to, he could not keep
a spark of life in Beowulf's body
or unmake what the Almighty had willed.
(God's hidden fiat determined the fate   2750
of every man, as it does today.)
Then the brave soldier fiercely rebuked
his friends, who had betrayed their trust.
Wiglaf, son of Weohstan, spoke out,
sad at heart, when he saw those cowards:
"One who wishes to speak the truth
must say of him who gave you these gifts,
this well-wrought war-gear that you have been wearing

healsittendum   helm ond byrnan,
þēoden his þeġnum,   swylċe hē þrȳdlicost
2870   ōwer feor oððe nēah   findan meahte—
þæt hē ġēnunga   gūðġewǣdu
wrāðe forwurpe   ðā hyne wīġ beġet.
Nealles folccyning   fyrdġesteallum
ġylpan þorfte;   hwæðre him God ūðe,
sigora waldend,   þæt hē hyne sylfne ġewræc
āna mid ecge,   þā him wæs elnes þearf.
Iċ him līfwraðe   lȳtle meahte
ætġifan æt gūðe,   ond ongan swā þēah
ofer mīn ġemet   mǣġes helpan;
2880   symle wæs þȳ sǣmra   þonne iċ sweorde drep
ferhðġenīðlan,   fȳr unswīðor
wēoll of ġewitte.   Werġendra tō lȳt
þrong ymbe þēoden   þā hyne sīo þrāg becwōm.
Nū sceal sinċþego   ond swyrdġifu,
eall ēðelwyn   ēowrum cynne,
lufen ālicgean;   londrihtes mōt
þǣre mǣġburge   monna ǣġhwylċ
īdel hweorfan,   syððan æðelingas
feorran ġefricgean   flēam ēowerne,
2890   dōmlēasan dǣd.   Dēað bið sēlla
eorla ġewhylcum   þonne edwītlīf!'

Heht ðā þæt heaðoweorc   tō hagan bīodan
up ofer ecgclif,   þǣr þæt eorlweorod
morgenlongne dæġ   mōdġiōmor sæt,
bordhæbbende,   bēġa on wēnum,
endedōgores   ond eftcymes
lēofes monnes.   Lȳt swīgode
nīwra spella   sē ðe næs ġerād,

when he gave his best men upon the mead-bench
helmets and mail-shirts, the most superb   2760
that he could find anywhere, near or far—
that he utterly wasted these weapons on you,
all this fine gear, when the fight began.
Our bold king had no reason to boast
of his comrades-in-arms. Yet God granted
that he was able to have his revenge
by himself, with his knife-blade, when courage was needed.
I could do little to save his life,
and yet in the struggle, beyond my strength,
I did what I could to help my kinsman.   2770
When I stabbed that noxious beast with my sword,
a weaker fire flashed from its maw,
but too few defenders rallied round
to support the king in his time of crisis.
   "Now all comforts shall cease for your kin—
the receiving of golden treasure and swords,
all happiness in your belovèd homes.
Stripped of the rights to your rich lands,
each of you now shall go into exile,
and foreign nobles shall learn how you fled   2780
as cowards do. Death would be better
for any good man than such disgrace."
   He ordered then that the battle's outcome
be proclaimed at court, up toward the cliff-edge
where the counselors sat, heavyhearted,
wondering whether their noble king
had died that day or would come back home.
The herald who quickly rode up the hill

ac hē sōðlīċe   sæġde ofer ealle:
2900 'Nū is wilġeofa   Wedra lēoda,
dryhten Ġēata   dēaðbedde fæst,
wunað wælreste   wyrmes dǣdum;
him on efn liġeð   ealdorġewinna
sexbennum sēoc;   sweorde ne meahte
on ðām āglǣċean   æniġe þinga
wunde ġewyrċean.   Wīġlāf siteð
ofer Bīowulfe,   byre Wīhstānes,
eorl ofer ōðrum   unlifiġendum,
healdeð hiġemǣðum   hēafodwearde
2910 lēofes ond lāðes.
                    Nū ys lēodum wēn
orleġhwīle,   syððan under[ne]
Froncum ond Frȳsum   fyll cyninges
wīde weorðeð.   Wæs sīo wrōht scepen
heard wið Hūgas,   syððan Hiġelāc cwōm
faran flotherġe   on Frēsna land,
þǣr hyne Hetware   hilde ġenǣġdon,
elne ġeēodon   mid ofermæġene,
þæt se byrnwiga   būgan sceolde,
fēoll on fēðan;   nalles frætwe ġeaf
2920 ealdor dugoðe.   Ūs wæs ā syððan
Merewīoingas   milts unġyfeðe.
    Nē iċ te Swēoðēode   sibbe oððe trēowe
wihte ne wēne,   ac wæs wīde cūð
þætte Ongenðīo   ealdre besnyðede
Hæðcen Hrēþling   wið Hrefna Wudu,
þā for onmēdlan   ǣrest ġesōhton
Ġēata lēode   Gūð-Scilfingas.
Sōna him se frōda   fæder Ōhtheres,
eald ond eġesfull   ondslyht āġeaf,

188

announced the news, and they listened closely:
"Now the giver of joy for the Geats,   2790
our belovèd lord, is laid on his deathbed,
taken down by the dragon's attack.
Beside him his enemy also lies,
slain by a knife; with his sword alone
the king could not wound him. Wiglaf sits there,
the son of Weohstan, watching over
Beowulf. By his lifeless body
he holds his vigil, heart-weary,
guarding them, both the loved and the loathed.

    "Now there will come a time of trouble   2800
and warfare, when the fall of our king
is known among the Franks and Frisians.
This quarrel began against the Hugas
when Hygelac's fleet sailed off to Frisia.
There the Hetware troops attacked
and overwhelmed him once he had landed;
he lost that battle and fell in the lines
and gave no more war-gifts to his retainers.
Ever after, the king of the Franks
has acted toward us with hostile intent,   2810
and I do not expect from the Swedish people
peace or good faith, since far and wide
it is known that Ongentheow put an end
to the life of Haethcyn, son of Hrethel,
near Ravenswood, when we, in our pride,
first attacked the Scylfing forces.
Ongentheow, old and deadly in war,
struck back and slew our noble king,

2930 ābrēot brimwīsan,   brȳd āhredde,
gomela[n] iōmeowlan   golde berofene,
Onelan mōdor   ond Ōhtheres,
ond ðā folgode   feorhġenīðlan
oð ðæt hī oðēodon   earfoðlīċe
in Hrefnes Holt   hlāfordlēase.
Besæt ðā sinherġe   sweorda lāfe
wundum wērġe;   wēan oft ġehēt
earmre teohhe   ondlongne niht,
cwæð, hē on merġenne   mēċes ecgum
2940 ġētan wolde,   sum' on galgtrēowu[m]
[fuglum] tō gamene.   Frōfor eft ġelamp
sāriġmōdum   somod ǣrdæġe,
syððan hīe Hyġelāces   horn ond bȳman,
ġealdor onġēaton,   þā se gōda cōm
lēoda dugoðe   on lāst faran.

Wæs sīo swātswaðu   Sw[ē]ona ond Ġeata,
wælrǣs weora   wīde ġesȳne,
hū ðā folc mid him   fǣhðe tōwehton.
Ġewāt him ðā se gōda   mid his gædelingum,
2950 frōd felaġeōmor   fæsten sēċean,
eorl Ongenþīo   ufor onċirde;
hæfde Hiġelāces   hilde ġefrūnen,
wlonces wīġcræft;   wiðres ne truwode,
þæt hē sǣmannum   onsacan mihte,
heaðolīðendum   hord forstandan,
bearn ond brȳde;   bēah eft þonan
eald under eorðweall.   Þā wæs ǣht boden
Swēona lēodum,   seġn Hiġelāce[s]
freoðowong þone   forð oferēodon,
2960 syððan Hrēðlingas   tō hagan þrungon.

rescued his queen, who had been captured—
Onela's and Ohthere's mother—   2820
and then chased after that desperate army,
which barely could escape from the battle
to Ravenswood, bereft of their king.
Then he besieged the sword's survivors,
wound-weary, and all night long
he shouted threats to those wretched thanes;
he promised to hack each one to pieces
in the morning—that some would swing from the gallows
to feed the birds. But at first light
when their hearts were desperate, help arrived: 2830
they heard the sound of Hygelac's trumpets;
he had followed their track with his own troops.
   "The bloody trail that these two peoples
had left behind, the horrible slaughter,
was known far and wide; it was no secret
how they had stirred up strife between them.
Then the old king went with his kinsmen,
in great sorrow, to find a stronghold
on higher ground. He had heard much
of Hygelac's pride and his prowess in battle,   2840
and he did not trust that his troops could hold out
against the Geats or that he could defend
his wife and sons from the fierce sea-fighters,
so he sought safety behind his earth-wall.
Then Hygelac's men swooped down on the Swedes;
with banners aloft, they soon broke through,
overrunning that place of refuge.

Þǣr wearð Ongenðīo   ecgum sweorda,
blondenfexa   on bid wrecen,
þæt se þēodcyning   ðafian sceolde
Eafores ānne dōm.   Hyne yrringa
Wulf Wonrēding   wǣpne ġerǣhte,
þæt him for swenġe   swāt ǣdrum sprong
forð under fexe.   Næs hē forht swā ðēh,
gomela Scilfing,   ac forġeald hraðe
wyrsan wrixle   wælhlem þone,
2970   syððan ðēodcyning   þyder onċirde.
Ne meahte se snella   sunu Wonrēdes
ealdum ċeorle   ondslyht ġiofan,
ac hē him on hēafde   helm ǣr ġescer,
þæt hē blōde fāh   būgan sceolde,
fēoll on foldan;   næs hē fǣġe þā ġīt,
ac hē hyne ġewyrpte,   þēah ðe him wund hrine.
Lēt se hearda   Hiġelāces þeġn
brād[n]e mēċe,   þā his brōðor læġ,
ealdsweord eotonisc   entiscne helm
2980   brecan ofer bordweal;   ðā ġebēah cyning,
folces hyrde,   wæs in feorh dropen.
Ðā wǣron moniġe   þe his mǣġ wriðon,
ricone ārǣrdon,   ðā him ġerȳmed wearð,
þæt hīe wælstōwe   wealdan mōston.
Þenden rēafode   rinċ ōðerne,
nam on Ongenðīo   īrenbyrnan,
heard swyrd hilted,   ond his helm somod,
hāres hyrste   Hiġelāce bær.
Hē (ðām) frætwum fēng   ond him fǣġre ġehēt
2990   lēana (mid) lēodum,   ond ġelǣste swā;
ġeald þone gūðrǣs   Ġēata dryhten,
Hrēðles eafora,   þā hē tō hām becōm,

Ongentheow was brought to bay;
hemmed in by swords, he had to surrender
his fate to Eofor. Furiously   2850
Wulf, the son of Wonred, lunged,
grazing his skull, and streams of blood
spurted out from under his hair.
But the old warrior did not waver;
he slashed at him with his sword and dealt him
a fiercer stroke than he had received.
The younger man was unable to answer
with a counterstroke, for the king had sliced
through his thick helmet. Drenched in blood,
he fell down, not yet fated to die   2860
(he was badly cut, but he recovered).
Beside him, his brother Eofor swung
his ancestral sword, which giants had fashioned,
brought it down on the huge helmet,
and split it apart. The old king staggered;
then he fell over, fatally wounded.
There were many who bandaged the brother's wound
and lifted him up, once they were left
in control of that blood-soaked field of slaughter.
Eofor plundered Ongentheow's body;   2870
he stripped off his armor—the iron mail-shirt,
the hilted sword, and the helmet too—
and brought the booty before his king.
Hygelac, pleased, took it and promised
a fitting reward to both the brothers,
and once they were home he kept his word.
Back at court in our own country,

Iofore ond Wulfe   mid ofermāðmum,
sealde hiora ġehwæðrum   hund þūsenda
landes ond locenra bēaga   —ne ðorfte him ðā lēan oðwītan
mon on middanġearde,   syðða[n] hīe ðā mǣrða ġeslōgon—
ond ðā Iofore forġeaf   āngan dohtor,
hāmweorðunge,   hyldo tō wedde.

   Þæt ys sīo fǣhðo   ond se fēondscipe,
3000 wælnīð wera,   ðæs ðe iċ [wēn] hafo,
þē ūs sēċeað tō   Swēona lēoda,
syððan hīe ġefricgeað   frēan ūserne
ealdorlēasne,   þone ðe ǣr ġehēold
wið hettendum   hord ond rīċe
æfter hæleða hryre,   hwate Scilfingas,
folcrēd fremede,   oððe furður ġēn
eorlscipe efnde.   Nū is ofost betost
þæt wē þēodcyning   þǣr scēawian
ond þone ġebringan,   þē ūs bēagas ġeaf,
3010 ond ādfǣre.   Ne scel ānes hwæt
meltan mid þām mōdigan,   ac þǣr is māðma hord,
gold unrīme   grimme ġeċēa(po)d,
ond nū æt sīðestan   sylfes fēore
bēagas (ġeboh)te;   þā sceall brond fretan,
ǣled þeċċean—   nalles eorl wegan
māððum tō ġemyndum,   nē mæġð scȳne
habban on healse   hringweorðunge,
ac sceal ġeōmormōd,   golde berēafod
oft nalles ǣne   elland tredan,
3020 nū se herewīsa   hleahtor āleġde,
gamen ond glēodrēam.   Forðon sceall gār wesan
moniġ morgenċeald   mundum bewunden,

he honored the warriors Wulf and Eofor
with lavish treasures: land and rings worth
more than a hundred thousand in money.   2880
No man on earth could call the king
too generous in his judgment; the brothers'
courage had earned these uncommon gifts.
He then gave Eofor his only daughter,
his pride and joy, in pledge of his friendship.
    "This long feud between our two peoples
is sure to flare up into new fighting;
their troops will attack as soon as they hear
that our king is dead, who guarded our country,
our lives and fortunes, against all foes   2890
after those battles with the bold Swedes,
and who worked so hard for his people's welfare,
doing so many heroic deeds.
Now let us hurry for a last look
at Beowulf, giver of golden rings,
and bear his body home to the pyre.
Not just a few of those fabled treasures
will melt with him, but the whole hoard,
untold treasure, dearly purchased
and at last paid for with his own life.   2900
The fierce flames will devour it all,
no warrior wear golden armbands
to remember his lord, no lovely woman
hang rich jewels around her neck.
Heavy at heart, bereft of adornments,
they will long wander in lands of exile
now that their dear lord's laughter and joy
are silenced forever; many a spear,
frigid at dawn, will be seized by fingers

hæfen on handa,   nalles hearpan swēġ
wīġend weċċean,   ac se wonna hrefn
fūs ofer fǣġum   fela reordian,
earne secgan   hū him æt ǣte spēow,
þenden hē wið wulf   wæl rēafode.'
    Swā se secg hwata   secggende wæs,
lāðra spella;   hē ne lēag fela
3030   wyrda nē worda.   Weorod eall ārās;
ēodon unblīðe   under Earna Næs,
wollentēare   wundur scēawian.
Fundon ðā on sande   sāwullēasne
hlimbed healdan   þone þe him hringas ġeaf
ǣrran mǣlum;   þā wæs endedæġ
gōdum ġegongen,   þæt se gūðcyning,
Wedra þēoden   wundordēaðe swealt.
Ǣr hī þǣr ġesēgan   syllicran wiht,
wyrm on wonge   wiðerræhtes þǣr
3040   lāðne licgean;   wæs se lēġdraca
grimliċ gry(refāh)   glēdum beswǣled;
sē wæs fīftiġes   fōtġemearces
lang on leġere;   lyftwynne hēold
nihtes hwīlum,   nyðer eft ġewāt
dennes niosian;   wæs ðā dēaðe fæst,
hæfde eorðscrafa   ende ġenyttod.
Him biġ stōdan   bunan ond orcas,
discas lāgon   ond dȳre swyrd,
ōmiġe þurhetone,   swā hīe wið eorðan fæðm
3050   þūsend wintra   þǣr eardodon,
þonne wæs þæt yrfe   ēacencræftiġ,
iūmonna gold   galdre bewunden,
þæt ðām hrinġsele   hrīnan ne mōste
gumena ǣniġ,   nefne God sylfa,

and held aloft; no harp music   2910
will rouse the warriors; but the black raven,
eager for flesh above the fallen,
will go to the eagle and tell the tale
of how he fared at the latest feast
when with the wolf he plundered the dead."
     The one who announced this hateful news
was telling the truth about past and future.
The men all rose, and miserably
they climbed down under Eagles' Cliff
to look at the wonder with welling tears.   2920
They found on the sand the soulless body
of the lord who once had given them gold;
the final day had come for the king,
who died such an uncanny death.
But what they saw first was something stranger:
the loathsome dragon lying there dead,
measuring fifty feet long at least,
scorched on its shimmering colored scales
by the fierce heat of its own flames.
Once, it had soared across the night sky   2930
joyfully, then returned to its trove;
but now that death held it, never again
would it guard its gold in a deep cave.
Beside it pitchers and cups were piled,
golden platters, precious swords
eaten by rust as if they had lain
in the earth's womb for a thousand winters.
The gold of the ancients possessed great power
and was bound by a mighty spell: no man
could ever enter that treasure-hall   2940
unless God Himself were to give permission—

sigora sōðcyning   sealde þām ðe hē wolde
—hē is manna ġehyld—   hord openian,
efne swā hwylcum manna   swā him ġemet ðūhte.

Þā wæs ġesȳne   þæt se sīð ne ðāh
þām ðe unrihte   inne ġehȳdde
3060   wrǣtte under wealle.   Weard ǣr ofslōh
fēara sumne;   þā sīo fǣhð ġewearð
ġewrecen wrāðlīċe.   Wundur hwār þonne
eorl ellenrōf   ende ġefēre
līfġesceafta,   þonne lenġ ne mæġ
mon mid his (mā)gum   meduseld būan.
Swā wæs Bīowulfe,   þā hē biorges weard
sōhte, searonīðas   —seolfa ne cūðe
þurh hwæt his worulde ġedāl   weorðan sceolde—
swā hit oð dōmes dæġ   dīope benemdon
3070   þēodnas mǣre   þā ðæt þǣr dydon,
þæt se secg wǣre   synnum scildiġ,
hergum ġeheaðerod,   hellbendum fæst,
wommum ġewītnad,   sē ðone wong strude.
Næs hē goldhwæte,   ġearwor hæfde
āgendes ēst   ǣr ġescēawod.
    Wīġlāf maðelode,   Wīhstānes sunu:
'Oft sceall eorl moniġ   ānes willan
wræc ādrēogan,   swā ūs ġeworden is.
Ne meahton wē ġelǣran   lēofne þēoden,
3080   rīċes hyrde   rǣd ǣniġne,
þæt hē ne grētte   goldweard þone,
lēte hyne licgean   þǣr hē longe wæs,
wīcum wunian   oð woruldende;
hēold on hēahġesceap.   Hord ys ġescēawod,
grimme ġegongen;   wæs þæt ġifeðe tō swīð

198

the true King and Protector of men—
for some great hero to open the hoard,
a warrior whom the Lord thought worthy.
    The daring venture had dashed the hopes
of the one who had cursed and hidden away
that brilliant treasure within the barrow.
The serpent had slain a man like no other,
who had paid it back with a deadly blow.
(It is a mystery how a hero   2950
comes to encounter his fated end,
never more to feast in the mead-hall.)
Beowulf, when he sought battle
with the cunning dragon who guarded the cave,
was ignorant of the ancient curse
placed on the treasure by princes who
had solemnly sworn that until doomsday
whoever plundered that place of its gold
would be guilty, imprisoned in pagan temples,
bound in hell-bonds, racked with torments.   2960
Instead of a spell, he had expected
the Lord's favor for fighting that beast.
    Then Wiglaf, the son of Weohstan, spoke:
"Often many must suffer great sorrow
because of the will of one man.
We could not persuade our noble king
not to attack that treasure-warden,
to let it lie where it had long been,
within its cave, till the world's end.
Beowulf held to his fate. The hoard   2970
is uncovered, but at a terrible cost.

þē ðone [þēodcyning]   þyder ontyhte.
Iċ wæs þǣr inne   ond þæt eall ġeondseh,
reċedes ġeatwa,   þā mē ġerȳmed wæs,
nealles swǣslīċe   sīð ālȳfed
3090   inn under eorðweall.   Iċ on ofoste ġefēng
micle mid mundum   mæġenbyrðenne
hordġestrēona,   hider ūt ætbær
cyninge mīnum.   Cwico wæs þā ġēna,
wīs ond ġewittiġ;   worn eall ġespræc
gomol on ġehðo,   ond ēowiċ ġrētan hēt,
bæd þæt ġē ġeworhton   æfter wines dǣdum
in bǣlstede   beorh þone hean,
miċelne ond mǣrne,   swā hē manna wæs
wīġend weorðfullost   wīde ġeond eorðan,
3100   þenden hē burhwelan   brūcan mōste.
Uton nū efstan   ōðre [sīðe],
sēon ond sēċean   searo[ġimma] ġeþræc,
wundur under wealle;   iċ ēow wīsiġe,
þæt ġē ġenōge   nēon sċēawiað
bēagas ond brād gold.   Sīe sīo bǣr ġearo,
ǣdre ġeæfned,   þonne wē ūt cymen,
ond þonne ġeferian   frēan ūserne,
lēofne mannan   þǣr hē longe sceal
on ðæs waldendes   wǣre ġeþolian.'
3110   Hēt ðā ġebēodan   byre Wīhstānes,
hæle hildedīor   hæleða monegum,
boldāgendra,   þæt hīe bǣlwudu
feorran feredon,   folcāgende,
gōdum tōġēnes: 'Nū sceal glēd fretan
—weaxan wonna lēġ—   wigena strenġel,
þone ðe oft ġebād   īsernscūre,

The destiny that had drawn him on
kept impelling him toward that place.
When I was inside it, I saw all
the cave's heaped gold when my path had been cleared;
not easily was I allowed
to make my way under that earth-wall.
I took in my arms as much treasure
as I could carry, and brought it back
to my dear lord. He was still alive   2980
and of sound mind. There were many things
that he said in his grief; he told me to greet you
and tell you to build a burial mound,
high and majestic, upon his pyre,
in his memory, since of all men
he was the worthiest warrior ever.
Now let us go quickly again
to see the treasure trove in the barrow,
the marvel within those ancient walls.
I will lead you straight there, and you will see   2990
the piles of priceless jewels and gold.
When we come back, let the pyre be built;
then let us bear his body to where
he must long dwell in the Lord's keeping."
    Then Wiglaf, the valiant son of Weohstan,
gave orders to all the principal men,
owners of land and noble lords,
to go to the forests, gather firewood,
and bring it to where Beowulf lay.
"Flames must engulf and fire consume   3000
the warrior who so often awaited
the iron showers our enemies shot,

þonne stræla storm   strenġum ġebæded
scōc ofer scildweall,   sceft nytte hēold,
fæðerġearwum fūs   flāne fullēode.'

3120   Hūru se snotra   sunu Wīhstānes
āċīġde of corðre   cyniges þeġnas
syfone (tō)somne,   þā sēlestan,
ēode eahta sum   under inwithrōf
hilderinc[a];   sum on handa bær
æledlēoman,   sē ðe on orde ġeong.
Næs ðā on hlytme   hwā þæt hord strude,
syððan orwearde   æniġne dæl
secgas ġesēgon   on sele wunian,
læne licgan;   lȳt æniġ mearn
3130   þæt hī ofostlīċ(e)   ūt ġeferedon
dȳre māðmas;   dracan ēc scufun,
wyrm ofer weallclif,   lēton wēġ niman,
flōd fæðmian   frætwa hyrde.
Þā wæs wunden gold   on wæn hladen,
æġhwæs unrīm,   æþeling boren,
hār hilde[rinċ]   tō Hrones Næsse.

Him ðā ġeġiredan   Ġeata lēode
ād on eorðan   unwāclicne,
helm[um] behongen,   hildebordum,
3140   beorhtum byrnum,   swā hē bēna wæs;
āleġdon ðā tōmiddes   mærne þēoden
hæleð hīofende,   hlāford lēofne.
Ongunnon þā on beorge   bælfȳra mæst
wīġend weċċan;   wud(u)rēċ āstāh
sweart ofer swioðole,   swōgende lēġ
wōpe bewunden   —windblond ġelæġ—

arrow-storms aimed at him by their bowstrings,
shafts that went soaring over the shield-walls
with feathers speeding the arrowheads home."
    Wiglaf summoned the seven best
of all the king's thanes. The eight went down
under the cavern's evil roof;
one of them walked in front, holding
a torch above him to brighten the path.   3010
They were all eager to loot that hoard;
they saw how the gold lay there unguarded,
heaps of it strewn over the hall,
all abandoned. Each man rejoiced
to leave the cave, carrying piles
of priceless treasures. They pushed the dragon
over the cliff-wall and let the water
enfold it and take it down to the depths.
Then they put all the precious gold,
that uncountable wealth, onto a wagon   3020
and carried the king to Whale's Rock.
    The Geatish people then built a pyre,
a huge one, for their belovèd lord,
and hung it with helmets, battle-shields,
and shining mail-shirts, as he had requested.
Then, lamenting, they laid in its midst
their heroic king, and kindled the greatest
of funeral fires. The black smoke rose
above the flames, whose ferocious roar
overwhelmed all the wailing voices.   3030

Beowulf

oð þæt hē ðā bānhūs   ġebrocen hæfd(e)
hāt on hreðre.   Hiġum unrōte
mōdċeare mǣndon,   mondryhtnes cw(e)alm;
3150 swylċe giōmorġyd   (Ġē)at(isc) meowle
(æfter Bīowulfe   b)undenheorde
(sang) sorgċeariġ,   sæ(id)e (ġe)neah(he)
þæt hīo hyre (here)ġ(eon)gas   hearde ond(r)ēde,
wælfylla wo(r)n,   (w)erudes eġesan,
hȳ[n]ðo ond hæf(t)nȳd.   Heofon rēċe swealg.
    Ġeworhton ðā   Wedra lēode
hlǣ(w) on h(ō)e,   sē wæs hēah ond brād,
(w)ēġlīðendum   wīde ġesȳne,
ond beti(m)bredon   on tȳndagum
3160 beadurōf(e)s bēcn,   bronda lāfe
wealle beworhton,   swā hyt weorðlicost
foresnotre men   findan mihton.
Hī on beorg dydon   bēg ond siġlu,
eall swylċe hyrsta   swylċe on horde ǣr
nīðhēdiġe men   ġenumen hæfdon;
forlēton eorla ġestrēon   eorðan healdan,
gold on grēote,   þǣr hit nū ġēn lifað,
eldum swā unnyt   swā hyt (ǣro)r wæs.
Þā ymbe hlǣw riodan   hildedīore,
3170 æþelinga bearn,   ealra twelf(e),
woldon (care) cwīðan   (ond c)yning mǣnan,
wordġyd wrecan,   ond ymb w(er) sprecan;
eahtodan eorlscipe   ond his ellenweorc
duguðum dēmdon—   swā hit ġedē(fe) bið
þæt mon his winedryhten   wordum herġe,
ferhðum frēoġe,   þonne hē forð scile
of l(ī)ċhaman   (lǣ)ded weorðan.

The wind settled; the searing fire
consumed the body; the heartsick thanes
grieved for the death of their dear lord.
A woman started to sing a dirge
for Beowulf, with her hair bound up;
over and over she voiced her dread
of conquering soldiers, cruelty, terror,
massive killing, mayhem, shame,
slavery. Heaven swallowed the smoke.

    Then they built, high up on the headland,   3040
a barrow that was lofty and broad;
sailors could see it from far away.
It took them ten days to finish that task.
They first surrounded the funeral ashes
with a stone wall skillfully fashioned,
as splendid as master craftsmen could make it.
Within this barrow they buried the riches,
the precious rings and finely wrought jewels,
which the thanes had carried out of the cave;
they gave that brilliance back to the earth,   3050
leaving the golden hoard in the ground
where it remains, as useless to men
as it was before. Twelve warriors rode
around Beowulf's barrow, chanting
solemn dirges and mourning his death.
They praised his nobility and his war-prowess
with the highest praise, as was only proper,
for a man should honor his own lord
on the day when he journeys forth from the flesh.

Swā begnornodon   Ġēata lēode
hlāfordes (hry)re,   heorðġenēatas;
3180   cwǣdon þæt hē wǣre   wyruldcyning[a]
manna mildust   ond mon(ðw)ǣrust,
lēodum līðost   ond lofġeornost.

Thus the Geats all grieved and lamented   3060
the noble lord whom they so loved.
They cried out that he was, of all the world's kings,
the kindest and the most courteous man,
the most gracious to all, and the keenest for glory.

Appendix: Genealogical Tables

THE DANES or Scyldings

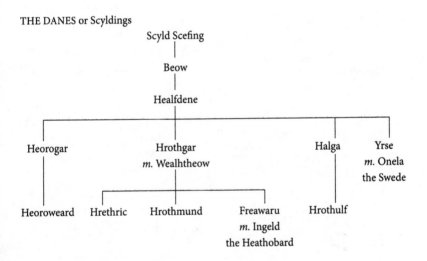

Scyld Scefing

Beow

Healfdene

Heorogar   Hrothgar *m.* Wealhtheow   Halga   Yrse *m.* Onela the Swede

Heoroweard   Hrethric   Hrothmund   Freawaru *m.* Ingeld the Heathobard   Hrothulf

Appendix: Genealogical Tables

THE GEATS

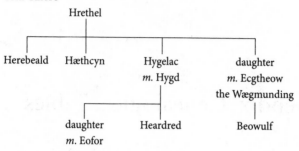

THE SWEDES or Scylfings

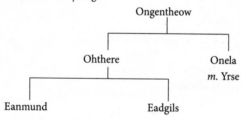

Notes

Unless otherwise indicated, line numbers refer to the Beowulf translation. All translations not attributed to others are mine.

Introduction

p. xi, *The single manuscript:* I have taken much of the rest of this paragraph from *Klaeber's Beowulf*, 4th ed., ed. R. D. Fulk, Robert E. Bjork, and John D. Niles (Toronto, 2008; henceforward abbreviated as Klaeber⁴), pp. xxvi–xxvii.

p. xii, *Among historians:* Ibid., p. clxxix.

p. xiii, *may have believed that these Geats:* At least one of his characters— Beowulf's king, Hygelac—is historical; the sixth-century historian Gregory of Tours mentions that he was killed in a raid on the Franks sometime between 516 and 531 (*History of the Franks,* III, 3).

p. xiii, *Tolkien was convinced:* J. R. R. Tolkien, *The Monsters and the Critics, and Other Essays* (London, 1997), pp. 42–43.

p. xiv, *What has Ingeld:* "Letter to 'Speratus,'" in R. M. Liuzza, *Beowulf,* 2nd ed. (Peterborough, Ontario, 2013), p. 154. The definitive pronouncement, made centuries later by an early Renaissance pope, expresses the Christian doctrine in language as clear as it is harsh: "All those who are outside the Catholic Church, not only pagans but also Jews or heretics and schismatics, cannot share in eternal life and will go into the everlasting fire which was prepared for the devil and his angels" (Pope Eugene IV, *Cantate Domino* [1441]). According to Christian doctrine, even the patriarchs and prophets of the Old Testament were trapped in hell and suffered unimaginable torments for hundreds of years until Jesus descended there after the crucifixion and escorted them to heaven.

p. xv, *The Beowulf poet was having none of this:* The greatest poet who wrote about the damnation of virtuous pagans was Dante. The locus classicus of his

Notes

distress is the fourth canto of the *Inferno*, where he encounters the most famous of the noble pagans—Homer, Horace, Socrates, Plato, Aristotle, and many others—who sit around in the equivalent of a vast waiting room, without anything to hope for, in infinite desolation. In the previous canto, Dante described the inscription over Gate of Hell—*fecemi la divina podestate, / la somma sapïenza e 'l primo amore* (iii, 5–6, "what made me was the divine power, the supreme wisdom, and the primal love")—using his incomparably beautiful poetry to express a lie as obscene as the *Arbeit Macht Frei* above Auschwitz. When Dante the character sees the virtuous pagans, who are sinless and condemned to eternal suffering only because they were unbaptized, he is filled with deep sorrow. Later in the *Inferno*, Vergil, his teacher and guide, who is himself one of the lost souls, warns him not to feel any pity at all for the souls in hell: "Are you like all the other fools?" he says. "Here piety forbids you from all pity. Who is more wicked than someone whose feelings contest the divine judgment?" (xx, 27–30). And Beatrice, a symbol of divine wisdom, who eventually leads the character Dante to heaven, says to Vergil, "I have been made by God in his mercy in such a way that your misery cannot touch me" (ii, 91–92). Whatever sympathy or compassion the character Dante is feeling for the damned is criticized as a weakness, even a kind of spiritual rebellion.

p. xv, *two other heroes:* Hama, who "fled from the hate / of Eormanric, wishing eternal reward" (1145–46; the Old English is *ġecēas ēcne rǣd*, which could also mean "obtaining enduring benefit"), and Beowulf's grandfather Hrethel, the king of the Geats, who "chose God's light" (2375).

p. xvi, *to seek the glory God holds for the just:* Sēcean sōðfǣstra dōm, literally "to seek the judgment (or glory) of the just." According to Tolkien (*Monsters and the Critics*, p. 39), "Sōðfǣstra dōm could by itself have meant simply 'the esteem of the true-judging,' that dōm which Beowulf as a young man had declared to be the prime motive of noble conduct; but here combined with *gewat secean* it must mean either the glory that belongs (in eternity) to the just, or the judgement of God upon the just."

p. xvi, *That there is one God:* Ben Franklin, *Autobiography, and Other Writings* (Boston, 1958), p. 87.

p. xvi, *righteous gentiles have a place in the world to come:* Maimonides, *Mishneh Torah, Hilchot Teshuvah* 3:4, based on verses in the Talmud.

p. xvi, *anima naturaliter judaica:* "A soul naturally Jewish," a play on the early Christian theologian Tertullian's phrase *anima naturaliter christiana*, "a soul naturally Christian" (*Apol.* 17.6; *Patrologia Latina* 1:377), which he applied to Vergil.

p. xvi, *the famous, heartbreakingly tender scene:* In Book 6. See *The Iliad*, tr. Stephen Mitchell (New York, 2011), pp. 105–8.

Notes

p. xvii, *the biblical patriarchs:* Abraham dies "an old man and full of years" (Genesis 25:8), Isaac "old and full of days" (Genesis 35:29), and Job "old and full of days" (Job 42:17).

p. xvii, *However Christian the poet may have thought himself:* Some scholars have argued that *Beowulf* is a Christian poem because the poet intended his hero to be a figure for Christ: just as the Jesus portrayed by the evangelists sacrifices his life for the salvation of humans (not all humans, but those who believe in him), so Beowulf, according to this theory, sacrifices his life to save his people. This has a certain element of truth to it, in that Beowulf's devotion to his people's welfare supersedes his own self-interest. But Beowulf never intends to sacrifice his life. His intention is to kill the dragon, and his death is a kind of glorious failure. Furthermore, though the dragon's death does save the Geats, it is only a temporary reprieve. (Beowulf's young kinsman and successor Wiglaf blames him, in fact, for making them all more vulnerable by engaging in the fight.) In the moral universe of the poem no savior is necessary. Virtuous men (and presumably virtuous women) go to heaven, whether they die in war or of natural causes or in the clutches of an ogre or incinerated by a sky-soaring dragon's flames, and wicked men (and women) go to hell. God is just. Faith in him leads to righteous actions, and it is people's actions that count. As King Hrothgar says, in what is often called his "sermon," it is within everyone's power to choose heaven and avoid the selfishness and cruelty that arise when conscience falls asleep:

> Guard against that pernicious evil,
> dear Beowulf. Choose the better way:
> eternal rewards. Turn from all pride . . . (1684–86)

p. xvii, *for people's delight:* Line 84.

p. xviii, *of the glorious deeds of heroes: The Odyssey,* tr. Stephen Mitchell (New York, 2013), p. 95.

p. xviii, *It is a fine thing:* Ibid., p. 109.

About This Translation

p. xxiii, *rum, ram, ruf:* Geoffrey Chaucer, "The Parson's Prologue," line 43.

p. xxiii, *wand tō wolcnum:* Klaeber⁴, lines 1119–24.

p. xxiv, *Before born babe bliss had:* In Episode 14, "Oxen of the Sun," in James Joyce, *Ulysses, the Corrected Text,* ed. Hans Walter Gabler, with Wolfhard Steppe and Claus Melchior (New York, 1986), p. 315.

Beowulf

1, *Spear-Danes:* The Danes. Though I have usually called them simply "Danes," in the text they are also called Bright-Danes, Ring-Danes, and Scyldings, after Scyld Scefing, their founder.

4, *Scyld Scefing:* The story of Scyld's miraculous arrival is attributed to Sheaf in Aethelweard's *Chronicon* (third book, A. 857): "And this Sheaf arrived with one light ship in the island of the ocean which is called Skaney, with weapons all around him. He was a very young boy, and unknown to the people of that land, but he was received by them, and they kept him with great care as one who belonged to them, and afterward they chose him as their king. It was from him that King Aethelwulf traced his descent."

72, *Heorot:* The word means "stag" and is a symbol of kingship. "An appropriate name for a building that probably was imagined as having projections atop the gables resembling horns, formed by crossing the elongated ends of the beams at the top of the endmost rafters" (R. D. Fulk, *The Beowulf Manuscript* [Cambridge, MA, 2010], p. 352).

76, *awaiting the fire:* The hall was fated to be burned down in a battle between Hrothgar and his son-in-law Ingeld in the feud between the Danes and the Heathobards.

94, *Grendel:* According to some scholars, the name is related to Old English *grindan,* "to grind," and hence may mean "destroyer."

99, *in revenge for the vicious murder of Abel:* Genesis 4:10–15:

And the Lord said, "What have you done! Listen: your brother's blood is crying out to me from the ground. Now you are cursed: cut off from the ground that opened to swallow your brother's blood. When you work the ground, it will no longer yield its strength to you. You will become a restless wanderer on the earth."

And Cain said, "My punishment is greater than I can bear. You have banished me from this land, and I must submit to you and become a restless wanderer on the earth, and anyone who meets me can kill me."

And the Lord said, "No: if anyone kills you, you will be avenged seven times over." And the Lord put a mark on Cain, to keep anyone who met him from killing him. And Cain went away from the Lord and settled in the land of Nod, *Restlessness,* east of Eden.

(*Genesis,* tr. Stephen Mitchell [New York, 1996], pp. 9–10)

104, *giants as well:* Genesis 6:4: "It was in those days that the giants appeared on the earth: when the gods slept with the women, and children were born to them. These were the heroes who lived long ago, the men of great fame" (ibid., p. 13).

"The story of a race of demonic monsters and giants descended from Cain comes from a tradition established by the apocryphal *Book of Enoch* and early Jewish and Christian interpretations of Genesis 6:4. . . . Early commentators traced the descent of Cain's unnatural sin through some of the separate stories in Genesis. Thus the 'daughters of men' in Genesis 6:2 were interpreted as Cain's descendants mentioned in Genesis 6:4, and their progeny were identified as the giants. These giants were taken to be wicked and were used to explain the following verses, Genesis 6:5–8, in which God, appalled at men's evil, decides on the Flood. From this traditional connection, presumably, came the legend that God vanquished the giants with the Flood" (Howell D. Chickering, Jr., *Beowulf: A Dual-Language Edition* [New York, 2006], pp. 283–84).

113, *thanes:* Old English, *þegna.* Men who held land granted by the king; noblemen. Technically, thanes ranked between hereditary noblemen and ordinary freemen, but the poet uses the term loosely, since in line 186 he calls Beowulf "Hygelac's thane," though he is of royal descent on his mother's side.

148, *make blood-payment:* The Anglo-Saxon practice, like that of some other northern European countries, was to make reparation for murder by paying money or property to the family of the slain man. The ancient Greeks had the same practice:

> And yet a man will accept due reparations
> for his brother or son, even from someone who killed him,
> and the killer stays on at home, having paid enough,
> and the family's anger is held back once they receive
> the blood-price.

> (*The Iliad,* tr. Stephen Mitchell [New York, 2011], p. 154)

186, *Hygelac's thane:* This is the first mention of Beowulf; he isn't named until line 324.

209, *sighted land:* They have sailed from the southern coast of Sweden to the Danish island of Zeeland. See map, p. xxxiii.

217, *Scyldings:* Danes.

235, *he must be not just a simple soldier:* This is a cherished belief in aristocratic cultures. Compare Menelaus's greeting of Telemachus and Pisistratus in *The Odyssey:*

"It is obvious that your lineage is distinguished;
both of you look as if you had royal fathers,
for no mere commoner could have begotten such sons."

(*The Odyssey,* tr. Stephen Mitchell [New York, 2013], p. 39)

286, *Boar-figures:* The boar was a symbol of strength and ferocity. Images of boars, sometimes clothed as human warriors, were placed on helmets in the belief that they would protect the man who was wearing it.

324, *Beowulf:* According to many scholars, the name means "Bee-wolf," hence "Bear," since the bear is a "wolf" (predator) to bees, ravaging their honey. Other scholars say that the element *Bēow* is the name of a pre-Christian god (*bēow* = "barley").

329, *Wendel:* A Germanic tribe, possibly the Vandals. Some scholars identify them as inhabitants of modern Vendsyssel in North Jutland.

395, *counseled me to go to your court:* This is consistent with 193–95, but not with 1911–16.

430, *Wayland:* A master blacksmith in Germanic mythology.

431, *Hrethel:* Hygelac's father and Beowulf's grandfather.

436, *the Wylfings:* "The territory of the Wylfings was in proximity to that of the Geats and the Danes; it may have been on the south of the Baltic Sea" (George Jack, *Beowulf: A Student Edition* [Oxford, 1994], p. 55). See map, p. xxxiii.

494, *Heathoreams:* A people of southern Norway.

495, *the Brondings' land:* Breca was the king of the Brondings.

592, *Helming:* The clan of Helm, the chief of the Wulfings, which Scandinavian sources define as the ruling clan of the Eastern Geats.

705, *a warrior sleeping:* This warrior is identified as Handscioh in line 1993.

732, *Both huge wrestlers:* There is a similar scene in *Gilgamesh:*

When Gilgamesh reached the marriage house,
Enkidu was there. He stood like a boulder,
blocking the door. Gilgamesh, raging,
stepped up and seized him, huge arms gripped
huge arms, foreheads crashed like wild bulls,
the two men staggered, they pitched against houses,
the doorposts trembled, the outer walls shook,
they careened through the streets, they grappled each other,
limbs intertwined, each huge body
straining to break free from the other's embrace.
Finally, Gilgamesh threw the wild man

and with his right knee pinned him to the ground.
His anger left him. He turned away.
The contest was over.

(*Gilgamesh*, tr. Stephen Mitchell [New York, 2004], p. 89)

832, *Sigemund's triumphs:* Sigemund is the hero of the Old Norse *Völsunga-saga* and the Middle High German *Nibelungenlied*.

835, *Fitela:* Sigemund's nephew. According to Scandinavian sources, Fitela is also Sigemund's son by his own sister, Signy.

858, *Heremod:* A Danish king, possibly the grandfather of Scyld Scefing.

859, *Jutes:* One of the most powerful Germanic tribes of their time, along with the Saxons and Angles. They inhabited the northern part of the Jutland Peninsula.

964, *Hrothulf:* The son of Hrothgar's brother Halga. According to Scandinavian sources, Halga begot Hrothulf by raping Yrsa, not knowing that she was his own daughter.

968, *disloyalty and betrayal:* According to many scholars, these lines suggest that upon Hrothgar's death Hrothulf seized the throne and killed the two young princes Hrethric and Hrothmund.

1014, *sang of Finn's sons:* "Much remains obscure and disputed about the story that the court poet narrates, the so-called Finnsburg episode; the following is probably the most widely credited reconstruction. Hildeburh, a princess of the Half-Danes [they are called "the Danes" in this translation], is married to Finn Folcwalding, king of the Frisians. During a visit to the Frisian court, the Half-Danes appear to have been attacked treacherously by certain Jutes either allied with or identical to the Frisian party. . . . In the attack, the leader of the Half-Danes, Hildeburh's brother Hnæf, is killed, as is her unnamed Frisian son. At a stalemate, the two sides agree to a precarious truce. In the spring, with the return of sailing weather, Hengest, who appears to have assumed command of the Half-Danes, goaded by some of his men, breaks the truce, and in the ensuing combat Finn is killed, the stronghold is plundered, and the visitors return home, bearing off the queen" (Fulk, *Beowulf Manuscript*, p. 354).

1033, *and the Jutes the other:* "Those with whom [the Danes] are to share a hall can hardly be Jutes among Finn's followers, against whom they have been fighting, and must presumably be Jutes from the retinue of Hnaef. So it seems that there were Jutes on both sides of the conflict" (Jack, *Beowulf*, p. 92).

1086, *the son of Hunlaf:* "The text is open to various interpretations. The one adopted here assumes that the Dane Hunlaf, brother of Guthlaf and Oslaf, had been killed in the fight, and that ultimately Hunlaf's son demanded vengeance

Notes

by the symbolic act of placing his father's sword in Hengest's lap, while at the same time Guthlaf and Oslaf reminded Hengest of the Jutes' treachery. It is not clear whether the subsequent fight in which Finn was killed was waged by the Danish survivors alone, or whether the party first went back to Denmark and then returned to Finnsburg with reinforcement" (E. Talbot Donaldson and Nicholas Howe, *Beowulf: A Prose Translation* [New York, 2002], p. 21).

1143, *the Brosings' necklace*: "The necklace of the Brosings, to which the poet compares the collar, is linked to a story of the Goths. In the thirteenth-century Old Norse . . . *Saga of Dietrich of Bern*, the fierce warrior Heimir (Old English Hama) takes sides with Þidrekr when he quarrels with his uncle King Erminrekr (Old English Eormanric). This king was the historical Ermanaric, king of the fourth-century East Goths. In the saga, Heimir is forced to flee the wrath of Erminrekr, and later the outlaw enters a monastery to make atonement for his sins. In doing so, he gives the monks all his wealth and armor. But there is no mention of a necklace, which, in the *Beowulf* version, Hama appears to have stolen from Eormanric. Perhaps two legends are already conflated here in the poem, since the closest parallel to the necklace itself is the Old Norse 'necklace of the Brisings,' made by fire dwarfs for the goddess Freyja and stolen from her by Loki" (Chickering, *Beowulf*, pp. 331–32).

1148, *on his last voyage*: We have historical corroboration for this story in Gregory of Tours' *History of the Franks*, III, 3, and the raid can be dated to 516–531. "The Danes, led by their king, whose name was Chlochilaichus [Hygelac], attacked the Frankish lands by sea. After they landed, they laid waste one district of the kingdom of Theudoric [king of the Franks], and carried off captives; and then, when they had loaded their ships with these captives, along with the rest of their spoils, they left for their own land. But their king stayed on shore while the ships were sailing onto the deep sea; he was to follow them in due course. When the news reached Theudoric that a region of his had been laid waste by foreigners, he sent his son Theudebert to those parts with a powerful army and a great supply of weapons. And he, after killing the king, attacked the enemy in a ship battle, overwhelmed them, and brought back all the plunder to his own land."

1327–28, *sooner or later / each man's life will come to an end*: The hero's creed is famously expressed in the *Iliad* by the great Trojan ally Sarpedon, who says to Glaucus, his comrade-in-arms:

"Glaucus, why is it that we two are held in the greatest
esteem in Lycia and honored with pride of place,
the choicest meat, and our wine cups always refilled,

and all men look up to us both, as if we were gods,
and we each have a large estate on the banks of the Xanthus,
beautiful tracts of orchards and wheat-bearing farmland?
It is so that we may now take our stand in the front ranks
and lead our army into the thick of battle
and fight with courage, so that the soldiers will say,
'These men who rule us in Lycia are not unworthy.
They may dine on fat sheep and drink the best of the wines,
but they are strong, too, and brave, and they fight in the front ranks.'
Dear friend, if the two of us were to survive this war
and could live forever, without old age, without dying,
I wouldn't press on to fight in the front lines myself
or urge you into the battle. But as it is,
since death stands facing us all in ten thousand forms
and no mortal can ever escape it, let us go forward
and either win glory ourselves or yield it to others."

(*Iliad*, tr. Stephen Mitchell, pp. 187–88)

1521–22, *one stupendous blow / that sheared off the monster's massive head:*
In some ancient cultures, having your head cut off was considered the ultimate
degradation. In one famous scene, Gilgamesh and his friend Enkidu cut off the
monster Humbaba's head:

Then the two friends
sliced him open, pulled out his intestines,
cut off his head with its knife-sharp teeth
and horrible bloodshot staring eyes.
A gentle rain fell onto the mountains.
A gentle rain fell onto the mountains.

(*Gilgamesh*, tr. Stephen Mitchell, p. 128)

In another, David cuts off Goliath's: "And David ran, and stood over the
Philistine, and took his sword, and drew it out of its sheath, and killed him, and
cut off his head with it. And when the Philistines saw that their champion was
dead, they ran away" (1 Samuel 17:51).

1531, *The ninth hour:* Three o'clock in the afternoon.

1613, *the Flood:* See note to line 104.

1762, *Seeing far lands:* "Because of the possibility of treachery in connection

Notes

with the succession of Hrēþrīċ to the Danish throne, conceivably Beowulf is not so much suggesting the benefits of travel as offering a safe haven in exile" (Klaeber⁴, p. 219).

1779, *the strife:* "The former 'hostile acts' between the Danes and Geats probably refers to the events described in Saxo Grammaticus's *Gesta Danorum,* where we read that the son of Scyld (Skiold) vanquished the Geats (Götar)" (Bruce Mitchell and Fred C. Robinson, *Beowulf: An Edition* [Oxford, 1998], p. 109).

1848, *Offa:* "He corresponds to the legendary, prehistoric Angle king Offa (I) of the Mercian genealogies. Being removed twelve generations from the historical Offa II, the old Angle Offa has generally been assigned to the latter half of the fourth century" (Klaeber⁴, pp. 222–23).

1885, *Ongentheow's slayer:* Ongentheow was the king of the Scylfings, a Swedish tribe who had a long feud with the Geats. The whole story is told below in lines 2378–93 and 2809–73. Ongentheow was actually killed by Wulf and Eofor, but Hygelac got the credit, since he led the attack.

1914, *I begged you not to attack that beast:* This account seems to contradict lines 193–95.

1944, *Ingeld:* See note to line 76.

1969, *Withergyld:* "We may imagine that the battle turned after Wiðerġyld, a leader, was slain. (It has been conjectured that he was the father of the young warrior . . .)" (Klaeber⁴, p. 232).

2102–7, *Yet in his youth . . .* : There is a discrepancy between these lines and 2335–42, which present an entirely different account of Beowulf's youth in the house of King Hrethel.

2115, *a thousand square miles:* The text says *seofan þūsendo,* "seven thousand"—that is, seven thousand "hides" of land. "The amount of land given to Beowulf would therefore be equivalent to that of North Mercia (2300 sq. km. [888.03 sq. mi.], though it is the number of families the land can support that the unit refers to, so that the area may actually be more or less . . .)" (Klaeber⁴, p. 237).

2121, *Hygelac fell:* See note to line 1148. After Hygelac was killed in a raid on Frisia (see lines 2266–77), his son Heardred became king. The Swedish king Onela later invaded Geatland and killed Heardred in battle (see lines 2293–95).

2274, *Hetware:* A Frankish tribe on the side of the Frisians.

2290, *Ohthere's sons:* Ohthere succeeded his father, Ongentheow, as the king of the Scylfings (Swedes), but when he died, his brother, Onela, seized the throne and drove Ohthere's two sons, Eanmund and Eadgils, into exile.

2300, *by supporting Eadgils:* Beowulf helped Eadgils, Ohthere's surviving son, in his successful attempt to gain the Scylfing throne.

2349, *that terrible wrong:* "It was long the view of scholars . . . that in the ancient Germanic world, even accidental homicide demanded vengeance. Hrēðel was thus held to be obliged to avenge the death of Herebeald but was unable to do so because he must not lift his hand against his own kin. It has recently been shown rather that the accidental nature of the killing is even likelier than the bond of kinship to have prevented vengeance for Herebeald" (Klaeber⁴, p. 245).

2352–53, *like an old man's / who sees his only son on the gallows:* "The basis for comparison is that in neither case may retribution be exacted" (Klaeber⁴, p. 245).

2380, *Ongentheow's sons:* Ohthere and Onela. (See note to line 2290.)

2383, *Hill of Sorrows:* In Geatland.

2398, *Gifthas:* An East Germanic people related to the Goths.

2405, *Daeghrefn, the Hugas' hero:* The warrior who killed Hygelac (see line 2268 and the note to line 1148). The Hugas were a Frankish people.

2407, *the looted collar:* See lines 1141–57 and 2091–93.

2504 *Weohstan's son:* Though "Wiglaf is said to belong to the family of the Waegmundings, the Geatish family to which Beowulf belonged, he is here called a Scylfing (Swede), and immediately below, his father, Weohstan, is represented as having fought for the Swede Onela in his attack on the Geats. But for a man to change his nation was not unusual, and Weohstan, who may have had both Swedish and Geatish blood, had evidently become a Geat long enough before to have brought up his son, Wiglaf, as one. The identity of Aelfhere is not known" (Donaldson and Howe, *Beowulf,* p. 44).

2513, *Eanmund:* See lines 2289–95 and the note to 2290. "Not only did Weohstan support Onela's attack on the Geat king Heardred, but he actually killed Eanmund, whom Heardred was supporting, and it is Eanmund's sword that Wiglaf is now wielding" (ibid.).

2584, *no better for bearing a sword:* Contrast lines 2403–4 and 2487.

2707, *the Waegmundings:* See line 2509.

2781, *Death would be better:* Tacitus (*Germania,* 6) tells us that "the greatest disgrace that can happen to them [the ancient Germans] is to abandon their shields. Someone guilty of this ignominy is not allowed to join in their religious rites or enter their assemblies. Many men, after surviving a battle, have ended their shame by hanging themselves."

2803, *This quarrel:* See lines 1147–57 and 2266–70.

2816, *first attacked the Scylfing forces:* There is a contradictory account in lines 2380–83.

2828, *some would swing from the gallows:* "Apparently Ongentheow is telling the besieged Geats that after he has defeated them[,] the next day he will sacrifice them to the war god. There are numerous reports of pagan Germanic troops sacrificing some or all of their vanquished enemies to Woden or Tiw following a battle" (Mitchell and Robinson, *Beowulf,* p. 151).

2961–62, *Instead of a spell, he had expected / the Lord's favor for fighting that beast:* These two lines are obscure and probably corrupt. I have followed the interpretation of Klaeber[4], p. 266: "He had not by any means sought out (or expected?) a curse on gold, rather the [O]wner's favor."

3036, *voiced her dread:* Hector's great farewell to Andromache in the *Iliad* imagines the same kind of misery:

> "But however it is, deep in my heart I know
> that a day will come when the sacred city of Troy
> will be devastated, and Priam, and Priam's people.
> And yet it is not their anguish that troubles me so,
> nor Hecuba's, nor even my father, King Priam's,
> nor the blood of the many brave brothers of mine who will fall
> in the dirt at the hands of their enemies—that is nothing
> compared to your grief, when I picture you being caught
> by some bronze-armored Achaean who claims you and takes
> your freedom away and carries you off in tears.
> Then, all your life, in the Argives' land, you will work
> long days, bent over the loom of some stern mistress
> or carrying water up from her well—hating it
> but having no choice, for harsh fate will press down upon you.
> And someone will say, as he sees you toiling and weeping,
> 'That is the wife of Hector, bravest of all
> the Trojans, tamers of horses, when the great war
> raged around Troy.' And then a fresh grief will flood
> your heart, and you will start sobbing again at the thought
> of the only man who was able to ward off your bondage.
> But may I be dead, with the cold earth piled up upon me,
> before I can hear you wail as they drag you away."

(*Iliad,* tr. Stephen Mitchell, pp. 106–7)

Bibliography

Bammesberger, Alfred. "Old English *wæteres weorpan* in *Beowulf*," ANQ 19, no. 1 (2006): pp. 3–7.

Chickering, Howell D., Jr. *Beowulf: A Dual-Language Edition*. New York, 2006.

Dobbie, Elliott van Kirk. *Beowulf and Judith*. New York, 1953.

Donaldson, E. Talbot, and Nicholas Howe. *Beowulf: A Prose Translation*. New York, 2002.

Falk, Oren. "Beowulf's Longest Day: The Amphibious Hero in His Element." *Journal of English and Germanic Philology* 106, no. 1 (January 2007): pp. 1–21.

Fulk, R. D. "Some Contested Readings in the Beowulf Manuscript." *Review of English Studies* 56 (2005): pp. 192–223.

———. "Some Emendations and Non-emendations in 'Beowulf' (Verses 600a, 976a, 1585b, 1663b, 1740a, 2525b, 2771a, and 3060a)." *Studies in Philology* 104, no. 2 (Spring 2007): pp. 159–74.

———. *The Beowulf Manuscript*. Cambridge, MA, 2010.

Fulk, R. D., Robert E. Bjork, and John D. Niles. *Klaeber's Beowulf*. 4th ed. Toronto, 2008.

Heaney, Seamus. *Beowulf: A New Verse Translation*. New York, 2000.

Jack, George. *Beowulf: A Student Edition*. Oxford, 1994.

Kiernan, Kevin. *Electronic Beowulf*. 3rd ed. Programmed by Ionut Emil Iacob. London, 2011.

Liuzza, R. M. *Beowulf*. 2nd ed. Peterborough, Ontario, 2013.

Mitchell, Bruce, and Fred C. Robinson. *Beowulf: An Edition*. Oxford, 1998.

Pfrenger, Andrew M. "Grendel's Glof: *Beowulf* Line 2085 Reconsidered." *Philological Quarterly* 84, no. 3–4 (Summer–Fall 2008): pp. 209–35.

Tolkien, J. R. R. *Beowulf: A Translation and Commentary*. Boston, 2014.

———. *Finn and Hengest*. London, 2006.

———. *The Monsters and the Critics, and Other Essays*. London, 1997.

Bibliography

Walkden, George., "The Status of *hwæt* in Old English," *English Language and Linguistics* 17, no. 3 (November 2013): pp. 465–88.

Weiskott, Eric. "OE *lændagas* in *Beowulf* 2341b." *Notes and Queries* 60, no. 4 (2013): pp. 485–87.

———. "Three *Beowulf* Cruces: Healgamen, fremu, Sigemunde." *Notes and Queries* 58, no. 1 (2011): pp. 3–7.

Wrenn, C. L. *Beowulf.* Rev. ed. London, 1958.

Acknowledgments

My heartfelt thanks to Claire Kelley, who planted the idea in my mind, to Her Astuteness Linda Loewenthal, my agent, to Eric Weiskott, whose scholarship helped improve several passages in the introduction and dozens of lines in the translation, to Jeff Ward for his handsome map, to my eagle-eyed copy editor, Juliana Froggatt, and, at Yale University Press, to the excellent Jennifer Banks, Heather Gold, and Ann-Marie Imbornoni.